Florida's Ghostly Legends and Haunted Folklore

Volume One

South and Central Florida

Greg Jenkins

Pineapple Press, Inc.
Sarasota, Florida

Inquiries should be addressed to:

Pineapple Press, Inc.
P.O. Box 3889
Sarasota, Florida 34230
www.pineapplepress.com

Library of Congress Cataloging-in-Publication Data
Jenkins, Greg, 1964-
    Florida's ghostly legends and haunted folklore / by Greg Jenkins.
       p. cm.
    Includes bibliographical references.
    ISBN 1-56164-327-0 (v. 1 : pbk.)
    1. Ghosts—Florida. 2. Haunted places—Florida.   I. Title.
BF1472.U6J47 2005
133.1'09759—dc22   2004025871

13-digit ISBN 978-1-56164-327-1

First Edition
10 9 8 7 6 5 4 3 2 1

Design by Shé Heaton
Printed in the United States of America

Contents

Central Florida

Appendices

Acknowledgments

This book is dedicated to all those who have the wisdom to look beyond the confines of conventional thought, for exploring the evidence with an open mind without undo judgment in order to find the truth. I wish to thank those personalities of the supernatural, the psychical researchers and paranormal investigators who have offered me a chance to explore beyond the regions of my own philosophies. For Drs. Hans Holzer, Tony Cornell, Loyd Auerbach, Barry Taft, Kerry Gaynor, and William Roll, who first sparked my interest in the paranormal, and Dr. Andrew Nichols, Florida's own expert on the paranormal, and everyone who keeps my interest alive and strong, I thank you all for the momentum you have afforded me. I also thank Kimberly Penkava for assisting me in my journey into the unknown this last year, and Jennifer Schneider for aiding me while creating this book. Thanks to the music group *Midnight Syndicate,* whose atmospheric music not only kept me awake those late nights, but also gave me the inspirational juice to keep searching for Florida's elusive ghosts. Thanks also to Pineapple Press for having the vision to explore such topics as ghosts and the unknown. And thanks to all the many people who have helped me to make this book possible: the witnesses, the faithful, those who believe in me, and those who continue to keep Florida's unique and diverse oral traditions and enchanting folklore alive.

The purpose of this book is to create a compendium of ghostly and haunted phenomena, as well as the many enchanted or creepy locations found in the great state of Florida. It is also a registry of some of Florida's strangest and most haunted places: preternatural locations found in our cities, towns, national parks, cemeteries, and even in our own backyards. In the interest of those who wish their anonymity secure, some information, such as names and private addresses, are omitted for the sake of privacy.

During my investigations, which have taken me from one end of Florida to the other, visiting every place from lonely cemeteries, old abandoned psychiatric hospitals, and even deserted stretches of road that seemed to be endless, I found myself in awe of Florida's uniqueness. After interviewing more than eighty people in the process, I have been fortunate to learn far more about Florida's legends and folklore than I could ever have hoped for.

Of the people I interviewed, many were more than cooperative, eagerly wanting to share their stories, delighted to be recognized in some small way. Others, however, were more reluctant to share their personal accounts, wanting to remain completely anonymous. The reluctance of the latter group of people is generally due to their livelihoods, positions in their towns or cities, or understandable insistence on not revealing their personal addresses. Other stories and locations, however, are revealed for the reader as an invitation to do his or her own ghostly investigations and to consider this book a personal guide to some of Florida's most haunted localities, where ghosts abound in very unexpected places.

Preface

When most people think of Florida, they may think of warm sunny beaches, vacation attractions, and the night life it has to offer. Perhaps they think of the cultural diversity, which has made Florida the unique, perpetually growing state it has become. Yet, if we try to think of Florida as a haunted place, where spirits do indeed roam, we may only equate that as a possibility if it were a ride in one of Central Florida's amusement parks, not really haunted at all. Florida, after all, isn't old enough to be haunted. Well, considering Florida has St. Augustine, the oldest city in the United States, I think happily to the contrary.

The idea for writing a book on this subject came after a first-hand experience with the unknown, which solidified my belief in ghosts and hauntings without question. This experience opened my eyes to much larger realities and possibilities, where before I refused seriously to entertain such notions outside a good horror movie, or ghostly novel at best.

In the summer of 1987, my uncle died of a massive heart attack in his sleep. He and my grandmother had been living in a small mobile home in Pompano Beach, Florida, at that time.

My grandmother was sick then and was staying at my parents' home in Boca Raton a few miles to the north. I was working the graveyard shift at the hospital and decided to stay at the mobile home, letting my grandmother have my room at my parents' so I didn't have to sleep on the couch. I would go directly to my grandmother's mobile home right after work, sleeping in my uncle's old room, in my uncle's old bed. This was all well and fine, but each afternoon when I awoke, the door to my uncle's bedroom was always halfway open. I couldn't understand why the door would be open when I knew I shut it when

I went to sleep. After the second afternoon, waking up to find the same thing, a strange feeling came over me, as if I were being watched, as if I were not alone. Although I quickly dismissed that feeling, I decided just to sit on the bed, close the door, and wait for it to open. Nothing happened.

The third morning when I was preparing to sleep, I decided to shut the door, lock it, and put a chair up against it, making sure that it would not open again. I tried to reason that the door was naturally opening as a result of, well, something natural. And for sure, this time it would not open again. . . . I was wrong. When I woke up that afternoon, the door was once again halfway open, and the chair neatly moved out of its way. Needless to say, that very strange feeling had come over me a second time, yet, it was not a feeling of dread or threat; it was, strangely enough, a feeling somewhat of amusement.

This event was not caused by the wind, nor the old mobile home settling in its foundation, even if it had a foundation, and I was unable to find a rational explanation for this occurrence. Moreover, deep down in my heart, I just knew it was my uncle.

As he was always protective of me, and good-natured in life, it somehow seemed logical that he would be that way beyond death. I think that this was his way of saying everything was all right and not to worry, and I can honestly say today, I no longer worry about death, as I now believe that it is just one more step into a much larger existence.

This event initiated my quest to research the many different paranormal occurrences, which go far beyond our society-made limitations, to open myself to the knowledge of all things being possible. This I happily do today.

As I listened to the many time-honored oral traditions from Florida's residents, the long-lasting folk legends that create the very spice of life here, I've heard a distinct earnestness that made me believe. From the huge metropolises like Miami and Jacksonville, to the quaint hamlets of Oviedo, Micanopy, and the Florida Keys, I have found a unique sincerity that explains the longevity of such folklore.

In my ghostly research and folkloric endeavors, I have found an almost unending supply of ghostly folk tales and haunted legends here in the state of Florida. Perhaps those reading this book will agree that ghosts are something scientific, something explainable. Perhaps some will see beyond the fringes of the rational, of what we consider reality, to look for the unseen. With that said, prepare to go beyond Florida's bright sunny days and vacationing spots, into the lesser-known, darker areas of our most haunted Florida.

Introduction

Legends and Beliefs

The oldest and strongest emotion of mankind is fear, and the oldest and strongest kind of fear is fear of the unknown. . . .
—*H. P. Lovecraft*

The horror novelist Howard Phillips Lovecraft understood the concept of fear. His novels show us that the fear of the unknown is one of the most powerful emotions people experience. He also understood that the time-honored legends and oral traditions we all know and love are based, in one way or another, on a factual event in history. He took the actual historical elements, mingled them with pure fiction, and ended up with a fantastic yarn that people believed as truth.

Perhaps the existence of dragons in medieval times, for instance, was to some degree true: the large frightening creature may in fact have been there, but it was significantly less than what the many years of time and oral tradition have made these creatures out to be. Legends like these have a way of enticing us because they remain in the realm of the unknown.

Sea serpents in Northern Europe or the Bigfoot creatures here in North America may all be based in some factual event, one way or another. Without tangible evidence to their existence, however, they will always remain in the ethereal realm of the unknown and within the obscure regions of our imaginations. This is the realm in which we place ghosts. Beyond all the paranormal elements, ghost stories point to the one thing that all of us question, regardless of race, religion, or social status: the enigma of death and what follows the death of our physical being. Do we simply cease to be, or do we go on to some elevated place of existence? Anthropologists tell us that human beings have always asked themselves, "What happens to us when we die?" If we do indeed go on to a higher plane of reality, why are some made to stay on earth, bound to unfinished business that acts as chains holding them here?

What exactly are ghosts and spirits, and why are some locations believed to be haunted by the souls of the dead? Do these shades of human past, these disembodied mists of a once-living being truly exist? The answer might surprise, as for sure, one day you and I will find out for ourselves.

The very concept of ghosts, spirits, or apparitions can be seen in practically every culture of man from the beginning of human existence. From the mountains of Tibet to the jungles of New Guinea, from the fjords of Scandinavia to the savannah's of darkest Africa, and even on the sunny beaches of Florida, people around the globe have believed, seen, and felt these vaporous entities in all their guises. Although no one truly knows for sure what these phantoms are, if they're just overworked imaginations or the actual residue of a disembodied souls, no one can be absolutely certain. Yet, many rational, down-to-earth individuals claim to have encountered these strange wonders of our human existence, these spirits of the dead.

Many scholars and religious leaders believe that the human spirit may separate from its mortal body and exist outside that physical confine for a particular period of time, be it a few moments or many centuries, each spirit with its own purpose and time among the living. These spirits may inhabit various forms and may be manifest for diverse reasons.

One classification of ghost is the "crisis apparition." This spirit is said to show itself to a family member or friend as a warning of danger to come, or to give assurance that the person represented by the apparition did indeed die. This spirit may be trying to tell the living not to worry, that he or she is content with the afterlife, and that the living should move on with their own lives. In any case, crisis apparitions have been reported for centuries all over the world, never to be thoroughly explained by scientist or layperson.

Other forms of ghosts or entities may seem to repeat a particular action. One example of this phenomenon is the clichéd legend of a lady in white seen walking up the stairs of an old English castle every midnight when the moon is full. . . . This variety of spirit—continuing to do the same thing repeatedly, not necessarily of an intelligent mind—has a need to express an action over and over again.

The poltergeist phenomena, although represented violently in most films and books, are actually quite harmless, historically speaking. The German word "poltergeist" literally means "noisy spirit," and the true representation of this phenomenon is more of a prankster, a maker of bumps or knocking sounds. Perhaps these spirits mysteriously move, levitate, or manifest objects as if from nowhere. Any or all of these enigmatic events may constitute the presence of a poltergeist. One of the most common beliefs regarding the poltergeist is that the unexplained events are actually projections from a psychic source, perhaps a prepubescent child or adolescent who acts as an agent, somehow affecting the delicate balance of the ethereal plain. In addition to this theory, there are those who believe that these fascinating—if not a little frightening—occurrences are indeed tied to an actual spirit or entity, thus giving the spooky events a more human feel.

Other varieties of ghosts appear to have definite intelligence, as if coexisting in our plane of reality or dimension but going about particular tasks unto themselves. Perhaps, as many scientists of the paranormal believe, the ethereal realm in which these entities exist is actually all around us, at all times, with just the smallest division between our reality and theirs.

The classic haunting may involve strange things like unexplained cold spots, a creaking floor board in an empty house, a door that slowly opens by itself, a rancid smell as if from decaying flesh, or perhaps the sound of footfalls where there should be none. Of course, these are stereotypical examples; there appear to be many other phenomena to warrant what we call a haunting.

Haunted locations can be a house or hotel, an apartment building or even a supermarket. Cemeteries and battlefields may have preternatural residues (the vibrations of tragic events from the past), creating a portal for ethereal entities like ghosts. Moreover, some believe that if you build a home over such a location, you might be inviting entities like the aforementioned into that home. . . . Perhaps your home is already haunted.

Many practitioners of the paranormal believe that the whole world is in fact a haunted place, filled with a complex array of supernatural highways, if you will. Then again, this all might be nothing more than a settling house, or the wind blowing through the attic. Perhaps it's just a good legend that originated during a thunderstorm, when the lights went out and the environment was just right for telling such a story. And then again, maybe the legend is based on a factual event that once took place, and over the years has developed into something just a bit more than it once was.

The paranormal investigator, the parapsychologist, the lay ghost hunter, and the psychic are today's experts in ghosts and hauntings. Who are these people? Belief in the supernatural is as old as mankind, and throughout history, there have always been those who have claimed to be "experts" or "professionals." Traditionally, the priest, rabbi, or other religious leader would be the person to turn to in the event of a haunting, poltergeist outbreak, or a demonic possession. Today, however, although still sanctioned and investigated by some religious experts, lay scientists and self-proclaimed psychics take the lead in the investigation of such curious phenomena.

The paranormal investigator or parapsychologist may be a professor at a college or university, most likely trained in academic sciences such as psychology, anthropology, folklore studies, or physics. This group of people studies the possible causes and effects of alleged hauntings and will use various scientific equipment and procedures to rule out the possibility of a more down-to-earth cause for the seemingly ghostly events. Many ghostlike occurrences may in truth have logical explanations; a house that shakes everyday at a certain time may be affected by a passing train or even a subterranean river. However, not all eerie occurrences have such logical explanations.

Most of these highly trained people may truly want to detect the presence of spirits and specters, but they will not be convinced until they find sufficient proof and scientific evidence for the existence of such entities.

The ever-popular ghost hunter, whose popularity continues to increase, is by most accounts a layperson who may work an average day job and hold no formal expertise in the study of psychology or parapsychology. Notwithstanding, the ghost hunter's devotion to the study of the unknown may be as real and as determined as that of the scholarly professor or the seasoned scientist. Ghost hunters may be office secretaries, delivery people, managers at a fast food chain, or security guards by day, but when night falls, they take part in a spookier activity.

You might find these people creeping through an old abandoned building or graveyard, equipped with digital cameras, video recorders, and a large array of pseudoscientific gadgets in hopes of finding proof of life after death. The ghost hunter today has a ready supply of electromagnetic frequency analyzers, portable temperature gauges, hygrometers, infrared goggles, and a variety of other strange, science fiction–like devices, all at their fingertips via the wonders of technology and the distribution marvels of the World Wide Web. Needless to say, the search for ghosts is not just for the Hollywood Ghostbuster anymore. . . . It's now a possibility for you or me.

Site Map

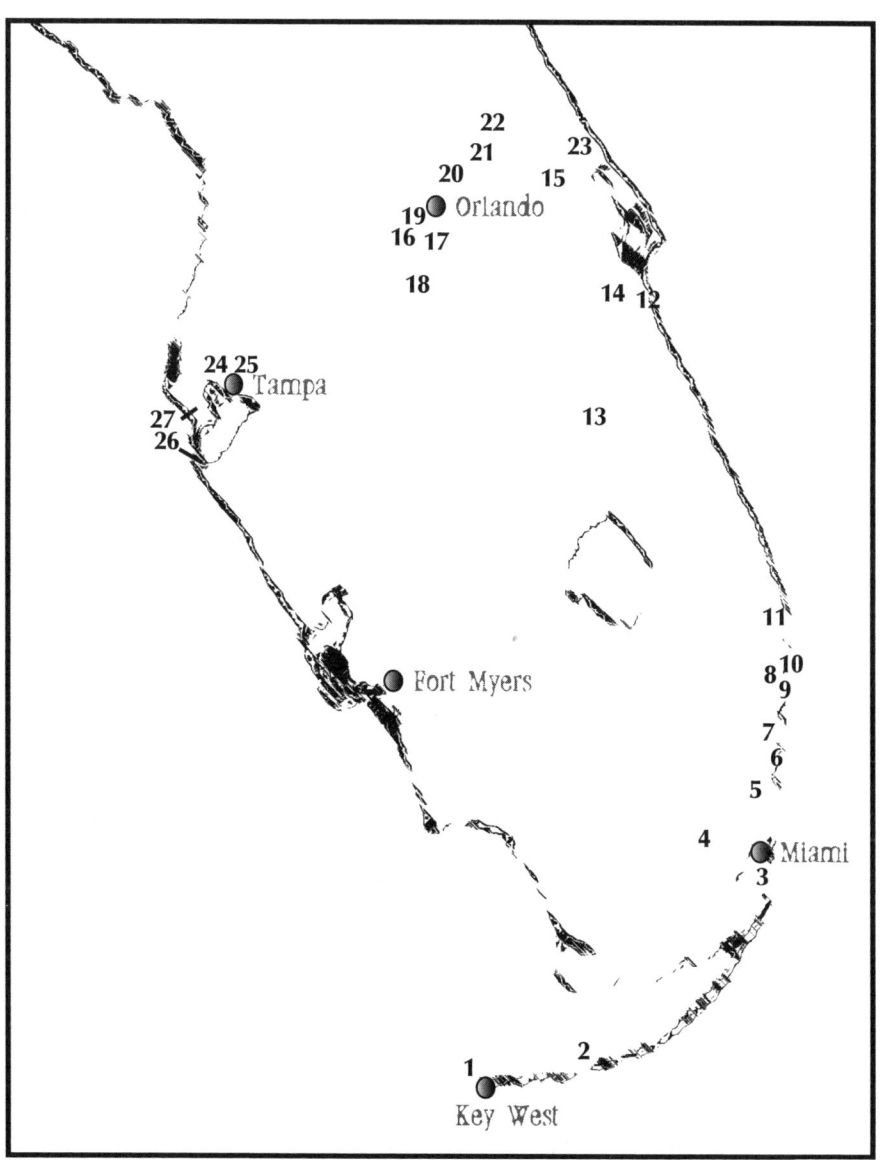

22
21   23
20   15
19 ● Orlando
16 17
18   14 12

24 25
● Tampa
27
26

13

● Fort Myers

11

8 10
9
7
6
5

4
● Miami
3

2
1
●
Key West

South Florida

1

La Concha Hotel

Key West

A Ghostly Waiter, a Lamenting Lawyer,
and Ernest Hemingway, too

A Little History

Built in 1924, the 160-room, seven-story La Concha Hotel is the tallest building in Key West. It has had an illustrious history entertaining all kinds of people, from European royalty and U.S. presidents to Pulitzer Prize–winning authors and even famous gangsters. The La Concha Hotel remains an icon of Florida's southernmost communities. During the 1920s and 1930s, famed author Ernest Hemingway frequently stayed at the La Concha and is known to have written many of his novels in one of the suites there. Having drinks on the rooftop bar or meeting his mistress in secret were among his pastimes at La Concha. Gangsters such as Al Capone and his cronies are also believed to have stayed there on occasion while on "fishing trips" in the Keys, and many other famous and infamous people have visited this charming hotel over the years.

The grand opening was in 1926, giving Key West its first elegant hotel. With marble floors, private baths, elevators, and other luxuries, it was no surprise that the La Concha was a success from the begin-

ning. In 1927, flights between Key West and Cuba began, and the La Concha was to become a major stop for travelers, who were delivered by the hundreds via Henry Flagler's East Coast Railroad.

After the stock market crash of 1929, the tiny island of Key West suffered, becoming one of the poorest cities in America. The hotel changed ownership in 1930 and was renamed the Key West Colonial. It struggled along until the Labor Day Hurricane of 1935, which destroyed most of the Overseas Railroad, cutting off Key West from the mainland until the Overseas Highway was built. Still, the hotel survived.

Over the years, the La Concha Hotel played host to many famous people. Ernest Hemingway was not the only literary hero to stay at the hotel: Pulitzer Prize–winning author Tennessee Williams completed his famous play *A Streetcar Named Desire* while staying at the La Concha in the mid-1940s. Sadly, however, even with such notable personalities the glory days of the La Concha Hotel were to go on an extended respite for thirty years. Within that time the once grand hotel became a victim of age and decay, while more modernized hotels and resorts gained the respect and esteem of Key West travelers. By 1982 the hotel's rooftop bar was the only part still operating; the rooms and suites had been boarded up, covered with dust and strung with spider webs.

Fortunately, the La Concha was about to find favorable fortune again as architect Richard Rauh was given the opportunity to restore the hotel to its former glory. Going by old photographs and interviewing many of Key West's old residents, Rauh spent millions in the process of orchestrating a major restoration. The La Concha Hotel became up-to-date, yet maintained an atmosphere reminiscent of its colorful past. It reopened with a gala celebration in 1986.

Because the La Concha is the tallest building on Key West, it offers a remarkable panoramic view of the entire island, from the Gulf of Mexico to the Atlantic Ocean and all in between. On the seventh floor, you'll find the wrap-around observation deck that makes viewing sunsets a memorable experience. The Crown Room restaurant with its 1930s décor, reminiscent of the hotel's heyday, gives one the feeling that Ernest Hemmingway is in some way still there, enjoying the luxuries of Key West and the beautiful La Concha he once knew. Listed on the National Register of Historic Places, the La Concha Hotel has the unique and somewhat spooky feeling of yesteryear, as if the famous and not-so-famous personalities of Florida's colorful past are still there . . . and many believe they still are.

Ghostly Legends and Haunted Folklore

The La Concha Hotel, steeped in Florida's history, is without a doubt one of our state's prized hotels, and although thousands of people stay here every year to enjoy Key West's beaches and jubilant night life, the hotel has a reputation for attracting another kind of population:

ghosts. Because the history of the La Concha is rife with dramatic events—including accidental deaths and suicides—it stands to reason that a few of the sad or lost souls who died here would choose to remain.

One ghost in particular is a tormented spirit who in life worked as a waiter during the early 1980s. It was New Year's Eve 1983 when this young man, a native of Key West, was picking up dishes from the fifth floor en route to the kitchen on the lower level. The festivities were well under way, and it was around 1:45 A.M. when the waiter was finishing up for the night. He was hurrying to get back to the kitchen to unload his cart, picking up the streamers and confetti as he went along, hoping to go home in time to celebrate for himself. Sadly, however, this was not to be. As he was pulling the heavy cart along, backing up to the elevator, and glancing over his shoulder to push the button to go down, he struggled to keep the dishes and trays from toppling over. Trying not to make a mess, he heard the door open behind him and backed up, cart in tow. In what must have been the most frightening moment of his abbreviated life, he stepped backward into an empty shaft, falling five stories, cart and all, to his death. You see, the elevator had not landed on the fifth floor but the sixth, one floor above him.

No one is quite sure why the elevator malfunctioned, but most speculate that something must have gone wrong during the restoration of the hotel a year earlier. Perhaps the wiring was old or the elevator just needed servicing; either way, a young man died in his prime. His dreams and endeavors, his loves, his hopes, and his future, were lost forever that early morning at the bottom of a long, dark shaft. It was not until an hour later, when a hotel resident complained that the elevator was not responding, that maintenance was sent to investigate. As the maintenance man pointed his flashlight down the dark shaft, he saw the lifeless body of the waiter below, the service cart covering the upper portion of his remains. The incident was kept as secret as it could be, and life went on normally in the hotel. The elevator was repaired and people came and went, and business moved along as usual. Nevertheless, something was different after the accident . . . something scary.

Almost immediately, the hotel's employees and guests started noticing strange occurrences. Many of the La Concha's staff reported feeling watched on the fifth floor, being tapped on the shoulder only to find an empty hallway behind them, or feeling a cold draft pass them as they walked through the hallway. To this day, many of the hotel's maids refuse to work alone on the fifth floor, demanding to have another maid work with them on their shift, then departing as fast as they can when they're done. Some of the kitchen staff claim to see the shadowy image of the waiter pushing his cart through an unlit portion of the room after hours. Others have found colorful streamers and confetti on the fifth-floor landing after there had been no celebration. When a janitor went to the supply closet to get a vacuum or broom, the party favors that were there only moments before would be gone.

On several occasions, some of the hotel employees, particularly the overnight staff, complained that their carts had been moved from where they were left, and each time the missing cart would be found sitting neatly by the elevator, as if someone were preparing to take it down to the kitchen. On more than one occasion, a guest reported seeing a waiter walking down the hallways late at night, moving slowly and stiffly as if he were intoxicated or dazed. When the guest asked the waiter a question, he would ignore the guest's inquiry and turn a corner, out of sight. If the guest were persistent enough to walk down the hallway to catch up, he would find no one.

In addition to finding a streamer or a light sprinkle of confetti on the fifth floor, sometimes hotel patrons hear strange things, too.

Returning from a late night of partying at one of Key West's many bars or clubs, a guest might hear the faint sound of laughter and an eerie echo of music from the 1980s, slightly muffled. And, when the kitchen is closing for the evening, it's not uncommon for the night staff to get the feeling that they are not alone, which makes some of them eager to pick up the pace and get out as quickly as possible. Is the waiter disgruntled for losing his life that early morning in 1983? Does he still walk the corridors looking for his cart? No one knows for sure, but if you're staying at the La Concha and hear the sound of a waiter's push-cart squeaking past your room late at night, you might want to let it pass before you open the door.

There appear to be several other spirits residing at the La Concha, as well. The presence of Ernest Hemingway has been felt by many who have stayed in the suite in which the author entertained his mistress in the1930s. He is believed to play tricks on those who spend the night in that suite, usually by moving things around. Known as "psychokinesis" or "PK" by paranormal investigators and parapsychologists, unexplained moving objects were once reported in the early 1990s by a guest in the hotel.

A man staying in the suite complained to the staff that someone was in his room the night before. Apparently, a videotape recorder, which was sitting on a dresser table, fell off by itself: not once, but three times. The first time the machine fell to the floor, the guest turned on the light and secured the recorder back on the dresser, then went back to bed. After it fell again, he got up and did the same thing; this time, however, he checked the dresser table to make sure it wasn't wobbly. The dresser was secure and stable, and the man went back to bed, this time letting his eyes adjust to the darkness. As he lay staring at the dresser, he noticed a shadow the shape of what looked like a man slightly hunched over, standing in the corner by the bathroom. He thought it was a trick of the light that barely emanated from Duval

Street, but as soon as he made this rationalization, the video recorder once again fell to the floor, this time spurring the gentleman to turn on the light in a hurry. He got up, not knowing what he would find, and walked around the room thinking for sure that someone was in there with him. But the room was empty and the door was locked and secure. Needless to say, the event was a complete mystery. Although no one is quite sure who the specter is, if it's the playful nature of Ernest Hemingway or that of another guest from the La Concha's past, one thing is for sure: this spirit revels in sending a chill up its victims' spines.

Another ghostly legend concerns the spirit of a man who led a life of lies and deceit, a dishonest lawyer who was staying at the La Concha in the late 1980s. According to the staff, this lawyer was being investigated for embezzlement and fraud, charges that would have sent him to jail and devastated his family. Fearing that a federal inquiry would soon find enough evidence against him, he decided to make one last desperate plan of escape, one last lie to clear his name. The hopeless lawyer decided that if he could make his suicide look like he was murdered, his family would get the insurance money. If it was obviously suicide, the insurance company would not pay. Accordingly, he took his hand-held tape recorder and concocted a story on the tape that would make him look innocent of the federal charges and, more importantly, make the authorities believe he was pushed from the balcony of the seventh floor. Talking wildly into his tape recorder, the lawyer paced the roof's balcony ranting and raving that his secretary was responsible for the embezzled money and that assassins were coming to kill him. He made a desperate plea for someone to look after his family and again stated that he was completely innocent. Then, tape recorder in hand, he leapt from the balcony to his death below. The recording survived, complete with four remaining seconds of the rushing wind and his final screams.

Sadly for the deceitful lawyer, his plans to fool the authorities failed. The federal agents were already aware of his crimes and had ample proof. The secretary was cleared, and the lawyer's family did not receive the insurance money. The lawyer went to his grave forever marked by his transgressions. Although the case was closed and the incident quickly forgotten, the furor of the lawyer's guilt seems to continue just as it did when he was pacing the roof's balcony that fateful evening.

On certain occasions, usually around sunset, some have claimed to see a middle-aged man walking back and forth on the balcony in a state of disarray, as if he were mentally ill. Because he was seen talking to himself frantically and looking over the balcony as if he were going to jump, the people who saw him would call hotel security for help. When security arrived, however, they would find no one, and no sign of anyone ever being there. Most of the time, witnesses only heard the pitiful ravings coming from the rooftop. However, on at least one occasion, a couple sitting in one of the rooms below frantically called the front desk to report what looked like a body falling from the roof. When the staff raced outside to see if someone had jumped, they found no sign of a body and no one on the roof. To this day, the lawyer is said to continue his painful vigil on the rooftop, doomed to retrace his last steps, which condemn him to this reappearing, residual haunting . . . forever regretting his final choices in life.

Afterthoughts

The La Concha Hotel has seen its good times and its bad. It witnessed the Great Depression and has catered to high society and the elite. It has ushered in happy newlyweds and carried out the dead, and it has seen Florida grow from grass shacks to a vacationer's paradise. The La Concha is in many ways representative of not only Key West's colorful past, but that of the whole of Florida as well. The spirits of this wonderful hotel seem to speak volumes of what they did in life, what they missed, or what they regret.

The ghostly waiter who will tap you on the shoulder may be trying to ask you why he cannot leave, or perhaps he is waiting for someone to show him the way out of the hotel so he can finally go home. The shadow in the corner of Hemingway's old suite might very well be the author's spirit, showing his playful side to the living. Perhaps, since his life was sometimes as dark and tragic as the characters he wrote about, his tormented soul chose to remain in this place of comfort after his suicide so many years ago. The La Concha was a place of refuge for him in life, and perhaps it is a refuge for him today, with the added consolation of playing tricks on unsuspecting guests in the middle of the night. And, what of the lamenting lawyer? Will he ever be set free from his earthly torment? Will he ever be able to forgive himself? Only time will tell.

Today, the La Concha serves as a place for many happy vacationers to get away from it all and enjoy the beauty and pleasure that Florida has to offer. But when visiting the gorgeous beaches of Key West, taking advantage of the island shops and the tropical environment, enjoying the many cafes and restaurants, try to remember the vibrant—and sometimes tragic—history many of the island's locations have seen. And when you're heading back to the La Concha Hotel for a night's rest, just remember to look over your shoulder when walking the quiet halls . . . you never know who might be standing right behind you.

2

Flagler's East Coast Railway

Islamorada

Phantom Trains and Ghostly Cars

Within seconds the rumbling was right over them, and the old train track foundation was vibrating, then rocking violently. The sound of a train whistle was so loud they had to hold their ears. As they looked ahead, they both realized that there was no track just beyond them. That was gone years ago; this train was going to crash!

—Old Islamorada Fisherman

A Little History

Henry Morrison Flagler, founder of Standard Oil, architect of the grand Ponce de Leon Hotel in Saint Augustine, and creator of Palm Beach Island's Whitehall Mansion, was one of Florida's most remarkable visionaries. By the 1880s, Flagler decided to extend his brilliance and wealth as far south in Florida as he could go, with visions of providing his hotels' guests with the most modern transportation available. In order to do this, he simply assembled an entire railroad system. He purchased existing railroads that ran from Jacksonville to Daytona Beach, then extended their lines and service all the way to Palm Beach, Miami, and eventually to Key West. From the beginning, Flagler considered all the possibilities for his railroad: With the construction of the Panama Canal going on at that time, if his railroad reached as far south as Key West, arriving and departing Panama workers would have better access to and from the mainland. However, because Key West is more than 100 miles off the coast, Flagler had to build a bridge. It would take seven years and close to 5,000 men to finish this modern achievement.

By 1912 the railroad and bridge were finished and officially opened to the public, realizing the final link in Flagler's railroad dream: The Florida East Coast Railway. Sadly, however, Henry Flagler only lived a year after his railroad was completed, just short of seeing the tremendous effect his dream would have on the people of Florida. But in spite of structure and architecture that appeared sound in every respect, Flagler's railroad dream would have no more than two decades of glory left, as there was something bigger, something horrific on its way . . . the 1935 Labor Day Hurricane.

It was during the morning of September 1, 1935, when the storm warnings were posted from Palm Beach to the Keys. People in Miami began boarding up their homes and securing their boats. In the Keys, the native Indians chanted and prayed while others in their tribe gathered food and made shelter for what they called "a big blow." Others in the area were having extra meals cooked, candles collected, and lamps filled with oil. The islanders prepared for the loss of electricity, which could last for weeks. They prepared for the worst. Meteorologists were sure that by Monday, Labor Day, the storm would hit the Keys.

By 1:30 that Monday afternoon, the local authorities called for the evacuation transport from Homestead, but they received no reply, just static. Sadly, there were no advance plans for such an emergency, no strategy for an evacuation. There was no passenger train—or fuel or cargo train—in Homestead at the time, so the town leaders had to send a message to Miami and have a train sent as soon as possible. Unfortunately, it was late in the evening before a train left the station, and it was close to 9 P.M. when it arrived to pick up hundreds of people from the upper and middle Keys. It had taken close to four hours to reach Islamorada. The storm became so strong and deadly, with such unbelievable winds, that the ten passenger cars were tossed off the track and onto their sides, ripping and twisting the tracks from their foundations. Meanwhile, a good number of the natives and migrant workers had hidden in huts and abandoned houses, some even strapped themselves to palm trees in the hopes of riding out the storm.

By Tuesday morning, in the wake of one of Florida's most devastating hurricanes, a category five storm, with winds over 180 miles per hour, many of the smaller keys had completely disappeared, and hundreds of people were reported missing. The survivors crawled out of their shelters and took part in the search. In the end, the islands were all but destroyed; the houses were now rubble and debris, and when the gruesome search for the missing was over, the death count was unbelievable.

The people who had tied themselves to trees now hung over the ropes, twisted and barely recognizable. Some of the victims floated out in the bay, some washed up on the shore, still others were pulled out of the swamps, and over 400 victims were never to be seen again. Some of the train's cars that were tossed into the water remain there today, as well as automobiles that were scurrying for safety. For the hundreds of men, women, and children who lost their lives that day, their final moments will remain a mystery.

The East Coast Railway was not rebuilt. The Overseas Road and Toll Commission purchased the railroad and converted the single-track trestles into a two-lane unbroken highway (U.S. 1) from Homestead to Key West in 1938. Although the march of progress continued with tour buses now bringing income and revenue to the islands, the trucks that carried in produce, meats, textiles, and cargo made the maritime shipping lanes almost obsolete.

With recovery well under way, life in the Florida Keys was beginning to move forward again. This was all well and fine, but almost immediately, strange things began to take place. The sound of a train whistle and the thundering of a steam engine passing could sometimes be heard late at night. Now and again, headlights from misty, antique cars could be seen silently rolling by in the wee hours of the morning. On occasion, and still to this day, the eerie shapes of people, literally hundreds of people, appear silently walking through the marshland swamps in the darkness. When the Labor Day Hurricane of 1935 took its toll on the Florida Keys that fateful Monday evening, leaving hundreds dead and hundreds more homeless or missing, it also left something even more terrifying . . . the restless roaming victims of that killer storm.

Ghostly Legends and Haunted Folklore

Talking with fishermen on the banks of the ocean near the Seven Mile Bridge, I was offered some frightening accounts of paranormal events that should not be left out of any collection of ghost stories—stories of phantom trains and vaporous cars, of eerie headlights and the shadows of people staggering through the swampy estuaries. They are, as one angler said, enough to "curl your toes."

As the old fishermen recalled, the first sightings began in the early 1940s, and one man was more than willing share one of his own experiences. It was around 1943, when he and another boy would fish under the remains of the original bridge that once held the tracks of Flagler's railway. They would cast their nets near the bridge's discarded wreckage because the fish and shrimp were more plentiful there. Although the majority of the original structure had been converted for vehicle use, there were remains of the original tracks and pylons that littered the banks back then.

As the story goes, while these two boys were shrimping under a section of the old bridge one evening, a storm was forming off shore. With flashes of lightning and what looked like a thick wall of rain closing in, it seemed like a good idea to pull in their nets and get home as fast as they could. But the storm, quickly approaching, altered the boys' plans.

As they were folding their nets and putting on their shoes, the first splattering of rain began, but within a few moments, the light rain had turned into a torrential storm. The two boys were now collecting their gear as fast as they could, hoping not to be struck by lightning. They started to climb the bank, but just as they were grabbing hold of an old iron track, a bolt of lightning seemed to hit only a few yards away. The lightning was so close they both could feel the hair on the backs of their necks standing on end, and with that, they decided to duck under the cement pylons, where there was a small, hollowed-out area surrounded by granite stones.

They had been sitting there for a few minutes, recalled the old fisherman, when they heard a train whistle in the distance. They both looked at each other in amazement, because there should be no trains there, not anymore. The boys knew a little about the train that once ran there and the hurricane that blew it off the tracks, but that was many years before. . . . Now there should be no trains at all!

The old man said that after a minute or two, his friend pulled himself up by the iron railing to get a good look at what was making the whistle noise. A moment later, he dropped back down with a strange, pale look on his face. The boy looked at him in a very weird way and said that he'd just seen a train light on the tracks heading right toward them. The two of them didn't know what to think, let alone what to do about the astonishing situation, but the sounds of a thundering locomotive were getting louder by the second. They were both too scared to respond, so they just sat there. Within seconds, the rumbling was right over them, and the old train track foundation was vibrating, then rocking violently. The sound of the train whistle was so loud they had to hold their ears. As they looked ahead, they both realized that there was no track just beyond them. That was gone years ago; this train was going to crash! The boys buried their faces in their laps waiting for the terrible collision . . . yet, the rumbling of the train just faded away, the whistle ceased, and the only thing they heard was the dying storm. They looked out and saw nothing but the falling rain and a few flashes of distant lightning. They saw nothing: there was no train.

Needless to say, this event spawned many ghost stories, and in the process, created a local legend that few outsiders have heard. The two boys witnessed a strange event indeed, and, although this is not, by far, the only phantom locomotive story today, it is uniquely Floridian.

If phantom trains aren't ominous enough, then ghostly cars passing by in the darkness surely are. On more than one occasion, old-fashioned automobiles have been seen slowly puttering by on the old highway in Islamorada. These cars are usually black, said to be like those driven in the 1930s or '40s, with only their dim headlights eerily shining through on foggy mornings, and making only the faint sounds of a distant motor. They make it past the first part of the bridge then dissolve away, as one witness put it, like an effervescent pill in water: blinking a bit, like a light losing its power, and then disappearing completely.

Years ago, a college student, while visiting some friends in Islamorada, saw a black phantom four-door car moving down the road around 3:45 A.M. As she was walking her dog, the student initially noticed the headlights, which were much dimmer than normal headlights, and at first she thought it might have been two bicycles. Then she heard the pitter-patter of an old engine. As soon as she heard this, her little terrier dog began to bark violently, as if something dangerous was approaching. Perhaps it was instinct, or just fear that made her pull her dog behind her, but the dog's barks soon became whimpers as the ghostly car passed her. At first glance she thought it might simply be an old antique car passing her, complete with the silhouette of a person in the driver's seat. But as the car neared the arch at the bridge's entrance, something strange happened. The sound of the motor seemed to grind, getting louder as it moved away, and the two red lights at the back of the car suddenly disappeared within the foggy mist. A moment of fear descended on her because she thought that the driver may have stopped and shut off his engine, but as she stared hard into the darkness, she knew the car was gone. She walked a bit further to see down the street beyond the bridge, but there was nothing . . . just empty road.

The ghostly car makes its run every once in a while, sometimes passing early morning fisherman, or lone pedestrians. Sometimes, the solitary automobile makes no sound at all as it passes over the bridge, only achieving a gasp from the observer when it fades and then disappears into thin air. Although many speculate whose car it once was, or why it is seen in this area, the best hypotheses for the phenomenon point to the Labor Day Hurricane of 1935. Many people were struggling to find shelter or trying to help those residents with no means of transportation. Perhaps this vehicular apparition represents one person's attempt to save someone else during that storm of so long ago. Perhaps that person died trying to help. Perhaps in one way or another, that person's love lives on in the retelling of that fateful day, the final attempts to save a life. And although this particular apparition, as well as that of the phantom train, may be the echoes of a race for survival, the last ghostly legend of Flagler's lost railroad refers to those who simply disappeared that dreadful Monday morning in 1935 . . . the over 400 people who are still missing to this day.

When Tuesday came and the storm was over, the search for the missing turned up grisly finds indeed. In fact, for the next three weeks the decomposing remains of hundreds of people were pulled from the nearby swamps and estuaries. As the torrential waves toppled houses and flooded buildings, the power of the surf was also strong enough to drown a multitude of people. Although the search was intense, many victims remained unfound, trapped under the huge roots of cypress trees or food for the abundant swamp life. To this day, government land workers or environmental laborers will still find the occasional skeleton lodged within the receding swamp beds, solemn reminders of that horrible hurricane of so long ago. And although such discoveries are alarming enough, they're not nearly as frightening as what some say they see near those swamps today.

Evidently, several of the locals have seen what appeared to be a mass of people roaming through the estuaries and wilderness late at night. Though these images have always been reported as anywhere from 50 to 500 people, all hunched over and shouldered together as if coming from a battle, they seem either to disappear into the thicket or simply vanish from sight. As local legend tells us, these shadowy people were spotted again shortly before Hurricane Andrew hit Homestead, Florida, in 1992. Always staggering to the north, as if to escape the doomed Keys, these ghostly figures seem to be reliving their last hours on earth. Perhaps these dark images are the remnants of those lost in 1935, or perhaps they're nothing more than an optical illusion for those islanders prone to fancy. At any rate, these shadowy people are part of south Florida's folklore.

Afterthoughts

When ghost hunters explore an alleged haunted location or reports of the supernatural, they will research that area in order to learn as much as they possibly can. They do this to piece together the possible reasoning for the presence of ghosts. When we look at the massive loss of life as a result of the 1935 Labor Day Hurricane, the possibilities are staggering. The phantom train and the ghostly car may represent the human spirit in its endless race to save those that are doomed.

Flagler's East Coast Railway failed its mission from the start, only to end up beached and tossed by nature's strong hand. The ghostly old car, although a mystery, may represent one man's attempt to save his family or a helpless neighbor . . . what may have been a doomed rescue mission. Although only speculation, the fact that this car is seen in the wee hours, when the weather is foggy or rainy, and only on certain occasions, may point toward a "place event," which would mean that the driver died near or on that location, perhaps while passing over the bridge or making the turn to get to the bridge, causing that action to be played over and over again like a recording. Who the driver was will most likely remain one of Florida's ghostly mysteries.

The corpselike crowd of people tottering through the marshlands late at night may also represent "place event" phenomena, where a horrific event replays itself repeatedly, signifying that tragedy. Yet, many paranormal investigators feel these spirits may collectively represent a "crisislike apparition." Most apparitions seem to have some sort of purpose; the crisis apparition communicates some sort of message. Although these entities usually appear during a severe family crisis, such as a recent or impending death, the ghostly marsh-people may serve to warn others of an approaching threat, like that of 1992's Hurricane Andrew, when this collection of spirits was seen. This event also suggests "collective apparitions," referring to a collection of ghosts seen by more than one person. In addition, though no one truly knows what these apparitions represent, for those who witness them, they represent a good fright for sure.

When visiting south Florida or the Florida Keys, enjoy the sun, the beaches, and the endless vacation spots this area offers, but also remember what was lost here so many years ago. Remember the lost dreams, the homes, and the businesses. Remember the fathers and mothers, the grandparents and the children. Remember that they died here one Monday in 1935 in a thundering wave of destruction. Try to remember the more than 400 souls lost in the murky swamps near the Seven Mile Bridge. When enjoying a leisurely walk in the evening or while fishing off the banks of this gorgeous paradise, keep a keen eye open for these dragging dead. If you spot the ghostly car crossing the bridge, wish him good luck in his efforts, and hope he finds his way home. And, if you get a glimpse of the phantom train's light during a thunderstorm, or hear its screaming whistle, don't worry about getting out of its way . . . that train hasn't been on the track for seventy years!

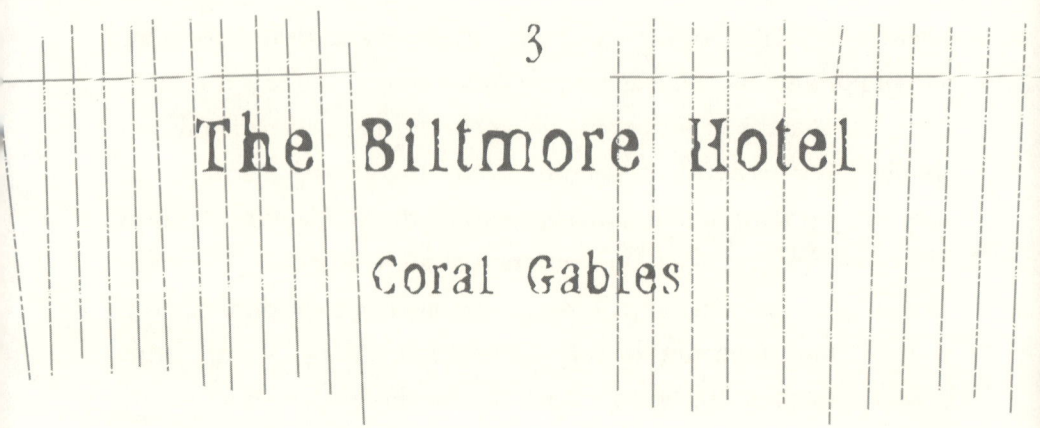

3

The Biltmore Hotel

Coral Gables

Fatty Walsh, the Ladies' Man . . . and He Still Is!

A Little History

The Biltmore Hotel is without a doubt one of the most magnificent hotels in the United States. Surrounded by beautifully landscaped boulevards, golf courses, and country clubs, and nestled amid Mediterranean-style homes, banyan trees, and tropical foliage, all on quaint, quiet streets, the Biltmore's very image is that of Florida in the grandeur of the Roaring '20s, like a scene from *The Great Gatsby*. The same designer and entrepreneur who brought Florida the city of Coral Gables and helped establish the University of Miami, land developer and tycoon George E. Merrick, joined forces with hotel magnate John McEntee Bowman in 1925. At the height of Florida's land boom, the two incisive dreamers decided to create a grand hotel, which would not only serve as the luxurious mainstay for the crowds that were relocating to Coral Gables, but would also be a center for education, sports, and fashion.

Oddly enough, construction for the Biltmore began on Friday the thirteenth, 1925, and the hotel was the signature of the south Florida

Florida State Archives

skyline from that day on. Inspired by the Giralda Tower in Seville, Spain, the Biltmore Hotel debuted in January, 1926, with a magnificent party that ushered in many Northerners on trains appropriately called "Miami Biltmore Specials." As soon as Biltmore's Giralda Tower had its lights switched on for the first time, the sound of the Charleston and the fox trot, as well as the laughter of society's elite, could be heard echoing through the quiet town of Coral Gables. It was at this moment that Florida gave birth to the legend that is the Biltmore Hotel.

The Biltmore was host to many of society's royalty, from Europe to Hollywood and all in between. Of the more notable guests were the Duke and Duchess of Windsor, the Vanderbilts, the Roosevelt family, Al Capone, Fred Astaire, Ginger Rogers, Judy Garland, and Bing Crosby, just to name a few. There were magnificent gala balls, fashion shows, and aquatic events that took place in the largest swimming pool in the United States, rightly called "The Grand Pool." And of course, what hotel of this magnitude wouldn't cater to the most extravagant weddings available? Or play host to world-class golf tournaments? All of which came nicely packaged with the popular big band and jazz groups of the day—top-notch entertainment for the world's wealthy in what was becoming known as America's Riviera Resort.

The Biltmore Hotel was able to survive the Great Depression by having the best—if not the only—aquatic sports shows in the world. People needed to take their minds off the Depression, so every Sunday afternoon the Biltmore would sponsor aquatic events like synchronized swimming, the ever-popular "bathing beauties," and even alligator wrestling! Professional swimmer and diver Jackie Ott would dive from an eighty-five-foot platform, amazing everyone. And then there was Johnny Weissmuller, the swimmer who broke a world record at the Biltmore's Grand Pool and would later become the famous actor of the 1930s Tarzan movies. All in all, thousands would come to the Biltmore, saving not only their own morale, but also the financial situation of the Biltmore. But the tide of good fortune was turning. . . .

All was going well until World War II broke out and the War Department converted the Biltmore Hotel to a military hospital. It became known as the Army Air Forces Regional Hospital, and the Biltmore was changed forever. Like a military barracks, or a navy warship, the windows were sealed up with concrete slabs, and the imported Italian marble floors were covered with a grayish, government-issue linoleum, hiding the very essence of Merrick and Bowman's dream. After the war, the beautiful Biltmore Hotel remained a hospital for Veterans Affairs, also serving as an early location for the University of Miami's School of Medicine. Hundreds are recorded to have died in the Biltmore, in addition to the lower levels being used as a morgue for the university's gross anatomy classes.

In the summer of 1973, however, the Historic Monuments Act and Legacy of Parks program granted the City of Coral Gables complete ownership and capital control of the Biltmore Hotel. But, as committees argued over the creepy eyesore that the Biltmore had become, and with the slow progress of political agencies that oversaw the future of trade and commerce, the now-looming, dark and foreboding Biltmore Hotel remained vacant and unoccupied for close to ten years. It wasn't until the fall of 1983 that city officials finally agreed to return the Biltmore Hotel to its original splendor. It took four years and close to $55 million to revitalize the hotel to her former state, and it officially opened the doors again December 31, 1987. There was a black tie affair honoring the Biltmore as it returned to the citizens of Coral Gables and reentered history as a world-class hotel. Nevertheless, the Biltmore Hotel although seemingly grateful to be reborn, appeared to have many stories to tell of the personalities who had entered her doors over the years . . . stories from beyond the edge of time and from beyond the grave!

Ghostly Legends and Haunted Folklore

The Biltmore Hotel, the jewel of Coral Gables and the pride of south Florida's hotels, has much to say indeed. As a war hospital, she held the wounded, healing some and shrouding others who would soon become the honored dead. As a VA hospital, she cared for the veterans who had fought bravely, sent to the Biltmore to fade away: the soldiers and the sailors with their depleted spirits, some gone mad from the sights of war, others forgotten by family and friends, left to themselves under the meager care of the government, alone and spiritually beaten. Then, as a hospital and morgue for medical students and future doctors, the Biltmore supposedly held the bodies of Miami's indigent and homeless dead for medical autopsy and experimentation. After that, she was abandoned and even despised by some as a blemish on their glorious city . . . forgotten, denied, and angry.

For years I have heard the stories of ghosts roaming the corridors of the Biltmore, not only today's stories, but those of the years when the hotel was abandoned. Many townspeople would stand on the adjacent golf course in the 1970s and 1980s and stare in awe at the haunted spectacle that went on inside the empty ruins. Sounds of music and crashing objects, and even eerie lights have been witnessed by hundreds of people, some who traveled many miles just to see these events take place. In fact, during the summer of 1979, Coral Gables and Miami police officers stormed the abandoned building expecting to find and arrest trespassers or drug dealers, but their raid turned up nothing.

Naturally, the police know how to stake out a location and prevent the escape of suspects for the most part, but on that early summer evening the police arrested no one . . . but where could they have gone? Some of the fourteen policemen and two detectives witnessed windows closing on the top floor, as well as the sound of glass breaking, and even figures running through the dark hallways. Outside, forty or so civilians gathered, waiting to see the big police bust, but there was nobody to arrest! The police found no one inside, and when two other patrol cars pulled up with two well-trained German shepherd police dogs, everyone thought for sure that even the most well-hidden vagrants or criminals would get caught under these circumstances. Well, both dogs came running out of that old building less than five minutes after entering, tails between their legs. Needless to say, the police bust was just that—a bust.

After refurbishing began in the 1980s, it seemed that more than just dust was being stirred up. On many occasions the nightly paranormal activities seemed to become more vibrant than before, and the floating lights or orbs and sounds of crashing coming from the blackened windows were too much for some. Some Latin- and Haitian-

American workers refused to work after dark, and some refused to go in the building altogether. Superstition or not, the Biltmore seemed slowly to come to life, little by little. As the dust settled, the new paint dried, and the new carpeting was laid, the old hotel seemed to become more and more dignified and stately. After the Biltmore opened her doors, the hotel's paranormal events didn't go away; they too became dignified, just as dignified as the many well-mannered, well-dressed people who have entered the Biltmore's grand entrance over the years.

The Biltmore Hotel seems to have a few ghosts within her stately halls—even hundreds, according to the psychics who have stayed there. Out of all these spirits, however, there are several in particular that are among the most vibrant residing at the Biltmore, ghosts that will almost always let you know they're right next to you. There is a lady in white who lingers in some of the guest rooms and is sometimes seen racing toward the balcony where she fell to her death many years ago. Then there are the playful spirits who constantly turn the lights on and off and are responsible for the sounds of doors opening and closing in the halls late at night. And then there's the granddaddy of all the ghosts there, Thomas "Fatty" Walsh: businessman, casino owner, and, oh yes, let us not forget that he was a gangster as well.

The lady in white, although sounding a little cliché, is based on a factual incident that took place in the late 1940s. The Biltmore has many ornate balconies on either side of the building, and to a young child, these may look like an inviting adventure indeed. According to the Biltmore's oral traditions, a family was staying on one of the upper levels, either the fifth or sixth floor. This family had a small boy around the age of six who, like most boys that age, wanted to have fun and climb on anything in sight, and the Biltmore's balcony's looked like a lot of fun. When his mother came to the doorway of her suite and saw her child standing on the railing of the balcony, struggling to balance, she naturally feared that the child would fall and sprinted toward him. Although she managed to grab the boy by his pant leg and pull him toward her, she was not as agile when it came to maintaining her own safety. As she turned in an instinctive response to make sure her child was safe, her momentum slammed her against the wall of the balcony and flung her backward over the edge. She fell the great distance to her death. Her child was left looking over the balcony, crying in horror at the sight of his mother's lifeless body below. Without doubt, this was one of the saddest incidents in the hotel's history.

Many parapsychologists feel that at the moment of the mother's tragic death, her mind and all of her emotions were focused on saving her child. Because she never truly knew that her little boy was safe before she died, even in death her concern and instincts repeat themselves. The woman's actions are what many parapsychologists refer to as a "residual haunting." In this case, the woman now known as the lady in white (most likely because that was what she was wearing the day she died) is seen running toward that very same balcony in hopes of saving her child. The lady in white makes no noise, but she has been seen with arms outstretched, her eyes and mouth agape in a stare of pure fear. The apparition is also seen walking through guestrooms from time to time, and it is not uncommon for the front desk to receive calls in the middle of the night concerning a strange woman walking through the hotel's bedrooms. Sometimes, a pale woman is seen sitting at the end of a guest's bed, only to vanish when that shaken guest turns on the light. Every report describes the woman as extremely sad and piteous. Although the hotel's staff is hesitant to divulge the name of this unfortunate accident victim, her identity can be found in the hotel's registry. If you should happen to see this tormented spirit, there is no need to be frightened; just remember what she sacrificed in life and the lonely vigil she now keeps in death.

The most notable ghost at the Biltmore Hotel is without a doubt that of Thomas "Fatty" Walsh. In the 1920s and early 1930s, Fatty Walsh was south Florida's equivalent to a big-time Chicago gangster. He was known by every bootlegger and crime boss that ever came to Florida, not to mention movie stars, sports stars, legitimate businessmen, and even the chief of police. Fatty ran an illegal—and quite profitable—speakeasy and casino on the thirteenth floor and was the talk of the town. Unfortunately, when a man runs a business like that, he not only makes friends, he also makes enemies, and the kind of enemies Fatty made were deadly.

No one seems exactly sure what went on the night Fatty was murdered, but it is suspected that it may have been a hired hit from a rival gangster. Another theory is that a sore loser at the gambling tables lost his cool and wanted revenge. In Fatty's business, you can make a lot of money or lose a lot of money, and in his casino, when you lost a game at his crap tables, you lost the game. But, someone didn't like those rules, got angry, and shot Fatty in the head, right there in front of about a hundred people . . . or so the legend goes.

Fatty Walsh was a ladies' man for sure. If you saw Fatty at the delicatessen, he would always have a beautiful woman next to him. While working the thirteenth-floor casino, he might have a gaggle of girls around him at one time. The man had only a few necessities in life: fine Cuban cigars, good liquor, and gorgeous women. His lusts for life and the finer things that go with it were always a concern for Fatty, as even in death, his spirit, although a little unnerving, is still largely friendly, especially if you're a woman. Because gambling and drinking were illegal, Fatty's murder was brushed under the table rather quickly, perhaps because there may have been people of political importance present, drinking and gambling. That certainly would not look good if the G-men were to investigate. So, after Fatty's murder, the body was removed and the casino closed and cleaned, just in case someone squealed. . . . But Fatty didn't want to leave!

To this very day, if you happen to be a young woman, preferably a pretty, young woman, the chances are good that you will meet Fatty Walsh yourself. The most common reaction Fatty has toward a young woman is to invite her to his casino. How does he do this? you might ask. Well, if you're getting into the elevator to go to your room for the evening and your room is on the fourth floor, the elevator might just pass the fourth floor and take you right up to the thirteenth floor, even if the thirteenth floor is key-coded for special guests. On many occasions, people go exploring the hotel, as one couple in particular did one late afternoon. Apparently, when they got in the elevator, pondering where to go first, the doors shut and the elevator automatically started going up, the numbered floor lights counting as it went upward until it finally stopped at the thirteenth-floor suite. The door opened and stayed open, the couple looking at each other in confusion as they waited for the door to shut. But the doors remained open for what seemed to be several minutes. They looked around to see if there were people there, but it was quite dark, just traces of the afternoon sunset shining in. So they decided that because no one was staying in the suite, they could venture in to take a look. As the young lady stepped out of the elevator, the doors shut quickly behind her, before her husband could step out. The elevator, now going down, passed every floor even while the husband was pushing the buttons to stop, and it took him right to the lobby. The elevator's overhead lights flickered on and off.

Now completely frightened, the man pushed the buttons to go up, but the elevator just sat there. So, he quickly ran out and told the bellhop, who used his special key to take the elevator to the thirteenth-floor suite. The two of them went up to find the man's wife standing at the elevator doors with a confused and frightened expression. As she got on the elevator and held her husband while descending to the lobby, the bellhop asked them how they got to the thirteenth floor without a key card. The husband replied that the elevator just took them there. When asked what had happened in the suite, the lady told them that it was very cold inside, and that she kept smelling cigar smoke.

After walking around and calling out "hello" to see if anyone was there, every once in a while she would hear the sound of small objects hitting the floor, and ever so faintly, she heard the sounds of people talking. Sometimes, she would hear what sounded like laughing in the distance, as if muffled, and she felt as though someone was always behind her, which made her to swing around from time to time to see if anyone was there. She said that the thing she remembered the most was the smell of cigar smoke, which she hated with a passion.

The three of them arrived at the lobby safely, but the bellhop only further shocked the couple when he told them about Thomas "Fatty" Walsh's murder and the thirteenth-floor casino. Needless to say, the couple decided to keep their exploring to the nearby malls and shops for the remainder of their stay.

The thirteenth floor is no longer a gambling casino or a speakeasy with homemade gin, although you're certainly free to gamble and drink there if you like, as it is still a very posh and expensive suite. Movie stars and rock stars stay there when they're in south Florida, and the occasional president has stayed there, too. Yet, social or political importance will make little difference if Fatty doesn't like you. One of the employees I spoke with told me of the time President Clinton was staying at the Biltmore. Finally the president had to leave the beautiful suite because no matter what he did, he just couldn't get reception on the television. There was a big football game on, one that he was anticipating. Of course, with the lousy reception he was said to be getting a bit angry, which in turn only got Fatty mad, and the gangster's spirit began turning off the TV every chance he got. Well, as the story goes, the Secret Service men looked at it, then the hotel's engineers looked at it, but they found nothing wrong with the television. It simply turned off as soon as the president sat down to watch the game. Maybe Fatty was just having a little fun with President Clinton, or maybe he didn't like his politics, but whichever is the case, the president is said to have stormed off, going to a friend's house to finish the game.

There are many accounts of lights turning on without the flick of a switch, which points to an electromagnetic charge, sometimes the distinct scent of ozone following the flickering light. Doors will sometimes mysteriously open and close right in front of guests and staff. These events are associated with Fatty and his playful antics. Although these aforementioned entities are the primary personalities seen and felt at the Biltmore, almost every psychic who has entered the hotel has reported a plethora of spirits within. Some well-noted psychics believe that the Biltmore's spiritual activity relates to its having seen so much grief in the past—most notably the cadavers that were once stored there for the medical school. Many of the vagrants and homeless died in a bad way, or were prone to living illegal or immoral lives, which carried on in death. The one thing that's for certain is that the Biltmore has a spirit all its own, whether created through the pride and glory of yesteryear or through the extravagant personalities that lived there. Either way, the Biltmore will remain one of Florida's top haunts.

Afterthoughts

If there's one place you absolutely must see while on your ghost hunt in south Florida, it's the Biltmore Hotel. Even if you can't stay the night, or if you can't afford the thirteenth-floor suite, go there for an up-close look into Florida's past. The Biltmore will remain one of my favorite haunted places just because of her grand spirit . . . or should I say "spirits"? When we look at the past this hotel has experienced, the good and the bad, one might even think that the building has a sentience to it. Tales like the lady in a white who fell off the tower balcony to save her child, and the phone calls from hotel guests complaining about a woman in white in their room, are particularly frightening circumstances indeed. And the legend of the Biltmore Hotel's most famous ghost, Thomas "Fatty" Walsh, the womanizing gangster who ran an illicit, thirteenth-floor casino in the 1920s, seems to indicate a building with a life all its own. . . . That's the Biltmore!

The Biltmore Hotel even has a resident storyteller and folklorist to entertain and educate guests and visitors. There is a meeting every Thursday night at 7 P.M. You will hear ghost stories of the hotel's illustrious spiritual personalities as well as other lesser-known Biltmore anecdotes. For more information on the Biltmore Hotel call 561-964-1234. And remember, the next time you take an elevator ride, you might not be alone.

4

Flight 401

Florida Everglades

Moans from a Swampy Graveyard

—*Well ah, tower, this is Eastern, ah, 401. It looks like we're gonna have to circle, we don't have a light on our nose gear yet.*
—*Eastern 401 heavy, roger, pull up, climb straight ahead to two thousand, go back to approach control, one twenty eight six.*
—*Twenty-two degrees . . .*
—*What? We're still at two thousand right? Hey what's happening here? Tower...Impact!*
Silence.
          —*Flight 401 Recorder, 11:34, December 29, 1972*

A Little History

Any person interested in ghosts and stories of the supernatural will most likely remember the famous plane crash of Eastern flight 401 and the amazing string of events that followed. It is without doubt one of the most frightening—and inspiring— stories to date. Tales of a benevolent spirit helping crews of other planes from crashing are certainly happy tales indeed; yet other legends of sad cries and moans and the eerie visions of faces in the murky waters where flight 401 crashed are tales of another type.

It was early in December of 1972 when a stewardess with Eastern Airlines had a series of what she believed to be psychic premonitions. She was having nightmares about a plane crashing, and she continuously heard sobbing and crying echoing in her head. The dreams were so vivid that she knew that this event was going to happen soon, and she began telling her friends and colleagues of her fears. Apprehensive, she told them that a Lockheed Tri-Star jet would be approaching the Miami International Airport and crash, killing everyone. The only part of her psychic dream that didn't make sense to her was that the passengers were fading away in what appeared to be "dark water," with hands stretched outward, then disappearing forever with muffled screams and crying echoing in the distance.

The disaster would happen around Christmas, she believed, because she kept visualizing holly wreaths and Christmas trees, in flashes. Strangely, on December 29, a last-minute change in crew schedules had the stewardess and some of her colleagues assigned to work on flight 401 from New York to Miami, and all but three would decline the assignment. The stewardess went home that evening, choosing not to work that night at all, hoping her dream was nothing more than that—a dream. Sadly, however, the events came to pass late that night. The stewardess received a phone call from a friend that flight 401 had crashed in the Florida Everglades near Miami, killing most of the passengers and the entire flight crew. Veteran Flight Captain Robert Loft and Second Officer Don Repo were among the ill-fated crew that night, both friends of the now-distraught stewardess. It was a night she will never forget.

After a close study of the black box flight recorder, investigators surmised that during flight 401's approach to Miami International Airport, Captain Loft noticed that some of the landing gear lights were not illuminated as they should have been. Captain Loft instructed his first officer, Al Stockstill, to check the gear and related equipment to see if maybe the lights were malfunctioning. After doing so, the officer informed the captain that the nose gear was not responding at all, either through the secondary panel control or by manual control. The captain radioed the MIA control tower and informed them of the situation. The control tower instructed flight 401 first to recheck the landing gear and the circuitry to make sure it was not sticking, then to ascend to 2,000 feet and swing back around for the final approach. Second Officer Don Repo was troubleshooting the circuitry box to see if the lights were nothing more than defective bulbs . . . no such luck. Captain Loft then instructed his first officer to engage the auto-pilot, while the control tower at MIA instructed 401 to check in the avionics bay to see if the position of the nose gear was correct and then troubleshoot the situation from there. After a while, the engineer reported that he noticed the aircraft's altitude had somehow decreased, and that they were not at 2,000 feet like they thought. The altimeter light on the main panel was on, the auto-pilot light was still engaged; yet their craft was descending . . . but how?

It was around 11:30 P.M. when the flight recorder offered these final chilling words: "What? We're still at two thousand right . . . Hey what's happening here? Tower . . . Impact!" Flight 401 was gone.

After a thorough investigation, the FAA subsequently determined that flight 401 was flying blind, and that due to instrument failure, the crew had no way of knowing their true altitude, or the horizon of their flight, meaning they had no way of knowing if they were flying level or not. The plane's right wing impacted the water of the Everglades while making its second approach, breaking the aircraft into several pieces and killing ninety-eight people in the process.

There were a few survivors found lingering in the swamps among the wreckage, and the legends would grow seemingly overnight. The crash was finally determined to be a mechanical fault, so the airline hoped to clean up the mess as best they could and move on with business as usual . . . but that wasn't to be. The remains of flight 401, the undamaged parts of the aircraft such as gears and engine parts, were recycled—either melted down or actually cleaned up as they were and used as parts for other Eastern planes. Saving money was especially important at that time and recycling was a necessary part of business. However, according to the oral traditions of Eastern's employees, their passengers, and even the airboat tour guides who show tourists the crash site, the recycling of these parts from flight 401 may have been beneficial, but it was also frightening from a supernatural point of view.

Ghostly Legends and Haunted Folklore

Since the crash of flight 401 in 1972, there have been a number of strange events directly related to the airplane, its crew and passengers. Perhaps the way they died had somehow made the spirits earthbound; perhaps the good nature of the crew lives on even in death in order to safeguard future flights from crashes. Whichever the case, the one thing that is for sure is that the refitting of 401's remains in other aircraft seems to be related to the strange events that soon followed.

Captain Robert "Bob" Loft was a jovial man in life. He was a hard worker and most of all, he enjoyed his work, and everyone knew it: colleagues and passengers alike. Having worked for Eastern for many years, and having been a seasoned pilot for years before that, gave him a standard of excellence that naturally stood out. Don Repo was also a man of distinction; years of service and devotion made him the best choice in his profession, and everyone knew it. The loss of these experienced men was difficult for everyone at Eastern Airlines, yet it seems that the particular love and devotion the crew had shown in life continued to be seen, felt, and heard after their deaths. Of course the crash was terrible, but life goes on, and no one gave it much thought

when 401's parts were scheduled to be recycled for use on other aircraft. It seemed like the logical thing to do, as recycling would save
money for the airlines, and it was considered a sign of reverence to
have 401's parts bestowed on one of her sister planes. This is when the
strangeness began.

One of the first ghostly events to take place was when a vice president with Eastern Airlines was enjoying one of his employment perks
and taking a well-deserved vacation. Apparently, this gentleman
boarded a Tri-Star Jetliner, a plane identical to that of flight 401 and
with several of the aforementioned recycled parts recently installed. As
the story goes, the VP was sitting in the first class section, traveling
from John F. Kennedy Airport in New York to Miami International
Airport, when he noticed one of Eastern's pilots sitting next to him,
his eyes apparently affixed on something outside the window. This is
not uncommon, as many airline personnel get free flights. Thinking
the pilot was on his way home, the VP decided to initiate a polite conversation, but the pilot didn't seem to want to talk, he just continued
to stare out the window. After a moment, the pilot slowly turned his
head toward the VP and stared at him with a sad, pale face. The VP
later said that he got the feeling one gets when discovering a dead
body or seeing a ghost. Well, that was it exactly, and at the very
moment the VP recognized the pilot as the late Captain Robert Loft,
the ghostly vision dissolved right before the man's eyes, as if no one
was ever there! The VP, needless to say, jumped out of his seat, mouth
gaping, and stared at the now-empty seat. The commotion alerted the
stewardess, and she came over to see what was wrong. With a moment
of hesitation, the VP told the stewardess what he had seen—the ghost
of Captain Loft!

This incident took place within months of the crash of flight 401
and marks the first of many such incidents. Captain Loft has made his
appearance on several other occasions, such as the time he had a con-

versation with crew members about flight safety and possible problems. The ghost covered problems that might take place if the crew didn't follow his advice on safety issues. After the spectral safety tips, the benevolent spirit once again vanished into thin air, raising the hair on the necks of the flight staff. This event led them to cancel their scheduled flight the next day. The reports of such visions would continue with various Eastern personnel and their patrons seemingly on a daily basis.

Although Captain Loft was the first to make visitations on the living, Don Repo later made his debut on an L-1011, flight 318, also making startling revelations from beyond the grave. A lady traveling to Miami thought she was sitting next to any old employee with Eastern Airlines. This gentleman, she thought, looked extremely pale and sickly, and she asked if he was all right. But the man just stared ahead, refusing to answer or acknowledge her in any way. So, the lady pushed the button to call a stewardess, who arrived in time to watch as the man completely disappeared right before their eyes.

It's not too hard to understand why the woman soon asked to find another seat, remaining stunned and relatively quiet for the remainder of her flight. When they landed, the stewardess was understandably curious about what she had seen, yet was pleased that she wasn't the only one to have experienced the apparition. She felt she had to do some investigating. So, she asked the passenger if she would look at some old photographs while at the airport. The lady agreed and followed the stewardess back to a lounge, where the two of them went through various photograph albums and pictures of Eastern Airline employees of the past and present. When they reached the photographs of Eastern's officers and engineers, the passenger recognized the mysterious man in the seat next to her as Second Officer Don Repo. It's not hard to imagine why they both got chills when they read the inscription, "In Memorial. Flight #401, Dec. 29th, 1972."

On one occasion, on a flight from New York to Mexico City, Mexico, a stewardess was preparing meals in the galley, when suddenly, while bending over to take the dinners out of the oven, she saw a man's head eerily illuminated inside, his eyes looking upward directly at the stewardess. Immediately, she jumped back away from the oven in shock. Again, she later recognized the face as that of the ill-fated Don Repo. On the same flight, two other stewardesses and an engineer saw the apparition of Don Repo and even heard him warn them to "watch out for fire on this plane." And sure enough, during the take-off on another flight the plane's engines malfunctioned, shooting out sparks and smoke, forcing the plane to return to the airport. If the problems had gone unnoticed, the plane would have certainly crashed.

On one final occasion, in his usual helpful manner, the ghost of Don Repo is said to have given one last statement to the captain of another Tri-Star Jetliner: "There will never be another crash on a Tri-Star. We will not let that happen." Without a doubt, this is the best thing the ghost of a dead aviator could ever tell a living aviator. Although this is believed to be the last reported sighting of flight 401's crew, many believe these guardian spirits still oversee the safety of others on Tri-Star planes.

There are other witnesses, however, that believe the other victims of flight 401, the passengers, are not so pleased in their resting place—the black, alligator-infested waters of the Everglades.

The Florida Everglades are an ancient and beautiful part of the Sunshine State. The wildlife and the wide-open spaces seem to call out for adventures, and this is particularly true for the airboaters who love to spend their weekends racing through the Everglades as fast as they can. Some have made a profitable business from airboating and have opened their own adventure tours to natives and visitors alike. On these two-hour trips, the airboat captains will show you all of Florida's natural wonders: wrecks of old boats, alligators galore—some the size of small cars—and oh yes, the faces of the dead . . . well, if you're lucky—or maybe not so lucky.

It all began around February 1972, while clean-up crews were still searching for human remains, as well as picking up any wreckage of flight 401 that may still have been lying around. Many of the retrievers would work late at night, with large searchlights shining down on the water, in hopes of quickening their work. From time to time, these investigators would hear what they thought were moans coming from the swampy marsh all around them. It would be hard to believe that anyone could survive after so long, especially with the alligators, but they looked anyway. Some of the clean-up crew would point their spotlights around the water, hoping to find an explanation for the sounds of whimpering and sobbing, but all they found was empty water.

Again, during another night of wreckage removal, the sounds of moans were heard from a large glade of grass and weeds growing out of the water. This time, however, when one of the crewman guided his small boat over to the area where the sounds were coming from, he found more than he bargained for. When he looked into the dark waters, he saw a most horrific sight: The bleach-white face of a man, his blank eye sockets staring up at him and his mouth opening and closing as if trying to scream! Well, it's not surprising when the crewman lunged back into his boat, screaming to the others, "I Found Someone! I Found Someone!" Quickly the other crew flocked over to the stunned and confused crewman to see what he had found. When they arrived there was nothing. No survivor . . . no body . . . nothing.

Reports of moaning seemed to be commonplace for the wreckage crew, and more and more of these ghastly faces were being seen in the water, sadly peering out. To this day, when airboat captains take passengers on night tours to this part of the Everglades, you can expect to hear a ghost story or two about the phantom faces beneath the waters and the moans in the night from the crew and passengers of flight 401. On occasion, the airboat passengers will hear and see these things for themselves, which only adds to the legend of the haunted Everglades. When we think of the agony the crew and passengers of flight 401 endured: the sheer horror of crashing into the black waters, and then to drown or be eaten by the alligators in the pitch-blackness of the Everglades night, as many did. . . . It is almost too terrible to consider.

Most of them died screaming, or slowly moaning until they could moan no more and their very spirits, tormented as they were, seem to continue to this day. So, if you're planning a trip to the Miami area for a vacation, or if you live nearby, schedule a night tour on one of south Florida's airboat rides. Ask the captain if he will take you to the spot where flight 401 crashed, and ask him if he's ever heard strange things about that place. Don't be surprised if he turns to you and tells you some of his own experiences about the haunted swamps and the ghosts of Eastern flight 401.

Afterthoughts

When we turn on the television and learn of a plane crash and all the lives that were lost, we cannot help but feel for the victims. We may wonder why this had to happen, or how it must have felt to die like that. We may not even think twice when boarding an airliner today, or seriously think of just how quickly our lives might end. Captain Loft, his crew, and passengers all thought they would make it back to the airport with few problems, transfer to another plane, and complete their mission, then go home or to a hotel and get some well-deserved sleep. But, that didn't happen. Some were lucky and died in the flash of an instant, while others lingered for days; others were to become food for the swamp life. They were planning their futures, but none of them were planning for that night.

The apparitions that have been experienced on Tri-Star jets over the years have played an important part for the living, as only their compassion was seen and heard by the witnesses, albeit, in a frightening manner indeed. And although Captain Loft and Second Officer Repo have made fewer visits to the passengers and crew of other airliners lately, there still are those who claim to have witnessed strange things. Sometimes, in the dead of night, the misty form of a man fitting the description of flight 401's captain is seen walking down the silent corridors of the Miami International Airport where the old Eastern Airline ticket counters once stood, then fading into what was once Eastern's concourse. Although Eastern Airlines closed its doors several years after the crash of flight 401, the crew and passengers seem to linger. Whether through the moaning in the darkness of the Florida Everglades and the occasional glimpse of a haunted face peering through the dark waters, or through the kind warnings of a phantom crew, the legend of flight 401 lives on.

Incidentally, I had the opportunity to speak with a former airline mechanic who worked on many Eastern planes. He told me that after Eastern folded up, their planes and all the parts were sold off to other airline companies, and he himself had worked with the old remains of the plane from flight 401. He claimed that he never felt easy working with the salvaged remains, as they were associated with so much tragedy, yet business is business, and spare parts are spare parts, regardless of his personal feelings. Strangely enough, his partner worked with a rescue team on another Everglades crash, which took place a few years ago; the plane, he says, was on a similar flight pattern with similar problems as those of flight 401.

It was the DC-9 ValuJet, flight 592 carrying 109 people from Miami to Atlanta, that plunged into the Everglades shortly after its takeoff one Saturday afternoon in May of 1996. It is believed that flight 592 experienced equipment malfunctions in the cockpit, which started to spew out smoke. The problems were much like those of the ill-fated flight 401. The communications between the tower and the plane were cut short by an eerie thud and then silence, but unlike the 401 crash, flight 592 completely disappeared into the dark, murky waters of the Everglade swamps, never to be found. Although both crashes, and the great loss of life, are officially believed to have been caused by faulty equipment and human error—roughly $12 in light bulbs for flight 401 and improperly marked oxygen canisters for flight 592—many that feel that these disasters were caused by the Florida Everglades itself. Perhaps these similar accidents are nothing more than coincidences, or perhaps they were caused by the mysterious swamps, already enchanted and cursed as many Native Americans have long believed them to be. Either way, this mystery certainly gives us something to think about the next time we board a plane that will pass over the dark, haunted swamps of the Florida Everglades.

5
Art Institute of Fort Lauderdale

Fort Lauderdale

The Ghosts of Sunrise Hall

A Little History

The subject of the Art Institute of Fort Lauderdale is especially close to me, because I graduated there in 1986 with an Associates Degree in commercial art and graphic design. Although I was later to devote my life to the research and practice of psychology and mental health (with a unique combination of art and therapy), I am grateful to the Art Institute for the special training I received there. I am also thankful for the introduction to artistic philosophy and art survey, which I now combine with many of my therapeutic approaches.

Back when I attended school there, in the early 1980s, the Art Institute was located in a portion of the Holiday Inn on Las Olas Boulevard off route A1A, but it relocated to 17th Street by my final year. Today, the Art Institute is as advanced an art- and technology-based school as one could possibly desire.

As the Art Institute matured and the number of students grew, the need for student housing became clear. Although many of the students secured their own living arrangements when they came to Fort Lauderdale, the Art Institute decided to set up a dormitory program

43

and co-leased an apartment complex off Sunrise Boulevard—"Sunrise Hall." The history of this building, however, has been subject to some conjecture over the years, as it holds a somewhat sinister past. Although stories differ from person to person, Sunrise Hall has a definite background in ghostly legend.

Apparently, as far back as the 1930s, eerie legends and ghostly folklore surrounded a wood-plank, three-story home that once stood in the exact place where the Sunrise Hall apartment complex now stands. The original home—which was, in truth, a brothel—was popular with much of Fort Lauderdale's seedier residents. With rumors of illegal gambling, drug dealing, and prostitution, this location was widely regarded as a den of filth. As with any rumor, however, finding the truth might be difficult at best, but with a little tenacity and a little more patience, I was able to uncover a few facts. The original building was a three-story wooden structure with surrounding balconies. In the late 1920s, it was officially used as a boarding house for travelers and wayfarers. Then it evolved into an apartment complex for nearby dockworkers and laborers.

During the Great Depression, it became a rundown, dilapidated dump for the city's down and out, a flophouse for the unfortunate. From the 1940s to the 1960s, the building, as well as its inhabitants, took on a less-than-pure persona. I had the opportunity to interview long-time residents of the Ft. Lauderdale area, and I was able to dig up a few interesting pieces of information, notwithstanding inconsistencies. Then again, there are some of these stories that don't differ much from teller to teller.

During the 1960s, the building's situation was so bad that the police visited at least once a day. Drug dealing and prostitution were the biggest complaints, although murder happened, too. According to one gentleman, there were several homicides in the old building—mostly prostitutes who were killed by the men they picked up or by pimps who demanding money. From drug overdoses to murder to the occasional suicide, many deaths took place there.

The old, tattered building sat as an eyesore to anyone who still remembered the class and charm Fort Lauderdale once had. Those in law enforcement, too, could only have wished to see this problematic building and its patrons just go away. Little did they know that they would get their wish. In the 1960s, late one evening, a fire broke out on the second floor, igniting the complex and burning most of it to the ground. Although some say that several people died in the blaze, I have found no evidence to support this belief. The old brothel was no more, save a small shed that sat in the nearby woods.

In the 1970s a small, apartment-style hotel was built on the spot where the old brothel once stood. Even though the neighborhood still left something to be desired, the hotel itself was pleasant enough: two stories, with quaint but accommodating apartments and a pool, close to downtown and the beaches. Information about the little hotel is sparse, but it had steady business over the years. Although guests usually didn't stay for more than a weekend, local legend tells us that many were never entirely happy with their stay. Some would complain of noises—sometimes people's screams—in the night, giving the fair city of Ft. Lauderdale a less-than-desirable appearance in the eyes of its visitors. It was not until many years later that Ft. Lauderdale regained its more pristine look and feel, when city officials and law enforcement took back their city from the aforementioned seedy elements and rebuilt Ft. Lauderdale to its former glory.

Unfortunately, though you may modify an old building from decay, or fancy up the landscape around a once-infamous location, it doesn't mean that location will be fresh and new. No, many psychical researchers believe that the spiritual residue of a place's past may indeed still linger there, despite physical improvements. The impressions of evil people may be left behind after their death. Some locations and places will not clean up, nor will evil histories just go away with a new building and a fresh coat of paint. The Art Institute of Ft. Lauderdale's Sunrise Hall is said to be such a place . . . a place where bad memories dwell.

Ghostly Legends and Haunted Folklore

The Sunrise Hall Dormitory is one of those places that will usually go unnoticed by the psychical researcher. Even unconventional ghost hunters and the paranormal investigation subculture overlook places like Sunrise Hall, and so it remains a mystery to all but a few diehard researchers. Because the dorms here are the private property of the Art Institute of Ft. Lauderdale, one cannot freely walk around in search of ghosts. Yet in my journey, I found many of the students to be very open-minded about their living quarters and their experiences.

Over at least the past five years, and most likely many more before that, this building and the area around it has had a strange reputation. Apparently, there have been numerous stories of strange sounds and displaced noises on the second and third floors of the dormitory, as well as reports of ghostly figures walking the halls late at night. One of the most frequently reported events at Sunrise Hall is the sound of someone moaning. These pitiful voices are always heard originating from the third floor, and almost always around 1:00 A.M. The moaning lingers for a few moments, as if the source of the noises is very close to the floor, somewhat muffled. Then, the moans begin to wane, drifting off to silence. As soon as things appear to return to normal, the moans begin again, erupting into crying and sobs, then abruptly stopping altogether . . . at least for the night. When students go to the third floor to investigate, they will find no source for the moaning, or any sign of trouble that would result in such lamentations. When they ask one of the student's living on the third floor, that student is likely to tell the intrepid investigators that he has heard nothing at all.

On nights when the moon is dark, in the wee hours of the morning, some students on both the first and second floors will report of hearing the sounds of metal objects, like tools or pipes being dropped. These objects seem to bounce a few times, roll across the floor, and then stop. Again, some of the students, understandably annoyed, will try to find out what's going on, only to walk away with no answers.

As if this weren't peculiar enough, residents sometimes hear the echoes of someone's high heel shoes clicking across the floor around 3:00 A.M. These ghostly footfalls begin as if someone is going to the door to leave, then silence. After a few moments the footfalls return, only now they sound as if someone is running for dear life, always running away from the door, to the interior of the room. Then, as quickly as it began, the footfalls stop. Such an occurrence should be enough to enrage any student trying to get a little sleep, and indeed, it's understandable that a few students might seriously consider living off campus. Yet these audible events are the lesser of the paranormal annoyances at Sunrise Hall.

Odd noises are one thing—pipes rolling across the floor in the middle of the night or the sound of shoes tapping across your ceiling is certainly unnerving—but these events are more annoying than scary. However, when a student actually sees an image through his or her window in the dead of night, well, that's another story entirely. On rare occasions, while a student is in bed for the night, he or she may be treated to a strange sight. Legend tells us that while students lie in bed with the drapes drawn, the outside lights cast shadows on the window when someone walks by. Sometimes, a shadow will stop in its tracks and appear to be looking at the student's window, as if trying to peer in. This may annoy some, but others naturally get a little frightened.

Upon seeing this, some students turn on their bed stand light, then turn it off again to alert the intruder outside their room. Most of the time this tactic seems to work, but sometimes the ghostly shadow just remains, unmoving and twice as scary for its determination. Sometimes, the student will rush to the door and open it quickly, preparing to confront the person outside. Strangely enough, when the door is opened, the student finds nothing but a vacant walkway; no person . . . not a soul.

Although events like this are rare, these stories have become legendary in some groups of students in the school, and they're now fixed within the annals of the ghost hunter subculture. Whether or not these events actually take place at the Art Institute is difficult to prove. And though no staff member has ever made such a claim of there being a haunting in the dorms, one student, who wishes to remain anonymous, was very open about her strange experience.

It was just before spring break a year ago when this young woman was one of only a few students still in the dormitory; most had already left for the holiday. She was still working diligently on her portfolio, preparing for her future as a production artist, but she decided to go to bed early with a cup of hot tea and a book. Her room was dark, aside from a small light attached to her head board. She sat propped by her pillows, now engrossed in her mystery novel. As she was reading, she noticed a shadow walking past her window. She paid no attention to it, thinking it was one of the other students still staying in the dorms. Then, the shadow walked past the window again, going in the same direction as before, but the young woman simply dismissed the event. A moment following that, the same thing happened. By this time, she was beginning to think it was a joke . . . she was wrong.

As the she got up to turn on the lights and open the door at the same time, hoping to startle the prankster outside, she half-expected the shadow to belong to a friend of hers, a known joker on campus. Instead, she only found a vacant walkway and a brisk wind blowing paper around the empty parking lot below. Because the dorms were almost empty as well, she began to feel threatened, as if someone outside knew she was alone in her room. She forgot her novel for the night.

After she locked her door, and turned on a closet light for an added feeling of security, she got into bed and prepared to finish her tea. This time, she would watch television for a while and hope to get to sleep. It wasn't long after settling down again that the elusive shadow walked by the window again, this time very slowly. Before it reached the other side of the window, the shadow stopped and became larger, as if whoever it was outside was trying to look inside. Understandably frightened, the student sat up, muted the TV, and grabbed her cell phone. She called another student on the other end of the building and asked him to walk over to her room. The boy listened to her scary experiences and agreed to come right over. Within a few seconds, the young man arrived.

Meanwhile, the girl watched the shadow slowly dissolve until it was barely noticeable. Soon following, her friend knocked and called out to her. The girl leaped up and opened the door to her friend who was noticeably confused. When she looked outside, again the hallway was empty. She asked her friend if he had seen anyone, but he swore that the hallway was completely vacant. Absolutely no one was there.

This student went on to tell me that she never had an experience like that again, and that she kept the experience to herself until she heard a similar story from another student later that year. Needless to say, she believes in ghosts today.

Afterthoughts

It is difficult to say for sure what is going on in the Sunrise Hall Dormitory. Are these events the psychic residue from the brothel of so long ago, or are they just the active imaginations of artists? We know that the original structure was a house of ill repute, and that many crimes took place there. But that structure was destroyed years ago, burned right down to the ground. How could a mere location be haunted without some kind of permanent edifice like a house or cemetery? Although this particular question has sparked much controversy in the realm of psychical research over the past one hundred years or so, there are only a few theories to explain the issue.

One of the most accepted theories is that a place—for instance, the old boarding house that once stood where Sunrise Hall now stands—was once occupied by evil people brimming with evil intentions, and so the place retains these experiences regardless of physical manifestation. People were raped there, and people were murdered there. Crime was a way of life at this location, right up until it burned to the ground. There are few records to tell us what happened in the years following the fire—

if customers at the small hotel were disrupted by paranormal phenomena or just the seedy neighborhood—but even today, Sunrise Hall dormitory does indeed seem to be haunted.

Perhaps the moaning that is faintly heard late at night is left over from a victim of long ago. Perhaps the clicking of the high heel shoes is from a prostitute who couldn't escape the wrath of her killer. What about the unnerving shadows that seem to play tricks on lonely students in the night? Are they the restless dead, too? Many think so. Whether or not the Sunrise Hall Dormitory is haunted must be left up to the students living there, as those not enrolled at the Art Institute will not be allowed to find out firsthand. We will have to rely on the tidbits of ghostly legends and haunted folklore that this school will offer us. One thing is for sure, however: there is at least one student who strongly feels that this dormitory is haunted by someone, or something.

6

Cap's Place
Island Restaurant

Lighthouse Point

Phantom Smoke and Dark Shapes

A Little History

Having grown up in south Florida, and having lived in Hollywood Beach and Lighthouse Point in particular, I have only fond memories of my childhood. I can recall many singularities about my youth, and one of those unique memories is Cap's Place Island Restaurant. For me, it was more an adventure than a restaurant, as taking a water taxi motorboat and running around the island were so much fun for me. Such adventures would be enjoyable for any eight-year-old boy, but it wasn't until I was much older that I learned to enjoy the finer things this rustic restaurant has to offer.

The restaurant and bar are located in separate wooden shacks, both resting on stilts, and they look as if they're right out of an old Hollywood film. The restaurant even slants to one side as if on a seaborne ship. Indeed, when I first walked in I expected to see Humphrey Bogart or Indiana Jones having a drink at the bar, as the atmosphere is truly reminiscent of a 1940s lounge. Cap's Place will always have a special meaning for me, as I'm sure it will for you, too.

Cap's Place is possibly the best-kept secret in south Florida. It has

been visited by presidents, prime ministers, celebrities, and sports stars for at least 75 years, and it remains popular today. It's listed as a historical site with the National Register of Historic Places and is one of Broward County's oldest eating and drinking establishments, dating back to the early 1920s. It was also one of the first bootlegging and gambling hideouts of old Florida, which was truly a hidden paradise back then. Even though the restaurant remains popular primarily through word-of-mouth advertisement (it's a favorite with the locals), people from around the world have enjoyed its excellent food and old Florida charm.

The restaurant and bar are located near Pompano Beach, between Fort Lauderdale and Boca Raton, right on the Intracoastal Waterway on a sand and coral island just off Lighthouse Point. Patrons can only get there by a water taxi that runs between the restaurant's single dock and Lighthouse Point Marina. It is very secluded, surrounded by Australian pines and cypress trees.

In the restaurant's heyday, Cap's entertained many of society's elite. Powerful social and political persons such as President Franklin D.

Roosevelt, Winston Churchill, Al Capone, Meyer Lansky, the Rockefeller and Vanderbilt families, and famous entertainers like Errol Flynn, Susan Hayward, and George Harrison, are just a few who have enjoyed Cap's Place over the years. They came to Cap's because of its reputation for fine cuisine as well as its historical uniqueness.

But who was "Cap," the man who started it all? His name was Eugene Theodore Knight, born in Cape Canaveral, Florida, in 1871. Growing up on the undeveloped beaches of old Florida, he learned about the sea at an early age. By thirteen, he ran away from home to work on ships, just as family members had done for generations before him. He gave thirty years to his profession and became a ship's master before retiring, earning the nickname "Cap" from his friends. After being a landlubber for a few years, doing meager jobs to make ends meet, Cap developed a new plan for his future. It was the 1920s and Prohibition was in full force, so Cap applied his seafaring background to rum-running outlawed liquors from the Bahamas back to the Hillsboro Inlet. He made a significant profit and was never caught (his brother sent warning signals from the Hillsboro Lighthouse). He became quite the local hero, establishing a broad base of customers for his burgeoning business.

In 1929 Cap opened a bar on an old barge he bought in Miami (the boat is rumored to have been used by Flagler to build his Overseas Railroad). He moved the rusty old barge to a tiny peninsula on the eastern side of Wahoo Bay in the Hillsboro Inlet, but due to the threat of hurricanes and flooding, he finally settled on a small piece of land on the west side of the canal, which he happily christened "Cap's Island."

He called his business "Club Unique," and it was an overnight success. Cap would bring gamblers and other folks who just wanted a stiff drink to his new club, using rowboats to cross the canal and pick up his customers. Whenever they flashed their headlights from across the water, Cap's little rowboat would arrive. The customers would even give a secret wave to prove they weren't G-men waiting to raid the place. Cap's Place soon became synonymous with excellent food, hard liquor, and all-night gambling, complete with slot machines, blackjack tables, and roulette wheels.

Cap's Place became so well known, in fact, that in January of 1942, some very famous and unexpected customers arrived for drinks and dinner. President Franklin D. Roosevelt and British Prime Minister Winston Churchill dined in Cap's famous "yellow room" and were served the best whiskey and a feast of steak, swordfish, and a rare Florida dish, hearts of palm salad, fresh from the nearby Okeechobee sabal palms.

By the 1950s, however, senate investigations into gambling, especially in Florida, forced Cap to give up the gambling business altogether, as well as the all-night drinking and partying that went along with it. South Florida's illegal nightlife departed practically over night, and an era was over.

Although Cap Knight died in 1964 at the ripe old age of 94, his legacy lives on, seemingly unchanged from the days of Prohibition speakeasies. Indeed, even for the many years since his death, Cap's Place has been known for its fresh seafood, steaks, chops, chicken, and of course, the hearts of palm salads. It's is one of those rare restaurants that one must visit at least once in a lifetime—if not for the fine food and ambiance, then for the history. And if that's not enough, you could always go to find the strange spirits that are said to roam this tiny island in the dead of night, as there seems to be a lot more happening on Cap's Island than just fine food and history . . . downright scary happenings.

Ghostly Legends and Haunted Folklore

Few have heard about the spirits of Cap's Island—perhaps a handful of the restaurant's patrons and maybe a few of the restaurant's employees. The legend of Cap's spirit and a few other unknown entities have, for the most part, eluded ghost hunters over the years. In spite of the fact that many Lighthouse Point residents know of Captain Theodore Knight, very few would ever entertain the idea that he may have chosen to stay and watch over his beloved eatery after his death. For those who have witnessed paranormal activity on Cap's Island, or felt Cap's gentle spirit, they know he is not dangerous, although some have still gotten a little spooked over the years.

Among the most common paranormal events encountered at Cap's Place are the echoes of footsteps on the dock and the smell of cigars where no cigars have been. Apparently, when it's late at night, heavy, deliberate footsteps can sometimes be heard along the docks leading to Cap's bar and restaurant. More than a few people have heard these strange footsteps while enjoying the view of the waterway, always turning around expecting to find someone approaching and finding no one even remotely near. Others, including a few employees, have heard the dock strangely creaking as they were preparing to go home for the evening, and on occasion, they have felt a gentle wind blow by, as if someone had just passed them. Of course, it could be the wind, and the sounds of footfalls might be nothing more than the old dock creaking as a result of the ebb and flow of the tide, but those who experience these odd events know better.

The docks are not the only locations for strange sounds or smells to take place. Other inexplicable events have occurred inside the rustic restaurant as well. According to several employees, footsteps have been heard echoing from the corners of the restaurant long after closing, as well as silverware and other restaurant paraphernalia falling off the tables of their own accord. For many skeptics the sounds of footsteps are not strange and for the most part can be attributed to some natural cause; they can be connected to the simple laws of physics, not to ghosts. The restaurant is slightly tilted to one side and is indeed sinking at one end due to the entire foundation sitting on pylons and the ground being made mostly of sand and coral. This could explain the falling items, but the items in question have all fallen against the slope, meaning that they have all fallen upward. . . . Are the laws of physics different on Cap's Island?

Other inexplicable events that occur in Cap's Place include the sometimes overpowering scent of cigars wafting through the restaurant and around the grounds. Now, the scent of cigars is certainly no peculiarity, as many people smoke cigars today, but when the scent comes from nowhere and then goes in a matter of seconds, the account naturally becomes a bit curious. Captain Knight loved his cigars; in life, he was rarely seen without one in his hand or sticking out of his overalls.

Almost all of the employees here have heard stories of the phantom cigar smoker who lights up a stogie in the restroom or the kitchen when no one is there. Sometimes a patron might catch a whiff of a strong cigar while having dinner and, turning around to the next booth to scowl at the culprit, will only to find an empty table. Sometimes the cigar smoke is just that—regular cigar smoke coming from a regular man smoking it. But, as many of the employees and diners will tell you, it's just as frequently Cap's cigar smoke, his spirit enjoying a fine Havana just as he did in life.

Though creaking footsteps and the scent of phantom cigars are, for the most part, common events, several people have claimed more unusually to see the dark shape of a slightly bent-over man standing near the waterway behind the restaurant. This particular image has occasionally instilled a good deal of fear in more than one person when visiting the secluded island restaurant. According to one witness, while she and a companion were having a drink at a picnic table behind the bar, she noticed something move behind a bush. She described it as looking like a man, hunched over, and staring at her, but because it was long after sunset, it was too dark to make out his face. She asked her companion to look over his shoulder and see if he, too, could see the dark figure standing in the bushes, and sure enough, he did. After a moment or two, the man decided he didn't like being stared at, and he told his companion he was going to address this man and see why he was spying on them. As soon as he started toward the dark figure, however, it seemed to move further behind the bush. As the man walked around, he noticed the shrubbery, the ebbing water from the Intracoastal, and a few rocks on the sand, but no man. He walked around the entire bush and looked in all directions, but saw no one. Whoever this person was, he escaped . . . but how?

Dark figures have frequently been reported over the years at Cap's Place, mostly on the southern part of the island, which is devoid of structure apart from a few cement pylons. And although no one seems to know who or what these dark shapes are, some have credited them to the spirits of the island's past, and Cap's Place has had many, many spirited people visit throughout its history. Nowadays, everyone who comes to the restaurant must take the water taxi, and the boat's pilot keeps a record of guests when they arrive and depart, so any unknown visitors either swam there or arrived via their own boat. These dark figures have never been identified, and the mystery continues to this day.

One can certainly understand why so many get an uneasy feeling from seeing such a thing, especially when there is no logical explanation for its existence. Though many have speculated, none have found a solid answer—an unfortunate side effect to the supernatural. One popular theory is that these dark figures are what many pop-parapsychologists refer to as "shadow people"—dark, wispy creatures that seem to have a malignant nature. Moreover, because these shadow people are said to inhabit places where evil things have taken place, one must wonder if some of those people who frequented Cap's Place in the early years were in fact evil. Perhaps the gangsters of long ago have somehow left their impressions on Cap's Island, or perhaps these entities are nothing more than shades of once-potent personalities that have chosen Cap's Place as their haunting ground. Either way, the mysteries of these dark shapes walking the island, the creeping footsteps in the night, and the phantom cigar smoke will most likely remain just as remote as the famous Cap's Place Island Restaurant.

Afterthoughts

Cap's Place truly is a uniquely Floridian restaurant. The atmosphere practically shouts out history yet maintains a level of comfort you can find only in Florida's natural paradise. Nestled between A1A and a marina and harbor, Cap's Place continues to achieve the look and feel of a 1920s speakeasy, like a vestige of yesteryear.

If there are ghosts on Cap's Island, finding out who they once were might be a difficult task, as there have been so many personalities to have graced this restaurant over the years. Are the dark shapes lurking behind the bushes and the footsteps on the dock the spiritual echoes from the restaurant's past, or just the wood planks cracking with age? And the phantom cigar smoke? Is this a sign that Captain Knight is still watching over the restaurant and bar in which he spent most of his life? Many believe so.

Although no formal investigation has yet occurred at Cap's Place, such supernatural reports seem to point to the classic haunting, and perhaps more. As the dark figures have no formal paranormal category, the mystery thickens. They are in some ways like the rare entities known as "shadow people," those evil humanlike shadows with seemingly sentient behaviors. If these figures are indeed shadow people, then Cap's Place has a much darker presence than most suspect. Still, these shadows seem to be benign, and one must ponder who they could have been in life. As so many gangsters and other personalities of ill repute spent a good amount of time on Cap's Island over the years, the mystery will remain a mystery until a worthy paranormal investigator or genuine psychic visits to find out for sure.

Cap's Place Island Restaurant is located about 8 miles north of Fort Lauderdale off U.S. 1. Take U.S. 1, also known as Federal Highway, to NE 24th Street, and go east to the Lighthouse Point Yacht Basin & Marina. Park your car in the parking lot and take Cap's own water taxi to and from the restaurant. For more information and for reservations, call 954-941-0418.

7

Hillsboro Ocean Club

Hillsboro Beach

Water Spirits

A Little History

The Hillsboro Ocean Club is a quaint, medium-sized condominium that is quietly nestled off A1A, between the Intracoastal Waterway and the beautiful beaches of the Atlantic Ocean. Hillsboro Beach, also known as Florida's own "Magnificent Mile," is located on an island north of the Hillsboro Inlet, which stretches about three miles from Pompano Beach to Deerfield Beach. Although the town of Hillsboro was officially settled in 1939, German cartographer William Gerard De Brahm mapped this gorgeous section of the Treasure Coast in 1770, naming it "Hillsboro" in honor of Lord Wills Hills, the Earl of Hillsborough.

Today, Hillsboro Mile is A1A's gateway to Boca Raton and Ft. Lauderdale. It has only a few secluded mansions buried within the thickets of sea grapes and palms, plus high-priced, exclusive, condominium high-rises for Florida's elite and retired citizens. The Hillsboro Ocean Club is one of these exclusive condominiums. No more than thirty years old, it offers several floors of spacious homes and many amenities. It has a certain charm that only Hillsboro Beach can offer—

61

a peaceful seclusion from life's hardships and stresses, surrounded by lush palm trees, a gentle sea breeze, and mature folks who like it that way.

Because the staff and residents of the Hillsboro Ocean Club would prefer to remain anonymous, I will only relate the ghostly legends, bypassing names and occupations. Also, because this is indeed a private residence, sightseers and ghost hunters will have to do their investigating from afar, as the residents here would not likely appreciate ghost hunters roaming the halls in search of spirits and specters. The beaches, however, are still open for the public, if of course you don't mind walking a few miles from the public parking lots at the Deerfield Beach Pier.

All in all, the Hillsboro Ocean Club is a beautiful condominium, which affords an element of both the stately and the eerie. Surrounded by scrub bushes and sea grapes, the building will always have the gentle sounds of swaying trees and whistling wind from the ocean. The private beach behind the building is long and winding, with only the towering condominiums as silent neighbors, offering an exclusive feeling, if not a bit lonely. On the inside, the dim lighting that glows from the wall lamps and the ambient, ethereal music that echoes from the ceiling speakers give a sense of class, with just a touch of something foreboding. Although the Hillsboro Ocean Club serves as a unique residence for the living, some believe that this place is also a residence for ghosts.

Ghostly Legends and Haunted Folklore

I first learned about the Hillsboro Ocean Club in 1985 while I was attending the Art Institute of Fort Lauderdale. My friend John, who was taking classes with me, worked part time for the now-defunct C.P.I. Security firm, a company that at that time had a contract with the Hillsboro Ocean Club providing in-house security guards. John worked in the evenings, usually on the third shift—the graveyard shift. He would invite me to visit him at work so we could do homework together, which was advantageous since we were taking the same courses. When I arrived the for first time, one late evening around 12:45 A.M., I immediately knew there was more to the Hillsboro Ocean Club than met the eye, yet I could not place the feeling. My first impression was that this place was too quiet; the entire atmosphere was very still and a little creepy to boot. John told me that it was always quiet inside the Ocean Club, although he would complain of sometimes hearing strange sounds throughout the night. Outside of these odd noises, only the occasional sounds of the underground garage door opening or closing, and perhaps a resident coming or going through the front doors, constituted the nighttime events of the serene interior. The whole place was as still as a morgue . . . which is not a happy image when working the graveyard shift all alone.

During my visit, John and I talked about what it was like working at the Hillsboro Ocean Club. He relayed many stories in those few hours, mostly about the residents, who included famous lawyers, executives, and other important people. He told me about his duties working as a security guard, taking me on a brief tour of the inside and outside while he made his rounds. We talked about school and our future plans and things like that, but our conversation really didn't get interesting until he told me about a few strange things that taken place here. Incidents like an alleged ghost on the second floor, and the nocturnal spirits that were seen on the surf one early morning. From that moment on I knew the evening was going to be interesting.

According to John, while he was working late one night, a female resident from the second floor came downstairs to the security desk. She asked him to accompany her upstairs to her apartment and look around because she'd had a scary experience. Apparently, the slightly frightened woman had not only heard an odd noise emanating from her bathroom, she had also momentarily seen a female figure with long hair walking around inside. John naturally followed this woman upstairs to investigate, flashlight in hand and ready for anything.

When they went into the apartment, they both noticed that the bathroom light was on, which the woman said was turned off when she left earlier. Both John and the woman looked around the entire apartment, in every closet and pantry, only to find everything in order and nobody inside. When John asked for an exact description of the person she had seen, the lady could only say that she was female with long brown hair, and that she had her hands up to her mouth, holding her face. This person had hair that covered a good deal of her body, and had walked very quickly from one side of the bathroom to the other.

Understandably, the resident was unnerved from her experience and chose to remain with John at the security desk for a while before returning to her apartment. Because it would be close to impossible to climb from the beach below to the second floor—namely because of the sawgrass there and the fact that there is only a wall leading straight up—the intruder in question would have to have amazing climbing skills to get to the second floor. Moreover, the fact that the woman's patio door was locked tight makes the situation more a mystery.

John wrote an incident report that evening describing the situation in detail, then gave it over to the supervisor in the morning. When he arrived the next night for duty, he was told that it was the second time someone made such a report at the Ocean Club, and there was no person living there or visiting who matched the description of the mysterious long-haired woman. The fact that anyone entering the Ocean Club has to have a garage door opener and key to get in the building, then walk past the security guard to get upstairs, makes the eerie female presence a little spooky, to say the least. As there are cameras all over the Ocean Club, both inside and outside, this "intruder" would need the magic skills of David Copperfield to get in unnoticed.

John's second story was even more unnerving. Late one November a year earlier, John prepared for another late shift. Books, drawing pad, artisan pencils, and other tools of the trade in hand, John was hoping for a quiet night of security work and the chance to get a little homework done at the same time. All was going well until around 2 A.M., when he spotted a policeman's patrol car shining a spot light in between the Ocean Club and the nearby condo to the south. John went to see what was wrong and introduced himself the officer. The officer told him that he'd gotten a report from a resident at the other condominium that there was a sailboat floating offshore with no lights. As John and the officer walked behind the Ocean Club, they both saw a single-mast sailboat, about thirty-five feet long, drifting, seemingly lifeless.

As the sailboat bobbed up and down in the rough waters, with no interior lights or running lights on either side, the officer was becoming concerned about the situation, fearing the worst. He called in to his headquarters for assistance, reporting that an apparently abandoned vessel was drifting north toward Boca Raton, and that the Coast Guard should be notified at once. When the officer was through with his radio report, he began shining his high-powered flashlight on the sailboat, hoping to get a name or vessel identification number. Though John and the officer could not find any way to identify the sailboat as they scanned the sea and beach, they both thought they'd caught a glimpse of what looked like a person dancing on the shore. Clearly, this was a bizarre scene, and both began concentrating their flashlights toward the shoreline, hoping to see survivors from the sailboat.

Keeping an eye on the beach, both John and the officer began to walk down to the shoreline. As they were walking, a call came in on the officer's radio informing him that a sailboat, originally from North Carolina and matching the physical description he'd given, had been reported missing from the northeast coast of Florida two months earlier. The husband and wife who owned this vessel had called in an S.O.S. in September of that year, but had not been found by the Coast Guard after an extensive search. With this news, both John and the police officer continued to approach the shore, scanning the area for people. Suddenly, John said he saw something like a human outline. As the officer flashed his light in that direction, both saw what looked like an adolescent child running past them about ten yards away. When they scanned that area again with their flashlights, the image was gone . . . as if it had never been there.

Because it was a particularly foggy morning, and doubly misty from the sea spray, the images could have been nothing more than a trick of the light, or perhaps just wishful thinking on the account of both John and the police officer. Nevertheless, both were certain that they had seen someone or something that early November morning. The officer went back to his car to finish his report, thanked John for the help, then promptly left.

The following night he returned to let John know that the Coast Guard picked up the abandoned sailboat, and it did turn out to be the sailboat in question, the one lost months earlier. The police officer continued to say that the sailboat was found empty inside, and that there was no sign of a fight or struggle, but it was completely water damaged. The tiny windows in the cabin were open, the tattered drapes proving that they had been getting wet for a long time . . . but there were no help messages, no bodies, and no clues otherwise.

Stories like this one are not as uncommon as we might think. Who the occupants of the sailboat were and what happened to them were never discovered while John worked at the Hillsboro Ocean Club. And, as for the dancing figure on the beach, well, that question will most likely remain a mystery forever. Many have reported similar images on the shores of beaches across the world, and mariners have seen such things for centuries. Perhaps this dancing image is the spirit of some victim lost at sea years ago, or perhaps it belongs in the realm of the fantastic. Perhaps this dancing water spirit was nothing more than the haze of the sea playing tricks with the bright flashlight beams on the mist and fog. Perhaps . . . .

Afterthoughts

Although I was not fortunate enough to have had a personal paranormal experience while visiting this condominium, my friend John did, and to this day he swears that what he saw that cold November morning can only be described as a water spirit.

The strange entity on the second floor of the Hillsboro Ocean Club was never identified, either in life or in death. Was she a former resident who died in that particular apartment? Was she a ghost who wandered in from the beach? There are some who feel that this tormented spirit is the ghost of an accident victim who was hit by a car between the Hillsboro Ocean Club and the Deerfield Beach Pier a few years earlier. The poor girl died while leaving the beach after an early morning swim. It was her nineteenth birthday. She is said to have been a beautiful girl who had long brown hair that fell below her waist. Coincidence?

What about these strange dancing ghosts, these water spirits? Are they apparitions of people lost at sea? Or are they sea imps, creatures that inhabit the realm of folklore and magic? Although these entities remain an enigma, my friend John and the police officer are not the only people to have seen them. Indeed, throughout history, stories of ghosts and spirits of people who died at sea have been told as a precaution to those who would venture too close to the rough waters of the ocean. Sometimes these stories are told to entertain children at bedtime, on stormy nights to give the kids a scare.

Today, the Hillsboro Ocean Club remains a beautiful and popular place to live. Although the history here is relatively short compared to other haunted sites in Florida, the accounts of its hauntings are certainly no less frightening. In the 1920s and 1930s, small shacks and cottages once stood where these monuments of wealth and status rest today. Therefore, it should not be inconceivable that a long-dead soul who once lived and died here would continue to walk the beautiful beaches that were cherished in life, or dance in the spot where once there was a wood plank floor in a rustic cottage of Florida's past.

Hillsboro Beach is a beautiful section of south Florida. Although its residences are reserved for a select few, you will enjoy seeing how people live there and why they call this part of Florida the Treasure Coast. Just south of the Hillsboro Ocean Club is Cap's Place Island Restaurant, another haunted location to explore. To the north a few miles, you'll find the Boca Raton Hotel & Resort, and the Boca Raton

Cemetery, fun places to visit and both homes to a few intriguing specters as well. If, when driving lonely A1A, you should spot a girl walking out of the Hillsboro Ocean Club, her head bowed low and long, flowing hair draped over her face, don't be alarmed, she's just the ghost from the second floor. And, if you come across a misty figure or two dancing on the shores of the beach here, don't be frightened, just remember the many families that once had their quaint little cottages where the large condominiums now sit. Once you see Hillsboro Beach, you'll know why a ghost would want to haunt such a paradise.

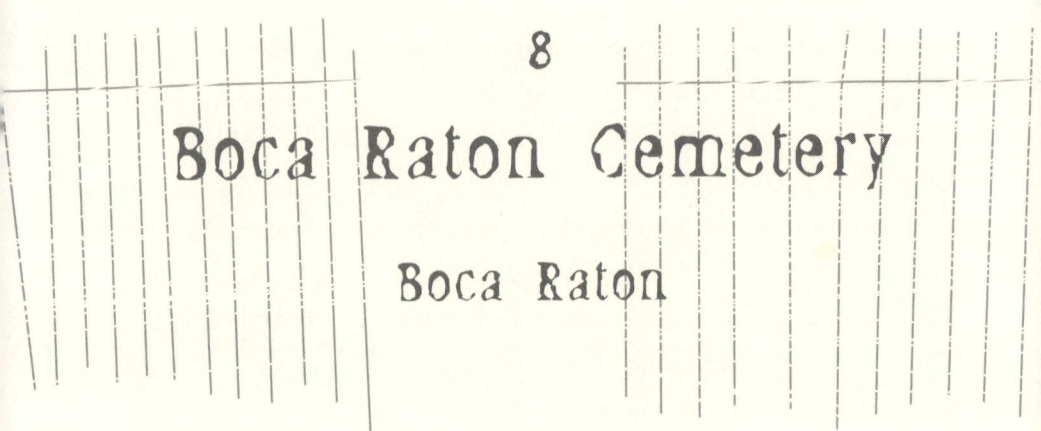

8

Boca Raton Cemetery

Boca Raton

The Screaming Man and Little Mary

A Little History

Boca Raton, known for its beautiful beaches and Spanish-style architecture designed by the famed architect Addison Mizner, is a renowned haven for the wealthy. But, under the glitter and high society, there seems to be something more . . . something supernatural. The Boca Raton Cemetery is the only cemetery currently operating in the city of Boca Raton, and although it is not an ancient place by any means, it seems to hold several active spirits. Located at 451 Southwest 4th Avenue, it is beautiful and well kept, complete with a memorial lawn and a mausoleum that serves as a gleam of pride for those residents of Boca Raton who have departed this world. Nestled between a synagogue and a Catholic church, this cemetery is a wonderful example of Boca's religious freedom and faith, and holds within it some of Boca Raton's elite and time-honored residents . . . and a few ghosts, too.

Ghostly Legends and Haunted Folklore

Having lived in Boca Raton for many years, I am well acquainted with the legend of the screaming man, even though it is rarely discussed. Apparently, from the direction of the cemetery in the dead of night, a man is sometimes heard mumbling, sometimes arguing, and sometimes yelling in a fitful rage. These screams have been loud enough to attract the attention of people living in the nearby apartment complex, who then alert the police to investigate. To date, there has been no one apprehended or questioned for the strange disturbances.

The screaming man was first heard in late 1991, the sound of painful crying coming from the inside the mausoleum's ornate atrium. At first, these cries and lamentations were considered the understandable response to the loss of a loved one, but as time went on, the sobs became louder and louder, culminating in vicious screams and curses against God. These screams continued for several months often on into the early morning hours, long after the cemetery staff and mourners had gone home for the night. It seemed that each night this event took place, the police would end up investigating the area only to find an empty cemetery and no one present. There was no evidence of any violence or vandalism inside the mausoleum and no trace of vehicles that may have belonged to the mystery screamer.

Although the police have made their presence known from time to time in the evenings, the park rangers are the ones responsible for making rounds and checking for unlocked doors throughout the night shift. One park ranger with over ten years of service, gave me a rather eerie account of the screaming man legend.

This park ranger (who asked to remain anonymous) said he had the scare of his life on one of his obligatory visits to the Boca Raton Cemetery. It was about 2:45 A.M. when he parked his car and began making rounds down the cemetery's long road. As he walked, he began to hear the strange crying, which seemed to be coming from the mausoleum about 100 yards away. He stopped to listen for a few minutes and then began to walk toward the massive marble structure to see who was there. After all, the cemetery was closed for the evening, and he had planned to ask whoever it was to leave the premises and return in the morning if he wished. When he got to the front entrance, the ranger noted that the sobbing and mumbling seemed to be moving away from him, as if this man were walking farther through the marble hallways, deeper into the massive edifice for the dead.

By this time, the park ranger told me, he was becoming a little concerned. The lights go off after 11:00 P.M. each night, and the many chambers and corridors of the mausoleum were dark throughout. It was at this time that he decided to go back to his car and drive around the cemetery using his spotlight instead of exploring by foot. It was a good idea, too, because when he began walking away, the sobbing began to get louder and louder. When the park ranger turned and peered down the corridors, with the help of the nearby streetlights, he saw the shadowy figure of a man flailing his arms in a frenzy, accompanying his painful and tormented cries. When he saw this, he quickly turned and picked up the pace, heading for his car.

When he finally reached his car, he could faintly see the shadowy figure dart from one part of the mausoleum to the other, waving his arms and shaking his hands in a fit of rage. By the time he was opening his car door, the sad pathetic cries were transforming into bursts of anger and fury. Needless to say, a cold chill ran down the park ranger's back, and it wasn't long until the Boca Raton Police came to investigate, only to find the usual—nothing.

This was the last time the park ranger ever saw or heard the screaming man, but some of the locals continued to tell stories of lonely cries in the night and sometimes frightening screams in the wee hours of the morning. One of the last times the screams received a lot of attention was during tropical storm Gordon in November of 1994. It has been said that while this storm was howling through the massive oak trees of the cemetery, so was the screaming man howling through the corridors of the huge marble mausoleum. Angry screams and cries of pain and sadness were heard by several people in the apartments close by.

The screams were so loud that two men from the nearby apartments, fearing someone was injured, decided to walk over and see if anyone needed help. But the closer they got to the mausoleum, the less they heard. Strangely, the lamenting sounds disappeared altogether as soon as the two men reached the gates of the structure, and after looking around, they found no trace of anyone ever being there. To this day, during thunderstorms or on moonless nights, the screaming man is said to walk through the lonely hallways and corridors of Boca Raton's mausoleum.

In contrast to the lamentations of the screaming man, there is another spirit, a peaceful spirit, who has been seen in the west wing of the mausoleum. This spirit is said to roam alone through the marble halls, strangely content. Known only as "Little Mary," this ghost is believed to be the spirit of a young girl who died from an illness at the age of thirteen. If you walk down the marble hallways toward the end, you might just feel the innocent, yet ghostly presence of a young girl.

According to local legend, Mary will sometimes appear to those who sit on one of the marble benches in the mausoleum, or to those who are grieving for a loved one interred there.

One witness I spoke to confirmed this legend. I was taking photographs of the mausoleum and cemetery when an elderly gentleman asked why I was taking pictures of a graveyard. Reluctant to tell him every detail of my mission, because the subject of ghosts might be upsetting to someone grieving in the cemetery, I told him I was researching Florida's folklore and urban legends, and was going to collect photos and stories from around the state. With a smile, the man turned and said, "You're in the right place, because there's a ghost in here." I asked for the story, and he was more than happy to tell it.

Once while this gentleman was visiting his wife, who is interred in the mausoleum, he decided to sit and reflect on his feelings. Out of the corner of his eye, he saw what appeared to be a young girl wearing a maroon-colored dress with white sleeves. Although the gentleman saw all of this in a matter of moments, he was able to say that this girl was kneeling in front of a tomb and was sweetly smiling at him. He was neither scared nor menaced by this youthful spirit. He simplify referred to the little girl as "comforting and content."

I have heard the story of a little girl spirit before from other paranormal investigators in that area. No one had ever mentioned the little girl's name to me, but I call her Mary for a good reason. When I walked to the back of the mausoleum where the old gentleman sat, and where others have reported seeing the young spirit, I found the tomb of a girl who died at the age of thirteen. There is no photo attached to her crypt, only a few toys left by her family and small flowers hanging from her nameplate. And, even though we don't know what she looked like, you get a warm feeling when sitting next to her resting place. . . . Her name was Mary.

Afterthoughts

The screaming man, whoever he is or was, may have died before his time, perhaps without the chance to say goodbye to someone who passed before him. Perhaps he wanders in regret of the things he had done in his life. Perhaps, but I doubt we will ever know his true anguish or why he screams. The only thing certain is that he has made himself known on many occasions and will do so again. As for little Mary, I can only say that her gentle spirit serves as a reminder to those who suffer, for those who have lost, that death is not the end, that there is nothing to fear in death. She seems to be a sign that there is always hope regardless of our fears.

When I made a visit to this cemetery, I was welcomed by a feeling of solitude and peacefulness while walking around during the daylight hours. However, when night falls and the shadows grow, the little things unnoticed during the day become something more. Perhaps it was my imagination or perhaps not, but the one thing I can say of this ornate mausoleum, this unique necropolis, is that there was something there . . . I felt it. I can also say that I am quite grateful the screaming man was silent and still that night.

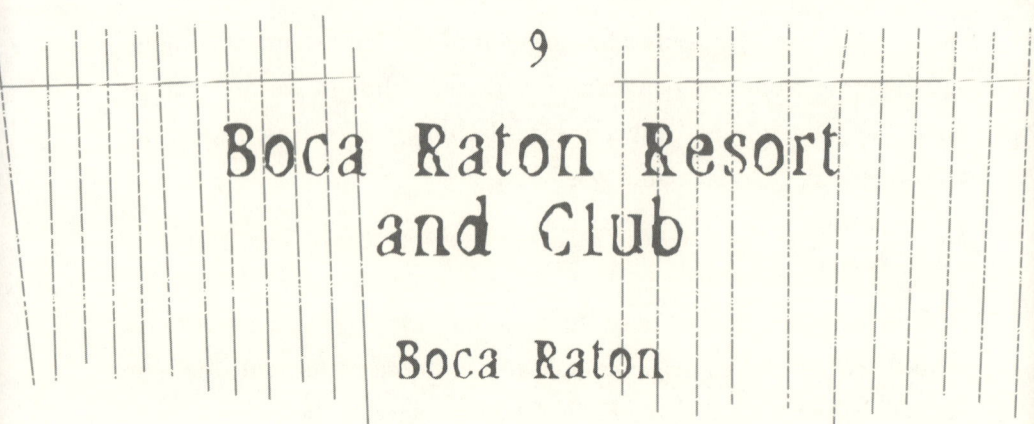

9

Boca Raton Resort and Club

Boca Raton

The Legend of Esmeralda

I am the greatest resort in the world . . . I am Boca Raton.
—Famous Addison Mizner slogan

A Little History

The Boca Raton Resort and Club was the dream of Florida's premier architect, Addison Mizner, and Mizner brought his vision to the people of south Florida. From the resort's beginnings in 1926, when it was known as the Cloister Inn, some of the world's most influential people have walked through its hand-carved archways and across its marble floors. From royalty to movie stars, from Wall Street moguls to land tycoons, this hotel has seen them all. There are few magnates, nobles, or celebrities who have not heard of the grand Boca Raton.

Since the days when Ponce de Leon sailed along Boca Raton's shores in 1513, when the Spanish conquistadors plotted the land, or when pirates and American Indians roamed freely within this tropical paradise, none were able to tame and cultivate this area like Addison Mizner. It's no wonder schools, office buildings, shopping centers, and condominiums have been named after him. But who was this man with such a beautiful dream? Addison Mizner was a self-taught architect with no formal education; he was an icon for the high society of his day, as well as an eccentric. He was a man who fell in love with Boca Raton when he first arrived in Florida for health reasons in 1918.

Over time, south Florida seemed to cure most of his ills. After a while, he found that life would never be the same anywhere else. As he recuperated, he had a marvelous vision and started planning to design a special convalescent home for officers and veterans of World War I. After receiving a small loan from a close friend, Mizner proved his architectural skills and constructed the ever-popular Everglades Club of Palm Beach. Mizner's creation was so well accepted, in fact, that Palm Beach's high society offered commission after commission to magnificent mansions and hotels that now define the Gold Cost. Mizner became the man about Florida.

It is said that when Mizner first ventured to Boca Raton in 1918, he fell in love with the land. He stood at the inlet, staring at the sea for a while, then turned around and looked at the lay of the land—mentally planning, as great architects do—and decided to build his dream. It was then that many believe he saw the future of the Boca Raton Resort and Club, and for that matter, Boca Raton as well. It wasn't long after that, around 1923, when Mizner and his brother fashioned the Mizner Development Corporation. Almost overnight the family-owned corporation purchased 17,500 acres of land in Boca Raton and began creating Mizner's dream, which would reflect an intriguing combination of European architecture, like that found in Venice and Florence, with styles reminiscent of Toledo and Greco-

Roman design.

In 1926, at a cost well over one million dollars, Mizner and his brother unveiled their creation, the Cloister Inn, a 100-room hotel of elegant structure resembling a popular Spanish style, complete with courtyards and tropical foliage. Mizner even furnished the hotel with rare antiques from his own private collection. It wasn't long before the Cloister attracted royalty, movie stars, and the social elite. Sadly, however, money problems began and signs of the Great Depression seemed to loom in the near future. By 1928, after many deals and alterations, Mizner sold the Cloister Inn to Clarence Geist, a millionaire from Philadelphia. Even though Mizner's original plans for Boca Raton were slightly altered, his impact was certainly felt and he did indeed accomplish his dream of a Golden City on Florida's east coast.

Addison Mizner, the consummate eccentric architect, was passionate in providing his guests with only the absolute finest experience possible. Antique collectibles gathered from around the world, from Central and South America, Spain and the Orient, were elegantly displayed throughout the hotel's unique structure. The food and libations had to be of the finest quality, too; if the King of Siam or the Queen of England were to drop in, they must be content. These were also the standards for hiring personnel. Therefore, in order to anticipate his guests' needs, the desires of the most discriminating clientele, Mizner hand-picked and developed a specialized staff compiled of men and women from around the world. These men and women were assiduously trained to provide a personalized hotel experience in the native language of each guest. Mizner's plan was quite successful, and his staff, whom he referred to as his associates, were well trained and attentive. Mizner had one caretaker, however, who outshined the rest. She was very special to the brilliant architect. Her name was Esmeralda.

Esmeralda was a chambermaid at the resort—but a chambermaid

truly devoted to only one person, and that was Addison Mizner. She was dedicated exclusively to the needs of her employer and his own personal guests, and her dedication resonated with respect as well as love. Esmeralda always went above and beyond her expected duties, and there was no amenity Mizner's guests were without. From fresh-picked flowers in the suites to fancy hors d'oeuvres during cocktail hour to taking care of the guests' pets, Esmeralda made sure that Mizner's visitors would return. In the end, the guests would speak volumes of praise about the Boca Raton Resort and Club and its creator. Esmeralda was as much a fixture of the resort as Addison Mizner himself, and everyone knew it. Sadly, however, that was about to change.

Ghostly Legends and Haunted Folklore

It was late one evening in 1926, after Esmeralda had finished making sure the flowers were in just the right vase and there was plenty of stationery at the desks. With everything put aside and ready for delivery the next morning, she finally decided to go back to her apartment in Old Floresta. Less than three miles from the hotel, Old Floresta consisted of several buildings built specifically to accommodate the employees of the resort. When Esmeralda got home after work, she would usually sit in her rocking chair, sip black currant tea, and read. On this particular night, however, when a gentle wind swept through her apartment, fanning the curtains from side to side, the breeze was so comforting that she fell asleep in her rocker without extinguishing the fire in her kitchen stove. After a few moments, a gust of wind blew the curtains across the stove and set them on fire. Within seconds the apartment was in flames—Esmeralda didn't wake up in time and died in the fire.

The staff and guests were saddened when they heard the news of Esmeralda's death the next morning, but they were not nearly as distraught as Addison Mizner. For several months after her passing, Mizner's exuberant nature seemed to dissolve; Esmeralda had been like a mother to him. But even this tragedy could not suppress the zeal of the architect, and his brilliance in running the resort soon continued. Although Esmeralda's personal touch was gone, many people, staff and guests alike, claim to have experienced something out of the ordinary from time to time.

Many believe that to this day Esmeralda's spirit continues to be welcoming to the guests of the resort. Her presence is sometimes felt on the third floor, where a cool breeze briskly blows through the hallways during the early morning hours, and throughout the lobby and patio the strong aroma of flowers is sometimes detected. Moreover, from time to time, usually during the spring months, freshly cut roses appear on the night tables of some of the regular guests. When these guests call down to thank the steward, the staff is baffled. When the chambermaids would not admit placing the flowers there, the mystery began and the legend of Esmeralda was born.

On other occasions, when guests pass through the dining room's French doors or look at the Cloister Museum's Mizner artifacts, they feel a comforting breeze. Sometimes this breeze carries the light scent of roses . . . Esmeralda's roses. When the guests look around to see who had walked past them, they find no one, only an empty hallway.

The courtyards and marble walkways at the west end of the resort are said to be haunted as well, especially during the graveyard shift. Apparently, more than one of the resort's staff members have claimed to have seen images. These images are fuzzy at best, but clear enough to recognize a female form walking silently, only to dissolve when looked at directly. Although there have been many to make such claims, none of them ever said they feared the apparition.

Esmeralda's presence has been the subject of polite discussion for many years at the Boca Raton Resort, and her spirit has become something of a mascot with the staff and select guests. Her spirit has never been angry with anyone here, only congenial and respectful. The lingering scent of roses and the strange appearance of freshly cut flowers on the night tables are fascinating to say the least. The spirit of Esmeralda appears to be content in her afterlife, and no one has ever made an ill comment against her. She remains the amiable servant of Florida's premier eccentric architect.

The gentle spirit of Esmeralda seems to be a mainstay of the resort, but what of the man who made Boca Raton the icon of class and luxury that it still is today? Has Mizner's vibrant spirit made a visit to his resort? Many say the answer is yes. Apparently, the kindly, whimsical ghost of Addison Mizner has been seen walking down the hallways dressed in his favorite blue silk pajamas with a monkey or a tropical-colored parrot on his shoulder. Some have claimed to see his spirit staring out to sea from the jetty across the Boca Raton Inlet. Though less jovial in this locale, in fact somewhat pensive, this specter is said to be standing in the spot where he first dreamt of the grand hotel. The distinct smell of cigars will be detected from time to time where there should be no such scent. But arguably the greatest proof that the wise, even humorous spirit of Mizner still walks the stately halls of the Boca Raton Resort is that this hotel has retained its charm and class through many years. To my knowledge, there has never been a report of a nasty spirit in the hotel, and this would seem to make sense, as Mizner would never allow such negativity to spoil his guests' good time.

Although a hotel like the Boca Raton Resort and Club can be a trifle expensive during peak seasons, the architecture and service at this resort make any vacation to south Florida complete. But if you happen to be catered to by the compassionate spirit of Esmeralda, then you may count yourself exceptionally lucky. When walking through the hallways, if you detect the scent of roses or see the image of a flowing gown through the corner of an eye, bow politely and say thank you to the resort's most caring chambermaid. If you detect the scent of a fine cigar where no such scent should be, then know that Mizner himself continues to make your stay the best it can possibly be in Boca Raton's enchanted hotel by the sea.

Afterthoughts

The Boca Raton Resort & Club holds a unique place in the realm of parapsychology. The roses or cut flowers that appear from nowhere signify the fantastic for sure. Parapsychologists refer to this event as an "apport," a phenomenon in which objects appear from out of nowhere. Apports have remained among the most extraordinary events in the history of psychical research. The detection of out-of-place scents or mysterious breezes are other oddities the Boca resort claims, phenomena that seem to have begun after the tragic death of Esmeralda. As for the convivial, eccentric spirit of Addison Mizner, his legend also continues at this wonderful resort, and why not? Anyone who would hold so dear the operations and continuation of a place— as Mizner held the Boca Raton—would surely continue to be as caring after death.

If you are fortunate enough to stay at the Boca Raton Resort and Club then by all means take advantage of all that this magnificent hotel offers. Enjoy Boca Raton's beaches, the world-class dining, and the nightlife, but try to remember that even in the loveliest of places there may be more than you bargained for. If you visit the hotel during October, be sure to take the self-guided "Esmeralda's Halloween Hunt." On this playful ghost hunt, you can visit all the places her spirit is believed to frequent. You never know when you'll bump into her.

Is the Boca Raton Resort and Club haunted? I would have to say yes, without doubt, as there have been far too many documented accounts of paranormal events over the many years.

The Boca Raton Resort and Club is located at 501 East Camino Real, in Boca Raton, Florida. For information on "Esmeralda's Halloween Hunt" or for reservations, call 561-447-3000.

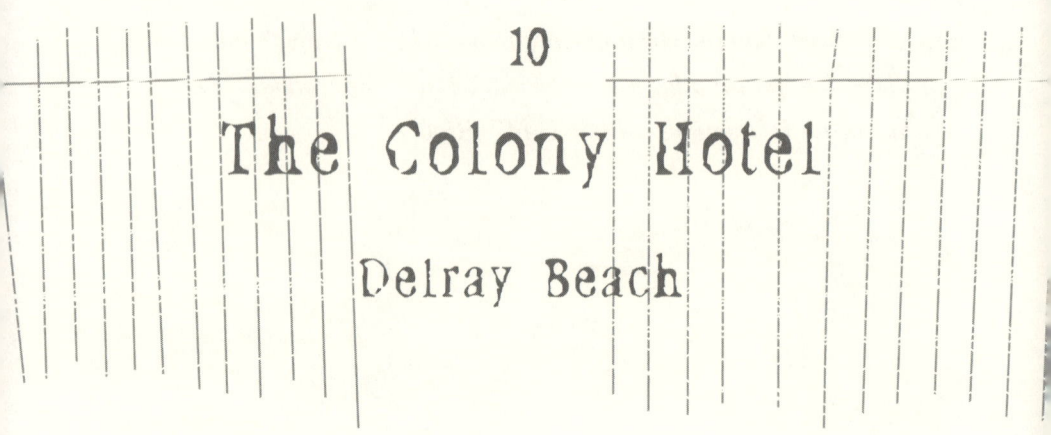

10

The Colony Hotel

Delray Beach

Strange Things

The Colony, Delray's oldest hotel, is one experience you won't want to miss. The lobby of the 1926 hotel is original, complete with wood burning fireplaces, white wicker furnishings and the original elevator still in use . . . and oh yes, there're ghosts. —The Waterfront News

A Little History

The Colony Hotel is one of south Florida's most beautiful hotels. Constructed in 1926 by Charles and George Bowden, it is a historic landmark in Delray Beach and is listed on the National Trust for Historic Preservation. During the 1920s, magnificent hotels like the Colony were built in warm locations like Florida because the wealthy and powerful wanted to get away from their frigid homes in the north and enjoy what we Floridians are entitled to every day. And so, guests came to Florida during the winter season to take advantage of the sun, the beaches, and the slow-paced atmosphere, and the Colony Hotel had just that.

When most of us hear the name Colony Hotel, we may think of former President George Bush Sr. and Kennebunkport Maine. And that makes perfect sense, because the Colony Hotel in Maine

has been the summer home for Delray's sister hotel for many years. It's a close-knit family of employees that work for the Colony Hotel, so dedicated that for years many of them lived in both states in order to create the best atmosphere a hotel can offer. The hotel's guest rooms are beautifully furnished with hardwood floors of Dade County pine, wood blinds, and art by local Florida artists. Although the rooms have a *Great Gatsby* charm to them, they have been updated for the modern vacationer or businessperson.

The huge dining room on the first floor is reminiscent of the Roaring '20s, the kind of room that would double as a ballroom in the evenings. There is a lounge across the hallway, just past the huge marble and coral fireplace. This is the famous Porch Bar that overlooks Atlantic Avenue. Here you can sit in the white rattan chairs and enjoy the best place for merriment and libation in the hotel. The Colony Hotel gives anyone staying there a glimpse into the past, almost as if time has stood still. The fast-paced world of today can offer even faster-paced things to do, but if you're looking to slow down a bit, this hotel is a good choice.

Until 1999, the Colony Hotel was closed a little more than four months out of the year, moving its staff and accommodations back up to Kennebunkport, Maine, during the summer months. It would sit alone, occasionally overseen by an outside caretaker during that time. The hotel was locked up, collecting dust and grit from the busy streets around it, with only a few faint wall lamps eerily illuminating the interior. Through the dark, foggy windows, the hotel looked as if it came from a Stephen King novel, complete with sheets draped over the tables and cobwebs in the corners. Most people who walked by it on a nightly stroll might have thought the hotel had been closed many years, waiting to be bought or scheduled for demolition, as lifeless as the cobwebs hanging from the dark hallways. Only the locals knew different.

For years, many of Delray Beach's residents spoke of odd things that would go on in the closed hotel, creating various ghostly legends in the process and culminating in a very spooky reputation. Many believe the old Colony Hotel is haunted by the several colorful guests who stayed there so many years ago. Today, the hotel is open year round, offering the same charm and amenities it has boasted since 1926. Moreover, the hotel stays relatively busy now that it's open twelve months out of the year, and some might think that the ghosts—if there ever were any—have moved out. Those who know better respectfully disagree.

Ghostly Legends and Haunted Folklore

The Colony Hotel has had a long, haunted history, according to many of the staff members and guests. In fact, the primary ghostly figures said to roam the hallways of the Colony are none other than Charles and George Bowden, the original builders and founders of the Colony Hotel. Apparently, the father-and-son team still watches over the many guests at the Colony, and for many years the two shadowy figures have been seen roaming around the hotel. For the most part, the spectral duo is quiet and usually only seen through the witness's peripheral vision, but on occasion the father, "Charlie," will show himself more boldly in either the lobby or the manager's office.

Justina Boughton, Charlie's granddaughter and a third-generation owner of the Colony Hotel, has had several experiences herself over the years. As a child, she would visit the hotel when it was closed during the off-season, running through the halls and playing in the old, deserted rooms. Back then she noticed how spooky it was, feeling that the first-floor rooms were the most haunted in the old hotel. As she got older, the experiences did not wane, but they did take on a more peaceful feeling.

She recalls several spooky, yet benign, incidents that took place in her adulthood. Most of the time, she would only catch a glance of a nicely dressed gentleman walking past her, or in a reflection in the glass of a framed portrait or painting. On rare occasions, she has heard the muffled sounds of a debate or argument coming from a back office or from the kitchen area. The ghostly presence is believed to be the gentle spirit of her grandfather just checking up on the family business. Although this particular variety of haunting is fairly pleasant, there seem to be other odd occurrences that are not attributed to the kindly grandfather. There is something else wandering the corridors of the Colony Hotel . . . something uncanny.

Of the many reports of strange and eerie events that go on in the Colony Hotel, the most frequent involves dimly pulsating lights in the second-floor windows and dark, shadowy figures moving about within the rooms. Although many have attributed the strange lights to passing janitors or others walking through the dark hallways with flashlights during the less active seasons, many paranormal researchers feel otherwise. Other events, like figures running through the main dining room, have been frequent enough to have the Delray Beach Police investigate on more than one occasion. Moreover, these dark figures have been observed by several people while going for sunset walks in the neighborhood.

On one particular night during the off-season in 1989, two people walking up the sidewalks on Atlantic Avenue noticed something moving inside the darkened windows of the closed Colony Hotel. As they strained to look through the foggy windows into the darkness, they agreed that kids must have broken in and were looting the place. This seemed logical, since the figures were moving quite fast, almost erratically, in the darkness. Believing that the hotel was being robbed, the couple stopped at a gas station across the street and had the attendant call the police. When the police arrived, they walked around the building and looked in all the windows, checking for obvious signs of a break-in.

The initial investigation turned up nothing, so the officers received permission to enter and explore the premises. At first, the only thing they found was a cobweb or two and a little dust. As they looked around, they checked the alarm system, which appeared secure, as well as the windows throughout the dining room, and made sure the French doors on the front side of the building were secure. Nothing appeared out of the ordinary.

As the officers were opening the doors to see if the alarm connections had been tampered with, the two people who had initially reported the strange event asked if everything was all right. Then, before the officer could reply, the elevator in the lobby made a rumbling noise. As the officer turned in amazement to see what was going on, a bell rang and the elevator door opened. The officer just stood in his place and stared at the open door, his right hand resting securely on his sidearm. The witness and his wife slowly stepped back and went down the stairs to the sidewalk, getting out of the officer's way in case something happened. The police officer called his partner on the radio and continued to stand where he was, as if waiting for someone to come running out. Though no one ran out of the elevator, the two police officers shut the doors leading to the street and continued to investigate inside. They left the building after a few minutes and proceeded to lock the doors behind them. They told the small crowd of onlookers that there was no one inside and that there may have been an electrical surge that tripped the elevator. Although this explanation sounded good on paper at the time, the witnesses had problems believing it was an electrical surge. And frankly, so do I.

In addition to the strange lights and the dark, darting figures occasionally seen inside the hotel, some have claimed that they have heard music coming from the dining hall late at night. The music is said to play on moonless nights, usually around 2:00 A.M.—jazz of the 1920s and '30s echoing as if from a little radio. Though music like this might have actually originated from a radio, no physical evidence has ever been found to support that assumption.

Even though no one has made any such claims lately, in the past the night staff has complained of noises coming from the kitchen, long after the cooks and kitchen staff have gone home. Some have claimed to hear voices coming from dining room, muffled voices, usually female . . . voices that fade away upon investigation into an empty dining room.

On more than one occasion a night watchman will be disrupted by the sounds of crashing pots or pans coming from the kitchen area or from the massive dining room. Unnerved, he will venture into the dark kitchen expecting to find the worst, only to find that everything is in order—no pots or pans thrown across the floor and nothing disrupted. When there is no staff to explain the event, and no sign of an intruder, the kitchen can be a spooky place to say the least. Although most of the staff is reluctant to admit to any haunting in the hotel, there have been some who tell a few stories. Eerie music where there should be none might be heard at any time, as well as disembodied voices from around dark corners and stairwells, but perhaps most unsettling is the enigma of floating, illuminated orbs in the second-floor windows.

During the summer months from 1985 to 1989, a plethora of witnesses came forward and reported seeing illuminated balls of light bobbing up and down in a chaotic manner throughout the upper windows as well as in the outside stairwells. Atlantic Avenue and Federal Highway are both busy streets, and many people claimed to see the lights during the late evenings and early mornings from around 11:00 P.M. to 3:00 A.M. Although these lights were bright enough to attract a few witnesses, most people didn't give them a second thought. Long before the word "orb" was in full use among paranormal researchers, people were referring to the strange phenomena as balls of dim light, or ghost lights. One witness noted, "It sure isn't swamp gas." However, the lights have not been reported since 1989.

Although the hotel staff might be reluctant to speak of such things as ghosts or orbs, you can always find out for yourself. Few paranormal researchers have investigated the Colony Hotel, but the ones who have all came away believing that this location indeed has something strange going on inside. A ghost hunter would most likely find the midnight hour and later the best time to search for ghosts, as these are the times when most of the activities have been witnessed. Because there is a night person working at the front desk, a ghost hunter could get permission to walk around the hotel. The ghost hunter could explore the massive dining room, walk the creepy stairwells where the floating orbs were seen, or just sit in the wicker chairs and listen for the ghostly music from another era. Who knows, perhaps those disembodied voices will call out while you're there. . . . Perhaps they'll call for you!

Afterthoughts

The Colony Hotel is open year round today, so you can enjoy its hospitality anytime you wish. The staff will make sure your stay is wonderful, but don't be surprised if they act ignorant toward your ghostly inquiries. Although one or two Colony employees might talk to you about some of the oddities that have taken place at the hotel over the years, for the most part you'll have to do your own research there.

The Colony has entertained several notable people since its early days, and it's been suggested that some nefarious characters have stayed there. People like Al Capone and Meyer Lansky are a few believed to have stayed at the Colony while on "fishing trips," and several Hollywood stars used this hotel to avoid the paparazzi. Whether to get away from it all or just avoid an ugly situation, the Colony seems to have been a secret retreat for some of history's most interesting people. With a past filled with such fascinating personalities, one must wonder how many decided to return long after they left this world.

I would recommend the Colony Hotel for those interested in experiencing Florida's old charm. As for ghosts, I would invite you to do your own investigations. You might be surprised what you find. According to several amateur ghost hunters who were being open about their findings, they have documented very interesting events such as major, high-level spikes on their electromagnetic detectors, anomalous readings in temperature, as well as strange, whispering voices on tape-recorded investigations. Though these ghost hunters found no obvious lighted orbs bouncing around inside the hotel, they did photograph several translucent orbs in the dining room and patio area. So something does indeed seem to be happening at the Colony . . . something strange.

The Colony Hotel is located at 525 East Atlantic Avenue, Delray Beach, 33483. For reservations and information about the Colony Hotel and Cabana Club, call 561-276-4065 or 800-552-2363.

11

Flagler's Whitehall Mansion

Palm Beach

Mary Lily Is Watching You

More wonderful than any palace in Europe, grander and more magnificent than any other private dwelling in the world . . .
—*New York Herald, 30 March, 1902*

A Little History

Henry Morrison Flagler, who founded the Standard Oil Company in the 1870s, was a remarkable man indeed. He was a visionary who seemed to have the Midas touch—wherever he went, he found fortune one way or another. After making millions in oil and Northern real estate endeavors, as well as other conquests, it was only a matter of time before he wanted to escape the snow and cold and discover the beauty and warmth of Florida.

There were also many family concerns, too, namely Flagler's wife at the time, who had been struggling with tuberculosis and other health problems. The idea of moving south seemed to be the most logical choice. Following a doctor's advice, the Flaglers visited Jacksonville during the winter in 1878, and instantly Henry Flagler fell in love with Florida. Sadly however, his wife's illness grew worse,

and she died May 18, 1881, at the age of 47.

It wasn't long after his wife's death that Flagler married her nurse, Ida Alice Shourds. The happy couple moved to St. Augustine, where Flagler recognized the city's potential for growth and began building an empire. Because there was a lack of proper transportation and hotels in St. Augustine, he decided to build them.

After Flagler completed the grand Hotel Ponce de Leon in St. Augustine in 1885, he decided he would need to build a better transportation system for his guests. He purchased an entire railroad system to compliment his chain of luxury hotels, which included the Breakers and Royal Poinciana Hotel in Palm Beach, the Royal Palm Hotel in Miami, and the Casa Marina in Key West.

During his travels throughout Florida, he found West Palm Beach delightful, particularly Palm Beach Island. He immediately began planning his future estate to sit next to the Intracoastal Waterway. Having divorced his second wife after she was committed to an asylum, he designed and built a fifty-five-room mansion on 60,000 square feet of property as a wedding present for his third wife, Mary Lily Kenan. Flagler commissioned the same architects he used for the Hotel Ponce de Leon to design his wedding gift, and he would christen it Whitehall.

Whitehall's stunning design includes substantial marble columns, red-barrel roof tiles, and a central courtyard surrounded entirely by the house—a mansion as elegant as any hotel Flagler would put his name on.

The grand public rooms on the first floor reflect the high façade trend in nineteenth century New York hotels. There are twelve guestrooms, as well as rooms for the house servants on the second floor, and even rooms for the guests' servants.

Whitehall mansion was so admired that many referred to it as a Taj Mahal-like structure. The *New York Herald* described it as "more wonderful than any palace in Europe, grander and more magnificent than any other private dwelling in the world." A world-class sentiment for a world-class wedding gift.

Henry Flagler, the man who had lived a life most of us can only dream about, the man with the Midas touch, eventually became old and tired. With his first marriage ended by tuberculosis and his second marred by insanity and institutionalization, Flagler had seen his share of failure and sadness.

In 1913, at the age 84, Flagler died from injuries resulting from a fall down the marble staircase in his beloved mansion. An American legacy and Floridian legend was dead. He was buried in St. Augustine alongside his first wife, Mary Harkness, and daughter Jennie Louise.

Mary Lily Kenan-Flagler, following in the footsteps of Flagler's second wife, is said to have ranted and raved, running through Whitehall screaming and cursing at the servants. When not enraged, she stared out of her second floor bedroom window for hours at a time, suspicious and jealous. She died alone and miserable.

Today, Whitehall mansion is a museum, listed as a National Historic Landmark and open to the public. It ushers in countless visitors wishing to see the home of such an industrious person. Some go to see the pride that went into the architecture of yesteryear, and some even go there in search of the ghosts of Whitehall. To this day, although long dead and buried, Henry Flagler and Mary Lily are said to walk the halls of Whitehall.

Ghostly Legends and Haunted Folklore

I have had many occasions to visit Whitehall over the years. I recall this stately mansion as something more than just a work of art; it's truly a masterpiece. I also remember the many ghost stories that went along with it, hearing from the staff the many testimonies of paranormal happenings.

Almost everyone in Palm Beach knows the legend of Mary Lily being seen on second floor, staring out the window at those walking on the quaint pathway below. Many know that she is said to stare with mean, judgmental eyes, making the witnesses feel like they're trespassing before they watch the angry vision dissolve into nothing.

Sometimes, Mary is seen running through the halls of the mansion after hours, complete with flowing dress and a large hat with a plume. Although it is more the shape of such a woman than a recognizable person, the image has certainly frightened a few people over the years. Whether or not the spirit of Mary Lily is happy or sad, one thing is for sure . . . she is still quite insane!

Although Mary Lily seems to get first billing at the Whitehall, Henry Flagler has also been witnessed from time to time, ascending or descending the massive marble staircase either early in the morning or late at night. Although Whitehall is now a museum, caretakers or Flagler family members will stay there from time to time. This select group of people has the greatest chances of witnessing the paranormal firsthand, and apparently some have.

Over the years, people have reported seeing a gentleman walking up the stairs, with his back turned toward them. He is reported to be an older man wearing period clothing and holding the handrail tightly as he climbs the stairs. When the witness tells a staff member or volunteer that there's an elderly man walking up the stairs, the staff naturally goes to investigate, to make sure this older gentleman isn't lost and to make sure he doesn't hurt himself. After a careful search in every room, however, they find no one . . . not a soul.

Although Henry Flagler has been seen walking through the hallways of his beloved Whitehall, he is most often seen walking on the stairs where he had fallen, the place that ended his life. Of course, he was 84 years of age and entitled to be weak and a little feeble, but that just wasn't Henry Flagler. Flagler was the kind of man who always had to be on top of things, and most of all, in control. In death, however, he seems to have lost most of that spirit entirely, leaving the paranormal events in the spectral hands of others.

Perhaps Henry is merely watching the living now in order to remember what he had once had in life, and what he can now no longer have. Perhaps he spends most of his time at the Hotel Ponce de Leon, now Flagler College, or visiting the many landmarks and palaces he created here in Florida. Either way, he seems to want little to do with the supernatural here at Whitehall.

During the 1970s, staunch non-believers in ghosts and hauntings reported a significant number of paranormal events, events that have been passed down from volunteer to volunteer at the museum. Evidently, plates and priceless utensils were found completely smashed within a locked glass cupboard. Many staff members and volunteers believed the breakage was caused by Mary Lily, who was showing her disgust and hatred for these heirlooms that had once belonged to the Flagler children, the children who had hated Mary Lily in life.

In addition to the broken heirlooms, the front door handles and locking mechanisms would sometimes look as though they'd been tampered with after a late night function or a family visit. Apparently, the door latch, which is a turn-of-the-century latch, will be found turned all the way around so that the handle will catch hold of the door frame and the door can't be opened.

The occupant is forced to go out another door in the rear section of the mansion, or through a window. When this unfortunate person goes to investigate the front door, he will find the latch in a strange position or back to normal, as if never touched. In these cases, the huge iron gates that surround the mansion are found closed and locked.

Once, when a family member was visiting, she brought her little dog with her for company, as she would be left alone in the mansion from time to time. She felt having her dog around might ease any apprehensions about being left alone in such a massive place.

One early afternoon during her visit, she heard the dog barking in the northern hallway. When she went to see what the dog was barking at, the woman found him sitting, wagging his tail and staring at a painting. She gave the dog a curious look, wondering why he was making such a fuss. When she looked closely at the wall where the dog was barking, she only saw a collection of paintings, and it was at this moment that she realized these paintings were of her dead relatives. The paintings were the kind commonly made at the time of funerals for remembrance of the dead.

As this guest was understandably unnerved, she calmed herself and prepared to go out for a banquet that evening. It was getting late, and she needed to go upstairs to get something from her garment bag. As she was getting ready to do so, she realized she was now the only one left in the mansion—all the volunteers and staff members had gone home for the evening. She started climbing the stairs and called for her dog to accompany her. The dog ran up quickly as usual, racing as fast as he could. The little dog was prone to winning this race with his mistress, so the woman just smiled at him as he passed.

The smile diminished, however, as the little dog reached the upper steps and stopped dead in his tracks. He began to growl, which was unlike him, and then he began to bark wildly. He seemed to be focused on the darkened hallways and rooms, places that are so bright and majestic during the day. Now, the woman knew no one was in the house, and she really had a hard time entertaining the idea of ghosts inside Whitehall, but when the dog turned around and ran away still growling, she decided to leave for her engagement without going upstairs. Probably a good idea.

There have been similar occurrences at Whitehall over the years, and most are attributed to Mary Lily Kenan. In addition to people witnessing this bitter, but apparently harmless, specter peering through the second-floor bedroom window, a few women have claimed to have seen her while using the ladies' bathroom.

On at least two occasions, Mary Lily has been seen staring into the bathroom mirror as if in deep thought. When a living female visitor was washing her hands, she saw this spooky image and politely asked if there was going to be a photo shoot that day, or perhaps a movie being filmed. When the pensive, costumed lady didn't respond, the visitor just left. When she asked a volunteer about actors working in the museum, they went into the bathroom to check the story out, but the bathroom was empty—just another mystery in the gorgeous but sometimes inauspicious Whitehall mansion.

Afterthoughts

When visiting delightful West Palm Beach, be sure to cross the bridge to Palm Beach Island. Make a date with the finer things in life. Be sure to visit Worth Avenue, where kings and queens have shopped, and dine in the restaurants that must be experienced to be believed. Enjoy the beaches and the nightclubs, and stay in one of the five-star hotels this luxurious island offers. But above all, visit the mansion that Henry Flagler called home.

When the sun goes down, take a stroll on the beautiful walkways leading around the stately Whitehall mansion. Gaze into the darkened windows of the mansion's second floor. Perhaps you too will catch a glimpse of the woeful Mary Lily staring down at you, accusing and wild.

When visiting Whitehall, be sure to take a look at the macabre paintings hanging on the walls of the northern corridors, and see if you can find out why the little dog was barking in this creepy hallway.

Climb the stairs where Henry Flagler fell and see if you too can feel the cold spots there, as so many psychics have over the years. Perhaps you'll find out why that little dog turned tail and ran down those stairs for dear life. Who knows, you might just meet Mary Lily Kenan face to face.

Flagler's Whitehall Mansion & Museum is located on the corner of Coconut Row and Whitehall Way in Palm Beach, Florida. The Museum is open year-round. The hours are Tuesday to Saturday, 10 A.M. to 5 P.M., and Sunday, Noon to 5 P.M. Closed on Mondays, Thanksgiving, and Christmas. For more information, call 561-655-2833.

Central Florida

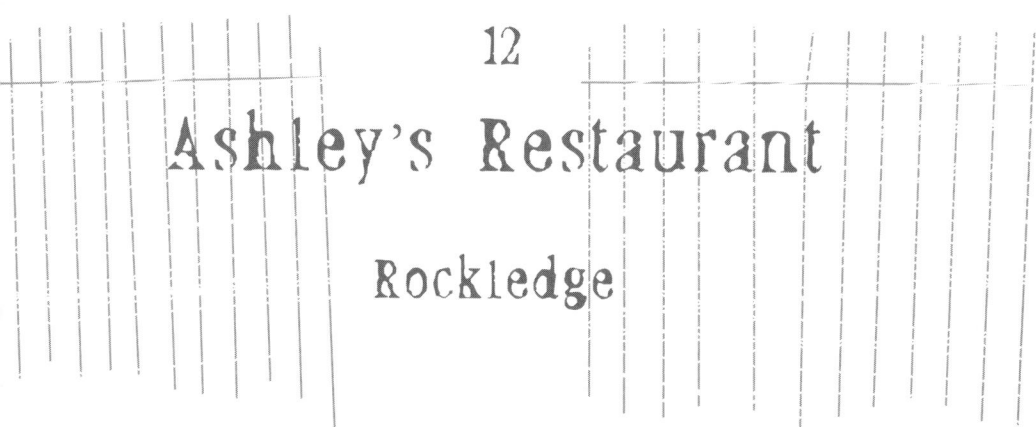

12

Ashley's Restaurant

Rockledge

Cold Ethyl

A Little History

Ashley's Restaurant, just south of Cocoa Beach near the old railroad tracks, is said to be one of Florida's most haunted restaurants. Although this location has been home to several restaurants in the past, including the Loose Caboose, the Mad Duchess, the Sparrow Hawk, and Gentleman Jim's, Ashley's has prospered, holding the same name for more than ten years. The architecture dates back to the late 1920s, and the restaurant sits a distance from the rest of the stores and businesses in the area, as if it wished to stand out from the others.

The two-story wood and stucco building has a European air to it, giving off a sense of nobility, albeit somewhat eerily. Inside, Ashley's has a pleasant, homey feeling—like a neighborhood bar and eatery where locals go to relax and watch a game—offering quaint booths on either side, tables, a bar in the center, and good all-American food. There is dining upstairs, too, with tables that look down onto the first floor. The dark wood, the old pane windows, and the antique pictures and mirrors hanging throughout the restaurant give the feeling of a safe and comfortable setting. Yet, there is also a noticeable impression that something more is there . . . in the dark corners or sitting at the tables behind you perhaps?

Ghostly Legends and Haunted Folklore

My interviews with the staff brought out some interesting ghostly legends indeed. One particular legend appears to date back almost to this building's beginnings. Apparently, there was a woman named Ethyl Allen, who, according to the oral traditions of Rockledge, was a local in the late 1920s and early 1930s. Ethyl is said to have run with a rather tough crowd, and it is widely believed that she got too involved with gangland thugs. As the legend goes, she was murdered in the building just in front of the main entrance, then carried off and left on the banks of the Indian River in the nearby town of Eau Gallie. Although there is some speculation to this legend, there are those who believe that Ethyl haunts Ashley's to this day, especially in the ladies' restroom.

Over the years, there have been many employees and patrons who have reported apparitions, and such ghostly sightings have steadily increased since 1979. The haunting events have caught so much attention that a series of psychical investigations were conducted and well documented during the 1990s. There has been an intriguing amount of evidence for spiritual phenomena, including the vortex phenomenon (which some believe to be a traveling form of ghostly energy) as well as orb activity that has been recorded on thermographic and digital cameras. Also, there have been several employees and patrons who have actually felt the icy hands of an unseen entity on their shoulders and back.

Judi Cowles, a manager of the restaurant from 1979 to 1984, tells of a ghostly experience she had late one evening while closing the restaurant. She went into the ladies' room to make sure no one was still there, and also to use the facilities herself. She was in one of the two stalls when she happened to note a pair of feet in the adjacent stall. She noticed that these feet looked rather odd because they were in high-heeled, buttoned, bootlike shoes that seemed to be from another era. She couldn't help feeling a little uneasy, yet she hesitantly said, "Hello? We're closed for the evening. . . . Hello?" But all she heard was silence. When she walked out, she noticed that the door to the next stall, where the strange feet were, was wide open and completely empty! Needless to say, a cold chill came over her, and she hastened to get home.

The shoes are believed to have belonged to the spirit of Ethyl Allen, or "Cold Ethyl" as she has been referred to over the years. Ethyl is reportedly more playful than threatening, turning on the water in the sink, closing and opening doors, and sometimes casting a faint reflection in the mirror to startle unsuspecting staff and patrons. The one thing that most of these unsuspecting ladies have complained about is not the appearance of odd-looking shoes under an adjacent stall, but never hearing anyone enter or leave the restroom, as the shoes appear and disappear without a noise. This is a chilling event to say the least, but there have been other events at Ashley's that are even more frightening.

History suggests that Ethyl Allen may have a darker side to her ghostly tricks. The first-floor corridor, the storage room, and the employee staircase that leads from the kitchen and bar area to the upper floor, all have a heavy sense of doom accompanying reports of actual physical attacks in those areas. According to Mrs. Cowles, there have been several accounts of female staff members feeling as if they were being choked from behind, and still others have claimed to feel an invisible push when climbing the stairs, almost making them lose their balance. Moreover, several servers have reported feeling a gripping sensation around their necks, or having the feeling of being suffocated while ascending or descending the staircase or while walking through the corridors. Some have said that at times they were unable to move forward, as if stuck in slow motion. Indeed, Mrs. Cowles said she also experienced various strange feelings in the corridor leading to the ladies room. When she put her hand up to the restroom door to open it, her hand would not push the door open, as if she were completely stuck. To be sure, the ladies' restroom is not the only source of haunted folklore in the restaurant.

Because such behavior goes against Ethyl's playful manner and demeanor, some believe that there is more than one restless spirit within the darkened corridors of Ashley's. In addition to the strangeness of Ethyl's ghost, some claim to have felt the presence of a child roaming the restaurant. The legend is that this child is a young girl who was struck and killed by a car near Ashley's in the 1950s. She left the scene of her earthly death and found her way into the already enchanted Ashley's. Many psychics who have visited Ashley's believe the child's spirit haunts most of the area including the outside of the building. Some claim to have seen her in the corners of their eyes, like a child dancing or playing. When they turned around expecting to see such a child, they found nothing, just empty space.

Over the years, there have been many strange happenings reported at Ashley's Restaurant. Lights have been seen flickering on and off in the dead of night, burglar alarms have gone off by themselves, dishes and glassware mysteriously break, objects move by themselves, and from time to time disembodied high-pitched screams have been heard long after closing hours. Because of such intense psychic activity, many paranormal investigators have visited the restaurant, all declaring the same bittersweet story of the playful Ethyl and even others who wander within this enchanting little eatery.

Local psychic Jean Stevens has visited Ashley's on many occasions and has had many visions in which she has seen a tall, thin man in 1940s garb being dragged down the main stairway near the front door, thrown or pushed into a patrol car by two police officers. The psychic image was detailed enough for her to notice how sparse and deserted the now very busy Federal Highway looked. She believes that the thin man in her vision had his daughter nearby, screaming and crying at the ordeal. In a fit of anger and fright, the young girl ran out in traffic, was stuck by a car and killed instantly. Ms. Stevens also believes that this young girl appeared to be a little off, as if mentally retarded or possibly autistic. Ms. Stevens said the incident felt horrible, and believes that this is the spirit or entity that is causing most of the paranormal turbulence. She believes that the psychic energy that is still lingering at Ashley's is generated by those traumatic events and emotional stresses that the child experienced here, leaving a psychic residue.

Billie Cox, a reporter for a local newspaper called *Florida Today,* heard many of the local legends regarding Ashley's ghosts and decided to conduct his own investigation in the restaurant over a period of several months. Mr. Cox admitted to recording the sounds of low whispers on his tape recorder, as well as loud, angry buzzing sounds while he was walking up and down the stairway where people have claimed to be shoved and choked. While on one such investigation, he decided to take photographs from the second floor. Standing on the second-floor landing and taking pictures of the first floor, he saw only one female employee near the bar, the rest of the area void of employees or patrons. When he got his film developed, he found the eerie image of an elderly man wearing black pants, a white shirt, and a small white towel over his left arm. Confused by this, he went to the manager and asked who it might be. He was promptly informed that there was no such man working there, nor has there ever been such a man since she began managing the restaurant.

Intrigued, Mr. Cox interviewed many of the police officers from the city of Rockledge. The police station is located directly across the highway from Ashley's, so it's easy for law enforcement officials to notice anything out of the ordinary. However, when burglar alarms go off when there has been no forcible entry, and lights go on and off inexplicably, and female screams come from within the restaurant in the dead of the night, well, even the police can get a little spooked. They could offer no explanation of the mysterious man in Mr. Cox's photograph.

Recent events suggest that Ashley's is still quite haunted, primarily in the early hours of the morning. Perhaps the building's location has much to do with this; perhaps it is the long-time ghostly residence of Ethyl Allen. When I questioned several of the regular customers, I found that this legend is more a matter of fact to them than simply a story. Almost all of them have claimed to see or feel something from time to time. Either way, the legend lives on.

Afterthoughts

I was fortunate enough to locate the grave of Ethyl Allen in a small cemetery on Merritt Island. The blackened stone sits silently under a large camphor tree almost segregated from the other headstones. In addition, although I did not experience her presence around me or a playful shove when walking past her grave, I did notice one strange thing. As it was a hot day in the middle of summer, I had noticed that the grave stones in the cemetery were quite warm. Nevertheless, when I felt Ethyl's gravestone, it was more than just cool, it was quite cold, as if chilled, as if it were empty. It just didn't feel right.

Ashley's Restaurant is one of those eye-catching landmarks. The elegance of this old building gives off an air of nobility, as well as spookiness, and it certainly seems to have the power to draw one in for a closer look. Once inside, you might be surprised how open-minded the staff is about their ghosts. When visiting, feel free to ask questions about their haunted events, and be sure to take a walk around this restaurant, for when you do, you may find some oddities in the architecture, both inside and outside. When you walk around the front of the building, you will notice a door toward the southern entrance, a door shaped like a coffin. This and other curiosities may give you some insight as to why many ghosts would wish to gather here in the first place. And who knows? You too may wish to join Cold Ethyl one day in Ashley's haunted restaurant.

Ashley's Restaurant is located at 1609 S. U.S.1 in Rockledge. Call 321-636-6430 for more information.

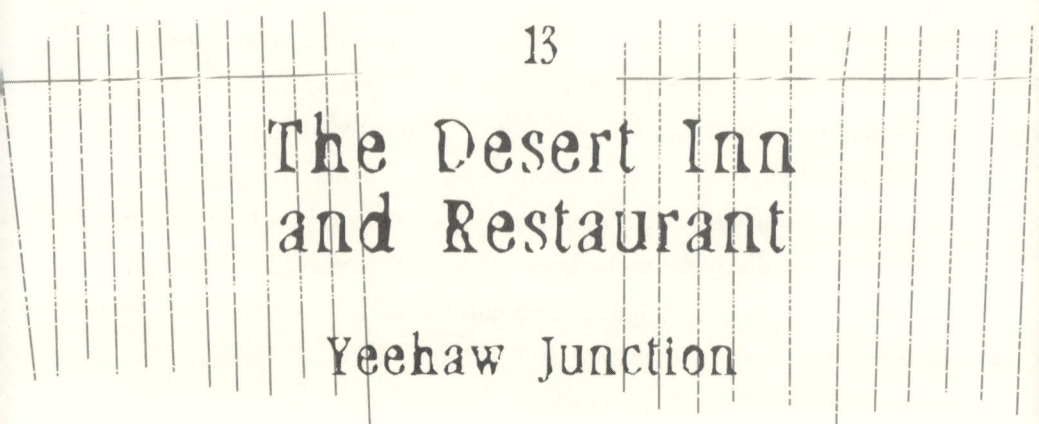

13

The Desert Inn and Restaurant

Yeehaw Junction

Ghosts in the Middle of Nowhere

A Little History

Since an early age I can remember traveling with my mother and father and sometimes my sisters on summer road trips to all areas of Florida. Whether going to Disney World in Kissimmee or visiting family in Gainesville, we would always take the Florida Turnpike to get to most of our destinations. The turnpike is one of the best ways of getting through long stretches of Florida.

I can remember my father always pointing out Yeehaw Junction as the middle of nowhere, and most of the time the middle of our journey. He would always comment on that little restaurant sitting off the turnpike, at the crossroads of Florida. I can remember thinking how odd and kind of spooky it all seemed, even as a little kid. And, as fate would have it, I would revisit this quaint and colorful little restaurant known as the Desert Inn many times after that.

When Florida became a state in 1845, Yeehaw Junction had already been there for a long time. By the 1890s this section of central Florida was a hub for cattle and oxen drivers, as well as a resting stop for travelers from the Flagler's East Coast Railway depot nearby.

Setting up lodging and limited amenities for the cattlemen and travelers was an obvious necessity.

The first structure was basically a glorified shack, which served as a watering hole and supply depot as well as a means for other "necessities" in the form of unsavory nocturnal activities that battled the problem of boredom out on the range, so to speak. The upstairs section was used not only as living quarters, but also as a bordello, complete with the ladies from near by towns, music, and flowing spirits to take the edge off a hard day's work. This footloose and fancy-free lifestyle lasted roughly until the 1930s when the roads started to be paved and a hint of civilization began to peek through . . . but just a hint.

Some speculate about when all this took place, and when the Desert Inn became what it is today, who built it and how. Although there are several theories about the historical roots, the best involves a railroad hobo by the name of Dad Wilson. Apparently, this hobo was kicked off one of the passing trains, landing close to where the Desert Inn stands today. It was at that moment that Dad Wilson decided to rebuild this time-honored watering hole, using "borrowed" railroad lumber to make it new and improved. And so, out of the proverbial ashes this unique landmark was born, and has remained relatively the same for many years.

In 1946, after several owners and managers had come and gone, Fred and Julie Cheverette bought the property and continued the legend of the Desert Inn at Florida's crossroads. The Cheverettes were as colorful as any of the many travelers who passed through this area since the start of it all, and most certainly the Cheverettes had the best sense of humor. When you go into the restaurant section, you will see the oblong bar complete with liquor and cigarettes and the usual tavern paraphernalia, but when you look up, you will see a web of fishing lines stretching out in all directions, over tables, and doorways. Attached to these fishing lines is an array of rubber spiders and creepy bugs designed to drop on unsuspecting patrons for a gag. That was the essence of Julie Cheverette.

After Fred passed on, Julie continued to run her restaurant and inn with the same colorful and humorous quirks, becoming a legend not only in that part of the state, but nationwide thanks to the numerous truckers and travelers. She died in 1986 at the ripe old age of 79. In 1987, the present owner, Beverly Zicheck, took the reins and continues this unique landmark in its traditional manner—all except the bordello of course, which remains simply as a little museum of Florida's less-advertised past.

While investigating the history and legends of the Desert Inn, I was fortunate enough to meet Bev Zicheck. I was able to hear many stories about the location and its past. I was especially fortunate to learn of the ghostly personalities that seem to have eluded many paranormal researchers and folklorists for years. When I began asking about the ghostly occurrences, I was worried that Bev, who is matter-of-fact and down-to-earth, would laugh at my inquiry. Instead, she explained with considerable ease that there were in fact ghosts in the

Desert Inn, that absolutely that her place was haunted. She said that there have been staff members over the years who refused to go upstairs without an escort because many people have had strange feelings and experiences there.

The upstairs section is now a museum and partial storage area that Bev occasionally shows to her friends and the curious. She asked one of her employees to accompany us upstairs to give me the grand tour. This special tour would offer me the chance to see a little-known piece of Florida's history. As my tour proceeded, there seemed to be a lot more than just history in this spooky restaurant and inn . . . there seemed to be a presence lurking around every darkened corner.

Ghostly Legends and Haunted Folklore

Because the Desert Inn is the only lodging for about 65 miles in any direction, and is positioned near the main turnpike, it is a logical stopover for many motorists who just can't go any farther without a rest. The old inn has even served witness to the last living moments of a few who have been involved in highway accidents nearby. According to the present owner, there have indeed been several deaths on the property and in the rooms upstairs, some fairly recently, so it stands to reason that a restless spirit may have made his or her home here at this little oasis. Now, it's important to realize that the Desert Inn is not a five-star hotel designed to attract traveling dignitaries or movie stars. No, the Desert Inn is a hometown lodging that serves everyone from truckers and weekend hunters and fisherman to genuine cowboys. On occasion, a traveler by foot may stay here for a week or so to catch his breath and then move on. Some of these weary travelers, however, may have decided to stay longer.

As my tour continued, Bev informed me of the deaths and the ghostly phenomena that have taken place over the past fourteen or so years of her management. Apparently, in the early 1990s, a traveler staying in one of the rooms upstairs committed suicide by hanging himself from an overhead pipe. Bev found the body the next day. There have been other deaths, too, in recent years, presumably by natural causes, not to mention the fatal gun fights during the early years of the Desert Inn. Bev ardently believes that there are indeed presences throughout the Desert Inn, especially upstairs.

As soon as we reached the top of the stairs and unlocked the door, the musty smell and humidity hit us in the face as if the room hadn't been opened in years. As this section of the inn is seldom used today (lodging for the inn takes the form of eleven cabins to the rear of the main structure), the upstairs now only serves as the museum and for miscellaneous storage. As our guide unlocked and opened the rear apartment door, she stepped back and said she'd heard a "shhh" sound, which sounded like someone was in the empty room ahead. For a second, she said, she thought she saw something in the darkened corner. This brief jolt was dismissed when Bev reminded her employee that, with the recent telling of ghost stories, the incident could have been all in her mind . . . perhaps. We were all a little amused with the event, but Bev went on to tell us of a couple of strange incidences that had taken place over the years.

One story Bev shared with us involved a desk, which is said to have moved from one end of an upstairs room to the other, seemingly by itself. Of course, something like this could have been done by the living, but Bev and others are certain that there was no mortal intervention taking place with the moving desk. There are some who feel this playful activity is the kind of behavior the patrons of yesteryear would expect from Julie Cheverette, just to get a chuckle out of someone. Remember those rubber spiders hanging over the tables and doors? It was Julie who once lowered them onto unsuspecting customers, so it wouldn't be too much of a stretch to believe that this prankster would continue her antics in the afterlife.

Then there's the alarm system which was once prone to going off by itself in the middle of the night. Bev said that after being awakened by the alarm and having to go upstairs in the wee hours of the morning, she decided to tell these ghosts to cease their noisy activities at once. Sure enough, the alarms stopped. Although this particular annoyance ended, sometimes late at night the employees and occasional patrons can hear the sounds of pacing back and forth, shuffling feet, and doors opening and closing by themselves. This happens when there's no one upstairs, with the doors locked to prove it.

Bev continued to tell of how at one time the staff were allowed to stay overnight in the upstairs apartments if they wanted. This was a kind gesture especially if they would have had a long drive home and were working early the next day. This was a logical choice after longer than usual nights, and several employees took advantage of the offer. However, they never stayed very long. The reason? There was just too much noise: sounds of moving around, walking up and down the stairs, and pacing on the creaky wooden floors. The spooky activity was altogether too much to bear. Some left the very first night because they were so frightened, and some to this day refuse to go upstairs for that very reason. And who could blame them? After all, this really is a spooky setting that could have anyone looking over his shoulder, especially at night in the middle of absolutely nowhere.

Afterthoughts

When you visit the Desert Inn you will meet only the most sincere and genuine people. Serving truckers, travelers, and tourists from around the nation and even the world, the Desert Inn is like a lonely beacon of civilization for the tired, hungry, and thirsty traveler. Those who visit are most likely hoping to find something unique, something genuinely Floridian, and the Desert Inn will definitely provide this. The food is great, too, resonating Florida in dishes like frogs legs, fried turtle, fried gator, or genuine Southern fried chicken . . . and you can throw in a few ghosts at no extra charge.

There is no doubt that the Desert Inn is a special historical landmark in Florida today, and with many such places disappearing in favor of new and improved modernized buildings, we are indeed fortunate to have such direct links to our history.

Is the Desert Inn haunted? Many people seem to think so. As this location was once home to rough people and rough situations, it's not unreasonable to believe that such powerfully spirited personalities might choose to remain at the place that was important to them in life. Other theories suggest that the paranormal activity might simply be psychic recordings playing over and over in a specific pattern, not actually coming from a sentient origin. Yet many at the Desert Inn feel otherwise, especially when remembering the antics of one of the late owners. As the Desert Inn and many locations like it were and are still active depositories of human emotions, both good and bad, the idea of such emotions continuing after death seem logical for many.

So, if you're traveling on the turnpike en route to Disney World or south to Palm Beach for the weekend, and you see the Yeehaw Junction exit, why not stop off and visit one of Florida's less-advertised restaurants and motels. Enjoy the good food and maybe have a drink, and keep your eyes on those hanging rubber spiders above you, as you'll never know when one might drop. Above all, keep an ear open for disembodied footsteps coming from the rooms upstairs. Although the atmosphere is both amusing and a bit creepy, you might just find there's much more than just history waiting to be found at this little place in the middle of nowhere.

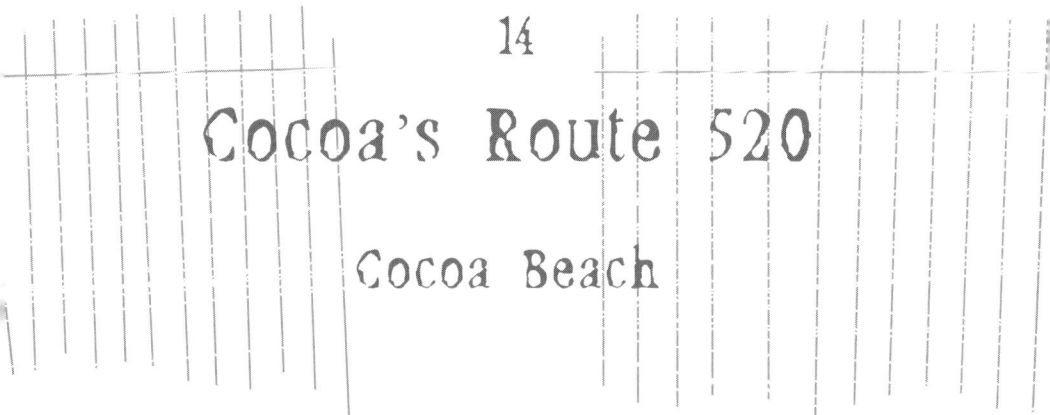

14

Cocoa's Route 520

Cocoa Beach

The Ghost Lights of Bloody 520

A Little History

Route 520 begins at Colonial highway, also known as State Road 50, and runs southeast to Federal Highway, US-1. Although a shortcut for many travelers, it is one of the most dangerous roads in central Florida. In fact, according to the Florida Highway Patrol, Route 520 ranks as the third most deadly road in the United States. Though speedy, 520 is only a two-lane road, which creates many fatal accidents and earns the name "Bloody 520." Long and winding, this stretch of road runs through an unlit, dense forest, so it stands to reason that accidents are even more likely here . . . and many an accident there has been.

Ghostly Legends and Haunted Folklore

Route 520 has had a long ghostly past, and many travelers have not heard of such legends, but if you ask some of the more mature or native Floridians, you may gain insight into this storied road. I have had the good fortune of hearing some of these legends firsthand from

several of the locals. It was a fine experience of rich oral tradition and ghost lore.

Route 520 appears to be home to arguably the oddest apparitions, known as ghost lights or spook lights. These spook lights are said to be greenish-colored, iridescent balls of light, which are sometimes seen floating on the sides of the roads. Sometimes, they are seen in pairs, and sometimes there is only one, but the most interesting aspect to this legend is the report that some of these spook lights have been known to chase people and even vehicles.

According to one gentleman who has lived in Cocoa Beach since the late 1950s, a spook light followed his wife home in 1977. Apparently, when his wife was coming home from a visit in Orlando, while at the midway point of Route 520, she saw a free-floating, glowing ball of light hovering near the passenger side of her car, keeping pace with her for several minutes. She tried to justify what she was seeing as a reflection of another car light hitting her window or maybe the light from her dashboard somehow casting the glow. Yet, no matter how hard she tried to find an answer, the light eerily continued to bob up and down, keeping up with her car as if it were alive.

Finally, this ghostly light slowed a bit and then was still on the side of the road. When she later told the story of how she was chased by the ball of light, the woman said she finally watched it disappear into the woods through her rear view mirror. Not surprisingly, the gentlemen who supplied this wonderful tale also told me that his wife would never take nocturnal journeys through Route 520 alone again.

Another story came from a cook at one of Cocoa Beach's roadside diners. According to this man, sometime in late 1990s, after closing the restaurant for the evening, he began walking home for the night. His home was about a mile and a half down Route 520, so being without a car was usually not too much of a problem. While walking on the left side of the road, however, he noticed a faint greenish light about fifty yards into the dense woods. This light was pulsating like a lantern, and so he thought it must be some local hunters looking for opossum or raccoons. Yet there was something about this light that didn't quite add up. As the man continued for home, the light seemed to be keeping pace with him, and then suddenly, as if out of nowhere, a second, dimmer light appeared behind the first. Now the weary traveler admitted that he was getting a little nervous and quickened his pace for home, all the time wishing the lights would just stop.

These lights continued to follow this gentleman for nearly twenty minutes, bobbing up and down just as if they were hunters' lanterns, which he hoped they were. No such luck. Within a few minutes, the first light seemed to move upward, as if climbing a tree, while the second light got very dim and finally faded to just a small dot of light. By this time our traveler was quite fearful, and so he crossed the road and quickened his pace even more, looking back only to find the floating ball of light now in the center of the road.

The cook confessed that when he saw this he decided to stop and hold his ground in case this was someone pulling a prank. He was ready to chastise the prankster, but when the light flickered and then extinguished all together, he changed his mind and raced home, never to see the ghostly ball of light again. Although the cook was quite jovial when telling this story, he admitted that he has a car now, and if for some reason he were to be stranded, he would not walk home at night alone again . . . not on Route 520 anyway.

Afterthoughts

In my quest for some kind of logical explanation for this phenomenon, I asked different people with various specialties, and each had different answers. When I asked a biologist and professor what these balls of light could be, he said that it is most likely swamp gas, the natural ignitions of decomposing methane. This sounded like a stable scientific explanation, yet I had to wonder if swamp gas could chase a car or follow someone walking down the road at night. His other response was even more scientific: he simply said that it was the witnesses' imaginations.

The second person I asked was an officer with the Florida Highway Patrol. He said that he'd heard similar stories from people over the years but had never seen these spook lights himself. He did say, however, that he has seen more than his share of fatal accidents on Route 520, and that if there could be a stretch of road that is haunted, it would be 520 for sure. This was an unexpected reply, especially from someone like a law enforcement officer, but it seems to make sense to me, as 520 is practically a graveyard.

Apparently, the most common time these spook lights are witnessed is between 10:00 P.M. and 3:30 A.M., so when you're driving alone on Route 520, remember to buckle up, keep your eyes on the road, and don't push the speed limit, because the Florida Highway Patrol may not be the only ones watching you.

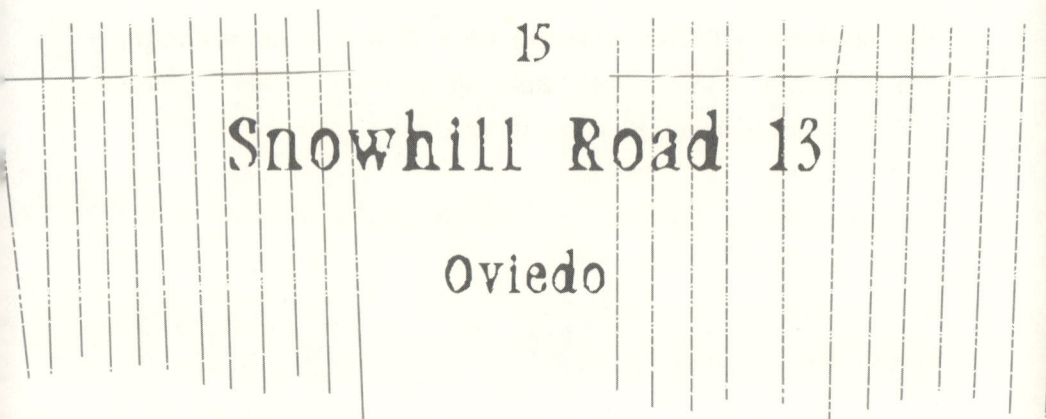

15

Snowhill Road 13

Oviedo

The Oviedo Lights and the Haunted Celery Fields

A Little History

The township of Oviedo, nestled between Orlando and Sanford and only minutes from the University of Central Florida, is one of the fastest-growing cities in the state. Oviedo was founded in 1875 by forty or so pioneer families who saw the rich soil and pleasant lakes as a potential agricultural hotspot for future farming and development, as well as a clean and safe environment for their children. With this simple philosophy and much effort, this quaint hamlet grew into the citrus and celery capital of central Florida and remained that way for many years. And, although Oviedo is rightly considered a city, it has managed to keep its old Florida township charm intact.

The Seminole Indians are believed to have lived in Oviedo's general area, including nearby Chuluota, centuries before the white settlers arrived. Evidence of this, including villages as well as several tribal burial mounds, has been discovered by archaeologists in recent years. Through the center of the ruins of an ancient village and burial ground runs the Little Econlockhatchee River, over which runs State Road 13, also known as Snowhill Road. Although a concrete bridge was completed in 1996, there once stood an old two-lane, wooden bridge that was used for many years, and it is at this site where several burial mounds once sat undisturbed, where the legend of the Oviedo lights is said to have originated.

Ghostly Legends and Haunted Folklore

The legend of the Oviedo lights has been told and retold throughout the years in both Oviedo and Chuluota, as far back as the 1880s, and the legend is faithfully kept alive even today. I first heard the legend of the Oviedo Lights while having breakfast at the Town Square Restaurant, one of Oviedo's time-honored eateries. One of the local people I spoke with, who had lived in Oviedo since the 1940s, remembered the legend well, especially the stories from teenage lovers who would go to the old Snowhill Road bridge on weekend nights to enjoy Oviedo's equivalent of a lover's lane. These stories featured greenish-blue orbs of light that would float up from over the river, bobbing up and down and fading away, or on some occasions, actually following cars and people as they crossed the bridge. To date, there continue to be reports of strange phenomena occurring at this same location. Many say these events are nothing more than swamp gas rising from the river, but many people from Oviedo know better—they're ghost lights!

Oviedo is certainly not alone in this phenomena, as legends of ghost lights, spook lights, *ignis fatuus* ("foolish fire"), and willow o' the wisps are all examples of these strange, luminous balls. These glowing balls of light have been seen all over the world, sharing similar qualities and behaviors, since ancient times. Moreover, even though scientists have tried to find the reasons behind these ghost lights—swamp gas, or reflections of headlights from distant cars—hard evidence of their true nature has never been conclusively established by anyone.

There have been many scientists and self-styled investigators over the years who have claimed that these lights are created as a result of the breakdown of various plant and animal deposits, thus creating a methane gas. When ignited through natural causes, methane generates an upward dispersal and instant glow, or "burn off," thus causing the spooky event. The process is usually instant and will reach up a few feet and fizzle out. This event is in fact a true scientific occurrence, which takes place in most swamps, estuaries, and other like bodies of stagnant water, but the Oviedo lights act differently.

The scientific process of burning swamp gas will usually take place within the summer months when it is balmy and humid, and even at night when there is a slight cool down in air temperature. Because of such explanations, it seems at first a logical assumption to believe these strange lights originate completely naturally. Swamp gas does not, however, float through the woods and follow cars or people as they pass, or in this case, float across the bridge on Snowhill Road. So the aforementioned scientific rationale, as far as the Oviedo lights are concerned, is insufficient.

The Oviedo lights have been reported to have a playful aura to them, almost like that of a child playing hide and seek. Sometimes these lights have been reported to sneak up behind those walking on the bridge, and although that might be a bit startling, there have never been reports of these luminous orbs causing harm to anyone. No, the lights appear to be more entertaining rather than anything dangerous or evil, and this particular aspect of the legend has remained the same for many years.

For years now people have gone to the old bridge on Snowhill Road for romantic endeavors. On many of those nights, some people will witness these eerie lights—sometimes bluish-green, sometimes yellowish-white in color—bobbing up and down over the river and up the banks. And sometimes, just sometimes, these lights cross the bridge as if alive, zigzagging in all directions. Sometimes these lights reduce to the size of a lemon and then expand to the size of a basket-ball, and then flicker like a Morse code signal, only then to dissolve altogether. One thing that always remains the same is that if you try to follow or catch the lights, they simply float away in a playful man-ner, as if they were a sentient life. That's some swamp gas!

The supernatural reasoning for these ghost lights varies from one legend to another, but one of Oviedo's more popular, time-honored theories says that these lights are the result of a suicide that took place on the old bridge many years ago. Apparently, there was a young man in post–World War II times who hanged himself off the railing of the bridge, the result of a broken heart and love lost. On occasion, his foggy spirit has been seen drifting under the bridge on moonless nights, head bowed and despondent. Although the specifics of this specter are questionable, many of Oviedo's and Chuluota's local peo-ple seem to follow this legend with great zest and acceptance.

Another legend of the lights involves reflections from a spectral locomotive, spiritually left over from the late Victorian Era. Some of the locals have been spinning yarns about a derailed train from Henry Flagler's Florida East Coast Railway that still steams and rumbles to an unseen destination. Some have even claimed to have heard the scream of a train's whistle in the wee hours of cold mornings, although there have been no trains in that area since the early 1930s.

The most readily accepted explanation today has gained ground with a greater awareness of the atrocities the Native American Indians suffered in our past. Archaeological discoveries have proven the exis-tence of burial mounds, which have been disturbed, built over, or completely destroyed by the advance of agricultural and industrial progress. It would stand to reason that the dead would be restless. To this end, many believe that these lights are the wandering souls of the Native American dead, whose graves have been carelessly desecrated over the years. While any of these legends may be true, the Oviedo lights have certainly found a place of wonder in the annals of Florida's strange and haunted history.

These ghost lights are so accepted in Oviedo that almost every resident who has lived there more than five years will have heard of them. And if you speak to long-time residents about this phenomenon, you might just hear a firsthand account of these odd, floating orbs.

Oviedo's agricultural history is quite impressive; it was known as the celery capital of the United States for a time starting in the 1880s, a profitable business that was to last for roughly forty years. As the land became less and less fertile, however, the farmers went north to grow their celery or started different crops altogether. By the end of World War II, most of the celery farms were gone completely, leaving barren, unattended celery fields growing wild. Today, there are streets and houses built where most of the crops once grew, but something from Oviedo's past remains in these fields. Several of the longtime residents of Oviedo relate another ghost story, which is rarely heard: the ghostly children of the celery fields.

The Oviedo settlement was in the early stages of becoming a genuine, thriving establishment. There was a general store, a town square, a common area where daily commerce took place, and a schoolhouse, as well as wood-plank homes sprouting up all over the area and farmers hard at work in the celery fields and citrus groves. Oviedo was looking very prosperous. According to local historians, around 1878 a family tragedy took place during the early morning hours, when there was a thick, low-level fog drifting over the moist ground. Although the name of the family and their position in the town is still a mystery, the legend of this tragedy and its aftermath has remained strong through the oral traditions of the people of Oviedo. Apparently, as the legend goes, a young widow and her three young children were riding in a horse-drawn carriage early in the morning, en route to the St. Johns River.

The fog was extremely thick that morning, and the mother and the horses could not see the road ahead of them. One of the wheels snapped while running over a rock, hurling the carriage down a watery bank. The mother was thrown from her seat, surviving the accident, but all three children were either crushed or drowned. Although the particulars of this story are as foggy as the morning that tore this family apart, the legend lives on. The children are apparently buried in an obscure cemetery in the town of Geneva, just northeast of Oviedo. The mother is said to have lived a short life after the tragedy. Then, consumed with sadness and guilt, she died a lonely and bitter woman. And they say the children now walk the celery fields looking for their mother.

Even though the area has grown considerably since the 1870s, there have been quite a few people over the years who have claimed to see three children, no more than eight years old, wandering a portion of these desolate celery fields in the early hours of particularly foggy mornings. Some have claimed that the children are happy, skipping hand-in-hand and giggling, while others claim they are visibly upset, crying for their lost mother. One longtime resident of Oviedo told me about a woman she knew for years, a coworker, who came to work one morning shaken and as pale as a ghost. The woman said that while she was traveling through Oviedo to get to work in Orlando one morning around 5 A.M., she saw what appeared to be three or four children dressed in white gowns, walking in an empty field near the road she was on. They looked very distraught, and she was concerned that they might be lost. She stopped her car, pointed her headlights toward the field and started walking where she saw the children. When she got in the middle of the field, however, an icy chill overcame her, and she finally noticed she was alone in an empty field. There were no children.

Afterthoughts

Ghostly children walking through empty fields during the wee hours of the morning or illuminated balls of light bobbing up and down near old bridges are just some of the sights you might find in little Oviedo. Similar legends can certainly be seen in many ghost stories from cultures all over the world. Legends like these have enticed kids to tell and retell their stories for many, many years: teenage lovers watch flickering lights in wonderment as they sit on the shores of the Little Econlockhatchee River. Perhaps these spooky lights are nothing more than swamp gas. Maybe there is indeed a logical, scientific explanation to this phenomenon. Yet, if you travel down old Snowhill Road late at night while driving through the little town of Oviedo, take a moment to park along the banks near this bridge and keep a keen eye on the river gliding silently past you.

With the dark, swampy woods surrounding you, filled with the sounds of Florida's own natural night life, try to remember that you are sitting on an ancient Native American burial ground. Try to remember the history that took place there and maybe you too will experience the wonderment of the Oviedo ghost lights. If you see three small children wondering through the empty celery fields early in the morning and stop to pursue them for their own safety, don't be surprised if you find nothing but a cool wind passing through your body and the echoes of giggling in the fog. Remember that even in a small city like Oviedo there may still be the ghostly personalities and the reflections of a simpler time.

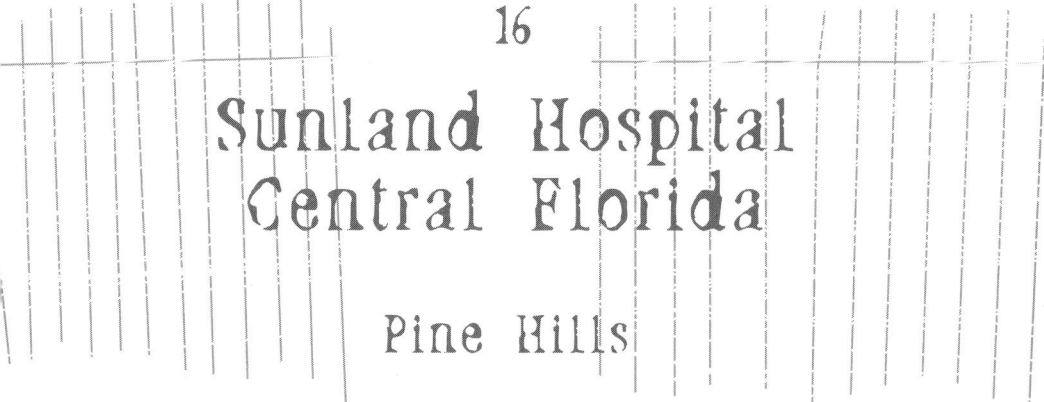

16
Sunland Hospital Central Florida

Pine Hills

Strange Lights, Eerie Cries, and Echoing Footfalls

When we arrived on the site, we knew it was bad. The kid was lying in a pool of blood with some of the metal parts from the elevator sticking through his right side. By the time rescue got him out of the shaft, he was slipping away, but fortunately he survived the fall down the shaft. I don't know about ghosts, but there was one weird thing: one of the other officers called in and said he saw a child, around ten or eleven, looking out the second-floor widow, so a few of us went to look, but didn't find anyone there. He didn't come from DCF. We checked, and no one reported a missing child matching that description, so that was kind of weird. . . . That place was always strange, even when it was a working hospital, so I'm glad it's finally gone.
—*Anonymous Orange County Sheriff's Deputy, 2001*

A Little History

Oftentimes known as "Sunnyland" or "Bellevue Hospital," Sunland Hospital, located off Laurel Hill Drive at 8800 Silver Star Road in Pine Hills, was synonymous with suffering and mistreatment for many years. Although Sunland's remains are almost completely gone today, the very name conjures thoughts of doom for the longtime residents of Pine Hills and of course, for any surviving patients that were unlucky enough to be placed there. The Sunland Hospital chain was run by the State of Florida and the Department of Heath and Rehabilitative Services (HRS), a program that could be as detrimental as it could beneficial. Of the many complaints Sunland administrators had, most were about financial problems. Because the state had only so much money for assisting the severely retarded patients at all the Sunland locations throughout Florida, the level of care and the number of qualified nurses and technicians were limited. As a result, these children were sometimes left alone for hours at a time, and many of them were forced to receive their food via feeding tubes instead of receiving meals from a caretaker.

Reports of children sharing rooms with violent offenders had been bad enough, but when a night orderly was accused in the mysterious pregnancy of a patient, Sunland Hospital was once again put under the spotlight. Moreover, a similar incident at the Sunland Hospital in Marianna, Florida, fueled a series of intense inquires by HRS and inspections of all Florida hospitals. Fortunately, these abuses finally came to an end in 1978 when the Association for Retarded Citizens (ARC) filed a federal class-action lawsuit on behalf of the Sunland patients for gross neglect and abuse. It seemed any hospital bearing the name Sunland would be cursed, especially the Central Florida Sunland Hospital and its sister hospital in Tallahassee. These hospitals, which both had ominous and sad reputations, would come to an end in 1983 and '84, only to leave a more frightening and even evil reputation years after they closed.

Three floors and 350,000 square feet of the Central Florida Sunland hospital were demolished in 1999 by Orlando Central Environmental Services, a demolition and environmental services company. Because Sunland had such large amounts of asbestos within its walls, the procedures for its removal and destruction cost the State of Florida around five million dollars. The land where the main hospital once stood has since been replaced by a large park and playground, but just to the east of the property lie the creepy remains of a sad and turbulent time. The original doctors' offices, a nurses' retreat, and several planning offices, as well as some of the transitional housing, still exist on that part of the property. There is a red-brick, two-story building that once served as an office and sleeping quarters for Sunland's physicians and nurses, and later became offices for psychologists, behavioral staff, and activity therapists. Today, the Department for Children and Families (formerly HRS) uses this building primarily for patient records and other file storage.

Overgrown with ivy and surrounded by oak trees, this colonial-style building, with its porthole windows and arched breezeways, stands silent. The windows are now dark with heavy deposits of rust, as are the large metal doors at the entrance. Sunland Hospital, thought by most to be dead, somehow continues to live . . . as if it were waiting for something.

Ghostly Legends and Haunted Folklore

When the main building still stood silent and alone, with its broken windows and walls covered with graffiti, it was certainly a foreboding image, and over the years, a strange fascination grew about it. Although most would just stand behind the ten-foot fence and gaze at the ominous grayish hulk, some were more inclined to break the law and enter the hospital's old and dangerous remains. Indeed, many of Orlando's youth have traveled inside the old hospital to hunt for macabre trophies, or to get a glimpse of the creepy interior. And oddly enough, some even went there to look for ghosts. Several of these brave explorers found more than just graffiti and old dusty hospital beds; they found something far more terrifying.

Over the years, many stories circulated about strange flashes of light coming from the third floor, as well as sounds of metal objects being dropped or thrown throughout the huge interior. There were several accounts of small children seen walking around inside the empty hallways or on the roof, which would at times alert the authorities to search the building. According to legend, the apparition of an hysterical young girl has been seen screaming on the third-floor landing, flailing her arms, her eyes closed in obvious pain. And of course, anyone who saw such a sight would run to her aid. But when she was approached, the child would stand up, still screaming, and jump off the third-floor perch. When the startled witness would run over to see where she had fallen, the child would be gone. This little girl in distress is said to wear a pale green dress, definitely of an older style. She was also described as having auburn hair tied in the back and freckles on her cheeks, making her look, as one witness said, "like a cute little kid who just got lost." No one has since offered a plausible explanation for this tormented spirit or any information of a suicide involving a young girl flinging herself from the third-story stairwell. However, while investigating the Florida Photographic Archives, I managed to find several interesting photographs of children from the 1960s or early 1970s. Apparently, the Sunland Hospital system allowed some of the higher-functioning, long-term patients to join chapters of both the Boy Scouts and Girl Scouts as a part of therapy. Interestingly enough, the Girl Scouts wore pale green dresses, much like that worn by the screaming spirit of the third floor.

There was another spirit witnessed within the creepy Sunland building, and although less frightening than the screaming girl in green, it does appear to be another lost child. Legends say that this child is forever searching for something. When two teenagers were wandering on the third floor late one summer evening in 1992, they met this ghostly inhabitant. As the two trespassers were climbing the eastern stairwell, they observed a boy, who at first appeared to be just another kid exploring the building until he walked through a half-opened door. This young boy, around ten or eleven, seemed to be desperately searching for something, as he would duck from doorway to doorway constantly looking around. The ghost was said to have stopped and looked directly at the two explorers for a few seconds, then continued his search, which took him straight through a large metal door that stood only partially ajar. Needless to say, the two teenage explorers hastily departed the old building and began a long line of haunted legends.

Local stories about the haunted Sunland Hospital continued throughout the years, igniting the adventurous spirits of countless central Florida teenagers. Most of the time, these kids would sneak in, although it was illegal, and tell ghost stories, then depart without incident. Sometimes local law enforcement would be waiting near the fence where these intrepid explorers entered and arrest them on their way out for breaking and entering. On one occasion, however, an accident took place. One humid and muggy summer morning in 1997, around 4:00 A.M., twenty-year-old Keith Murdock learned a painful lesson. While exploring the third floor, he thought he was entering a dark room, but it was actually an elevator shaft. He fell three stories with a loud crash. Murdock's friends, hearing the disturbance, became understandably concerned, and after searching several minutes for their friend, they found him lying unconscious in a pool of blood. They feared the worst, as a section of metal from the elevator's mechanisms was showing through his side. More than thirty minutes passed before rescue workers finally reached him, and although he sustained a fractured skull and extreme damage to his spine and stomach, he survived the accident. This was the incident that finally forced authorities to tear down the main section of the Sunland Hospital. An era of ghostly legends was over . . . or was it?

Most paranormal investigators and lay ghost hunters believe that Orlando's haunted Sunland is no more. Because the main structure of the hospital, its wards and patient rooms, the mess hall, and everything in between have been demolished, the hauntings must have stopped. After all, now that a quaint playground sits where the hospital's foreboding hulk once stood, ghosts like the screaming girl in green and the lost little boy must have moved past our corporeal world and on into the ethereal plane. Many feel otherwise, however, as sections of the original hospital remain just around the corner.

In the last few years, self-styled ghost hunters and paranormal investigators have visited the site where the hospital once stood. Taking many photographs with conventional 35mm cameras, digital cameras, and infrared video recorders, these investigators have found substantial—if not controversial—evidence of orb phenomena. These strange balls of iridescent light have been caught on film between the main site and the parking lot, and there have been reports of strong electromagnetic energy fluctuations. When searching around the parking lot, several of the investigators became aware of the aroma of roses, which in it itself is auspicious in the realm of psychical research. As the roses are associated with a blessing or a holy event, the presence of such a scent may refer to the release of the aforementioned spirits. Most investigation teams are not allowed to wear perfume or cologne, as it would distract from any olfactory phenomena, and so the scent of roses may be accounted as something significant to many professional researchers.

Most of the people who visit the location where Sunland Hospital once stood are unaware of the hospital's other sections, which still exist today. Just east of the parking lot and playground, behind a patch of tall pine trees, rests the two-story, red-brick doctors offices and clinic. Once used as office space for Sunland's physicians, psychologists, and therapists, this structure now sits lifeless. The metal doors are los-

ing paint and rusting, while the windows, covered in ivy and mold, stair blankly out at the street. The building serves no other purpose but to store outdated equipment and old medical records . . . but spirits are said to reside here, too.

Although there are only a handful of people who know the entire history of the Sunland Hospital system and the terrible reminders left in its wake, and even fewer who understand how the mental health system operates, it is no surprise that this last structure goes unnoticed. Although the building has not amassed many paranormal events as the main structure once did, strange things have been noticed on moonlit nights. Shortly after the destruction and removal of the old Sunland complex, those who once passed their summer nights sneaking around its dark and dingy hallways could only reminisce of their old escapades. As these one-time adventurers walk around the grounds, they sometimes stumble on the other building. During the day, this building looks pretty creepy. At night, however, it will absolutely send a chill up your spine. One group of teenagers walking around the old Sunland haunting grounds found much more than they bargained for.

Apparently, during the autumn months in 2000, four teenagers, in search of the haunted hospital their older friends had told them about, came across a pile of dirt and sand where it once stood. All the ghost stories they had heard when they were children dissolved to disappointment. Building up the suspense and mystery over the years made it unbearable when they realized it was no longer there. Downhearted, the four teens decided to walk down a nearby deserted street, which had obviously been there for a long time because it was riddled with potholes and overgrown with weeds and grass. As they walked down this street, they came across an old red brick building on their left. The building looked as deserted and as unused as the road they were traveling on, and with hopes of finding at least one ghost, they ventured up to the main entrance.

The boys tried looking in through the windows but it was completely dark inside, not even a glowing exit sign to cast some kind of light, and the windows were covered with soot and mold, which only added to the problem. They pulled on the doors to see if they were unlocked and sure enough, the door on the left opened with a reluctant thud. The boys, a bit startled, stood back and tried peering into the darkness, commenting on the musty smell of age. Without warning, they heard something fall within the black interior. Understandably, the four boys jumped back and started running toward the road. As they ran, the door, which was so rusted it stood open on its own, suddenly slammed shut.

The boys were sprinting back to the main road, but they managed to look back one last time to see if someone was chasing them. They saw nothing but the dark building, so they stopped to catch their breath. While standing there, breathing heavily, they noticed a brief flicker of yellowish light within the building. Suddenly, the flicker became a blindingly bright light, which glowed for a few moments and then stopped as suddenly as it had started. Needless to say, the four boys abandoned their search for ghosts and called it a night. It wasn't until much later that they discovered a strange footnote to their encounter: there has been no electricity running to that old brick building since 1985.

Afterthoughts

Although there have been other strange stories regarding the old building since that October night in 2000, from faces peering out of the windows to balls of light bobbing up and down within, the incident the four boys encountered was arguably the most frightening to date. Perhaps the spirits within, if any, were displeased with the lack of respect for the building. Perhaps these spirits were just giving the boys what they had wanted all along.

The true story of Sunland Hospitals, whether in Tallahassee, Gainesville, or Orlando, tells of sad and controversial circumstances to be sure. The lives that were lost during the many years were documented. And, although I have such documentation, I will omit it from this book for one simple reason: it is just too sad. If visiting the site where Sunland in Pine Hills once stood, keep in mind that this property is owned by the State of Florida's Department of Children and Families. The property is presently open to the public, but unlawful entry into any building will result in criminal prosecution, so keep your distance. Feel free to walk around the playground and park area. Take photos here in search of orbs, and see if you too can smell the light scent of roses. Take a stroll up the street where the old red brick building remains and see if you can catch a glimpse of a flicker of light, or perhaps you'll spot a face peering through the window right back at you.

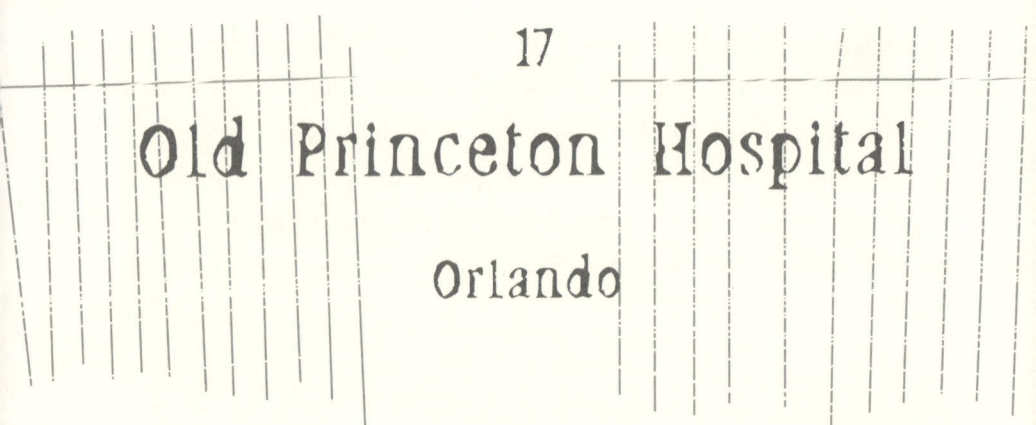

17

Old Princeton Hospital

Orlando

Dead Eyes on the Third Floor

A Little History

Located at 1800 Mercy Drive in Orlando, nestled behind tall trees and hidden within a thicket of beautifully landscaped gardens, rests a 140,000 square-foot building once known as Princeton Hospital. This rather plain structure, which sits on sixty-six acres near Lake Lawne, has a long history of helping thousands of people with mental illness since the 1960s. After years of service and dedication, suffering severe financial problems, the Princeton Hospital was forced to close its doors in July of 1999. The old and outdated building only sat idle for a short time, and it was soon reborn as The Lakeside Hospital, opening once again on September 1, 2000.

Devoted entirely to mental health patients, this psychiatric care hospital was able to offer a better place for recovery and rehabilitation than many hospitals today. Through advanced treatments, day and evening programs for the community, a specialized treatment center, as well as a medication trial center, Lakeside Hospital offers a great deal to those in need. Constant improvements in its system have dramatically enhanced the ability to better serve patients through superi-

or customer service and added conveniences, making Lakeside a great advancement since the facilities of Princeton Hospital's day.

Having worked in the psychiatric field for many years, I am familiar with the Lakeside Hospital system, which has attended the needs of many in central Florida for more than twenty years. Originally, Princeton Hospital was one of four separate mental health facilities in central Florida that merged with the newly formed Mental Health Services of Orange County in 1983. It then became known as Lakeside Hospital, and has grown to be among the finest psychiatric hospitals in the United States.

Because Lakeside Hospital today boasts better organization, an improved coordination of staff and healthcare-related projects, as well as the genuine respect for patients that all hospitals should have, there is both efficiency and quality of care for those in need of mental health services. With this mixture of medical knowledge and compassion, Lakeside Hospital offers aid for those suffering from emotional or psychiatric illnesses.

During my eight years in central Florida, I heard several stories about Lakeside Hospital from mental health technicians and nurses as well as from former patients. These events range from empty wheelchairs moving by themselves to the visible apparition of a doctor to a deceased nun walking around as if still working at old Princeton. Other events, such as feelings of dread when walking through the dark boiler room or the old morgue, are also common. Yet, the most upsetting event to take place has been the apparition of an unidentified patient who hatefully stares at the staff, as if moments away from trying to kill them. Although it was difficult to obtain some of the legends associated with the old Princeton Hospital, I was fortunate enough to have had friends working closely with the new hospital, thus receiving several intense and intriguing legends that would otherwise go untold. Because of the sensitive nature of this psychiatric hospital, or any hospital for that matter, I cannot refer to any employee or patient by name, but I will instead refer to witnesses by their position or status at Lakeside Hospital.

Ghostly Legends and Haunted Folklore

As with any hospital, the old Princeton Hospital's successor has seen its fair share of pain and misery over the years. Although many of the patients who have stayed here have gone on to find some degree of happiness in their lives, others have not been so fortunate, slipping through the cracks of our society and into the obscurity of institutionalization. Some of these poor souls have died in fits of rage and madness, creating many intensely negative feelings that apparently marked their fragile souls in the realms of our haunted world. In addition, even as the new and improved Lakeside Hospital offers much more than the psychiatric hospitals and mental heath clinics of years ago, some of these patients of long ago, now deceased, appear to be continuing their complaints. Indeed, some claim that in the dim halls of this hospital, there still echo the screams and torment of years ago.

I first heard about the haunted Princeton Hospital back in 1996 when I was working as a mental health technician with the University Center, a psychiatric hospital in east Orlando. A nurse there told me about Princeton's spooky side—strange things that have taken place on the second and third floors, which were later locked and off limits, where even the patients were unwilling to spend the nights. Apparently, the patients would be awoken by the sounds of things moving around, discovering a shadowy woman dressed as a nun walking across the floor in the dead of night. Although startled at first, some of the patients found comfort in knowing a representative of the church was there, only later to be surprised when they discovered that there was no nun in the hospital.

The nurse continued to tell me about reports of a phantom doctor who would be seen checking and rechecking his clipboard at the end of one of the closed-off corridors; then he would simply disappear. Interestingly enough, she said that there was a doctor back in the early 1970s who was so upset over the death of a patient of his that his mood changed dramatically and he became extremely depressed. It was rumored shortly after that that the doctor took his own life. Though this might sound like a popular ghost story told to frighten new technicians on the night shift, the nurse who told me the story swore by the legend and the many incidents that had taken place thereafter. After hearing some of these legends I became even more interested, and I began asking others working with me if they had ever heard of any haunted events over at Princeton Hospital, and sure enough, many had heard various ghost stories regarding the old hospital. The ghostly nun and the phantom doctor, for instance, have been seen on the second and third floors for at least a decade. Over the years, many creepy stories had been reported by nurses, technicians, and even a non-believing psychologist. Perhaps there is more to

Princeton Hospital's ghosts than mere legend.

Years passed since I had worked as a technician, and I had all but forgotten the ghost stories from old Princeton Hospital. I had known that the hospital closed a few years back, but didn't know that it had reopened and continued to function as a psychiatric hospital until recently, while I was working with a homeless center in downtown Orlando. I was taking one of my clients over to the Lakeside Hospital on Mercy Drive in Orlando when I remembered that the location was where old Princeton Hospital used to be. When approaching the main entrance, I saw a woman walk out, a woman I recognized as a former technician who had worked with me when I was at the University Center back in 1996. I told my client to go inside and sign in, while I stayed to reminisce happily with my old coworker. Seeing an opportunity to find out firsthand if there were indeed any ghosts reported in the hospital, I told her that I was writing a book on the subject. She exclaimed rather loudly that I had come to the right place. As she continued to tell me some of the paranormal events, I knew she was right: I had indeed come to the right place.

My friend told me of several events that were not only legend, but in her words, they were absolute fact. While working on the third floor, which was now used as a drug-testing center where volunteers were tested with experimental psychotropic pharmaceuticals, she had experienced several strange things. As she was sitting at the nurse's desk filling out patient reports one night, she heard a tapping at the double doors. Every employee has a badge to get through every door in the hospital, and if a patient or guest was visiting, they would have to be escorted by a security guard or technician, so she could not understand why someone would be knocking. It seemed strange.

Still, she got up to look through the porthole window at the door and saw no one. She thought this was odd, but started back for her desk, when once again there were three light knocks at the door. This time, somewhat disgusted, she headed back, hit the red release button, and opened the two doors, only to find a vacant hallway. Feeling a bit unsettled by the whole event, she stood back, let the doors close and lock, then headed back to her desk and called security downstairs to see if anyone had been allowed in the elevators. The two guards on the first floor informed her that no one was sent up the elevators or the stairs, nor had anyone been escorted anywhere in the last two hours. Knowing that there are security cameras on every floor, she asked if they would play back the surveillance tapes to make sure. They checked, but the security guards found no sign of anyone in the building that should not have been there and no one at all on her floor. It was an eerie mystery for sure.

My friend continued to tell me of a few other events that had her asking for a security escort when entering the dreaded second floor. For years, before the medication testing ward opened on the third floor, both the second and third floors were locked up and off limits to anyone but the building's engineer, security, and certain members of the administration. The floors had fully made beds and the normal accouterments of typical hospital rooms, left over from the early days of Princeton Hospital, even though these rooms had lain empty for more than a year and were now covered with a thin layer of dust and enshrouded in darkness. The empty hallways, with wheelchairs folded and lined up against the walls and full linen carts standing behind abandoned nurses' desks, only echoed a once-busy hospital ward. Today, although the third floor is busy again, the second floor remains empty, resonating something uncanny. And according to at least one late-shift security guard, the whole floor is unquestionably haunted.

According to my friend, the security guard who worked the evening shift reported a very frightening event, an event that had him requesting different hours. The guard had many duties as a security officer, namely watching his surveillance cameras, patrolling the floors, and making sure the patients were safe and under control during the night, and these were all usually easy tasks. On one particular night, the building engineer called in to have one of the guards go to the second floor to get some boxes from a storage room and bring them down to his office. The guard saw no problem with the request and headed for the second floor.

Because the hospital conserves energy, the lights on all unused floors are turned off, but with a special key, a maintenance man or security officer could turn them on when needed. The guard arrived on the second floor and fumbled with his keys and flashlight to turn on the main overhead lights, then put his key into the storage room door. As he did this, he heard the sound of someone talking from behind the doors. Understandably unnerved, he opened the door slowly with his flashlight raised high to scan the room before walking in to turn on the lights, which were located by the nurses' station. With only the hallway light barely lighting the ward inside, he took his flashlight and scanned the long corridor. Suddenly, he heard what sounded like a whisper, and from a darkened patient's room, an empty wheelchair slowly rolled out, then stopped when it bumped into the nurses' desk.

By this time, the security guard was thoroughly frightened, but he still thought there was a possibility that someone was playing a prank on him, so he closed the doors, locked them, and went to the elevator. He stood with one foot inside the elevator and one foot in the hallway, just waiting for something to happen. After a few minuets passed, he called the other security guard on his radio and told him what had just happened, then asked him if anyone else was on the floor and more importantly, if anyone was inside the locked area. The guard on the first floor responded that no one was there, and there shouldn't be anyone there. He also told him to wait until he could find someone to watch his desk so he could meet him on the second floor and they could both investigate. Within a few minutes, the other guard arrived and both opened the doors to search the almost pitch-black ward. Once inside they scanned the entire area. They went in every room and looked in every closet and storage room only to find empty rooms and nothing out of the ordinary, except the wheelchair sitting abandoned in the middle of the hallway. There was no one there, not a soul.

Whispers in a darkened, abandoned hallway and an empty wheelchair rolling across the floor might just spook two security guards, but when these two men were leaving the dark hallway and getting into the elevator, there was a faint rattling at the locked doors. Although they both heard this, they said nothing and continued downstairs. They omitted the last part of their experience in the security logs.

Once they had returned to the security desk, they decided to play back the tapes from the security cameras for that floor. They went back four hours and watched the tape at fast-forward on the monitor. During most of the video they found nothing, but toward the end of the tape, shortly before the first time the security guard went to pick up the boxes from the storage room, the lights went on inside the ward, then went off again. The next day, the engineer and the morning security guard made an investigation of their own. They checked all the rooms, the windows, and the fire escape, but all were locked and secure. They found nothing out of the ordinary and no sign of a forced entry or exit from the sealed ward.

This story is frightening enough, but compared to an experience a nurse had a few years ago, a wheelchair rolling across the hallway is child's play. As hospital legend tells it, the specter of a child has been seen from time to time in one of the hospital's de-escalation rooms. These de-escalation rooms are designed to restrain an unruly or psychotic patient to keep him from harming himself or others. Using a five-point restraint system, technicians and nurses would take the patient, most likely a violent patient, put him on a special bed, then restrain him with sheepskin-lined leather bands. The technician would observe the patient until he or she had calmed down enough to be released. Little by little, the patient would settle down and eventually be calm enough to return to the hospital community.

Although these restraint rooms may appear cruel or unethical to people outside the mental health profession, the truth is that they can be as important as medication to keep a patient safe and relatively content during his ordeal. Although sometimes necessary, hospital staff rarely wish to use such methods, and with the advances in medication today, many patients no longer need restraint rooms. Yet not too long ago, many hospitals had little choice but to help their patients in this manner. Apparently, one patient from this hospital's past never forgot his or her time in the de-escalation room, and an eerie image sometimes rears its ugly face to remind staff and patient alike that he or she had suffered here.

On certain days, usually overcast or rainy days, a face can be seen through the window of one of the hospital's restraint rooms. The person in the window has been reported as young, between seventeen and twenty years old, with stringy, wet hair that falls over the forehead and partially covers the eyes, which are said to be very dark. Because of the hair and slight of build, it's difficult to tell for sure if it's male or female—the main things the witnesses remember are the eyes. The eyes, they say, are intense—dark, staring eyes that never blink. The room where this specter is seen is usually dark, the lights off, so the details of the face are hard to see. According to legend, however, one technician saw more of the angry specter than he wanted to on a rainy day . . . the pale little face in the window had no eyes!

The idea of seeing a face behind the glass of an empty room is scary enough, but when the face stares at you from dark, empty sockets where eyes should be, that's downright terrifying. This technician is said to have stopped dead in his tracks and stared back at this oddity, waiting for something to happen. When the face in the window stepped back into the darkness of the room, the technician suddenly became brave. He was said to have slowly opened the door to the room, only to find it empty with no sign that anyone had ever been there. When the technician reported his experience to the nurse on duty, she simply smiled and said, "Again?" She told him that almost everyone working there had claimed to see the ghost with the blank stare in the restraint room from time to time.

To this day there are still those who claim to see this haunting figure, and many of these witnesses are said to quit shortly after their experience. As to who this ghost was in life, no one seems to know. Because there is no documented history of a patient dying in the de-escalation room and the names of hospital patients are kept private, it's hard to surmise who he or she once was. And this is information we will most likely never know. We may never know for sure why this specter shows itself to lone technicians and nurses when passing the old room, or why it appears on thundering, rainy days. But we do know that this spirit is very unhappy. Although we may never know this spirit's true identity, we will always know it as the "dead eyes on the third floor."

Afterthoughts

The pain, indignity, and humiliation of being placed in a psychiatric hospital could only be understood by someone who has experienced it firsthand, and we must take into account the feelings of such people. Working in such an environment, I have seen how the patients respond to their temporary home. Most will only see themselves as failures or as crazy instead of recognizing that they may simply need a break from life, need help through a life-altering problem, or need a little redirection in order to live what they feel is a worthwhile life. All too often, many of these patients never find the peace they deserve, simply falling through the cracks of society, becoming lost souls.

Some move on, some live in obscurity, and some believe they will never get better and end their own lives. And, although some think that suicide will release them from their torment and misery, many believe this action forces them to relive their pain over and over again after death. Psychical researchers and paranormal investigators feel that those who take their lives may be doomed in one way or another to repeat their actions via residual haunting. Others believe that, following suicide, the soul must be reincarnated and live through another life altogether, while others simply believe that the soul will never rest. In any case, the specter in the window seems to want attention, perhaps giving its witnesses some kind of message . . . a message no one has yet decoded.

The ghostly nun sometimes seen making her rounds may be nothing more than a myth to make a patient's life more colorful while staying in the ward, or perhaps a technician's job more interesting when working alone on the night shift. Perhaps she represents the remains of a pious spirit who only wishes to continue looking after those who are lonely and sad, as documentation shows that nuns had once worked in the old hospital. The incorporeal doctor who seems to be attempting to save the patient he had always regretted losing may be the spiritual accumulation of the passions he had in life. Though some of the longtime staff suspect the doctor's true identity, no one knows for sure who he was.

The second-floor wheelchair is said to have rolled by itself on other occasions over the years, leaving a legend in its wake. The face in the window, frightening to everyone who witnesses it, is believed by some to be a residual impression made by a person who either died in the room or was directly affected by that location before he or she had died. The fact that this spirit is reported to be missing its eyes only furthers the mystery of the ghost's identity.

Although Lakeside Hospital serves as a place of refuge for many of those who suffer beyond their own control, it also represents nearly every form of sickness and sadness known to man. It is a place of stored hardship, a building of collective pain and grief, a structure which may still hold many of the dark secrets past patients never had the chance to resolve. Is the old Princeton Hospital haunted? That may be hard to say for those who choose not to believe, but for the paranormal investigator, with the many legends that have continued over the years, this hospital is does indeed appear to be haunted. One thing is for sure, the security officers who heard voices echoing and the shaking of locked doors and the technician who saw the dead eyes staring through the restraining room's window, they believe . . . wouldn't you?

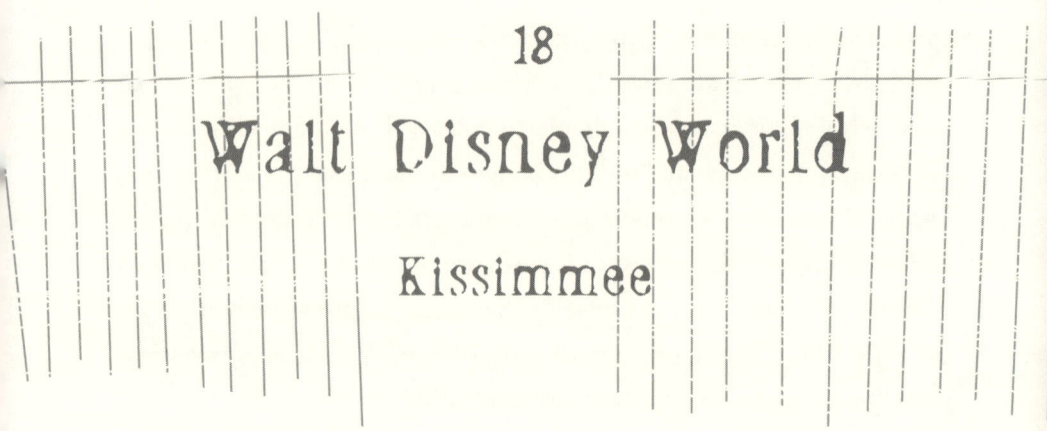

18

Walt Disney World

Kissimmee

Disney's Haunted Mansion . . . For Real!

A Little History

Walt Disney World, the sparkling gem that made central Florida one of the world's amusement park capitals, appears to have a few earthbound spirits all its own. And these spirits are reputed to dwell in a very logical place: the Haunted Mansion in Liberty Square.

As early as the 1950s, Walt Disney, along with Ken Anderson, one of his many "Imagineers," began mentally constructing his future haunted mansion exhibit. After some debate as to how the attraction would appear, the ride was eventually designed to look like an early nineteenth-century New Orleans mansion, complete with a spooky arboretum, huge oak trees with hanging moss, and of course, its own mausoleum and graveyard. Anyone who has seen it would agree that a lot of imagination went into this spectacular ride.

The mansion was originally created to be a walk-through storybook attraction where guests would enjoy the frights from several famed scary and macabre stories. But plans changed, as they usually do, and the walk-through idea was upgraded to a seated ride. The second half of the exhibit, with a stunning smoke-and-mirrors haunted graveyard, would be the ride's spooky climax.

Carriagelike transports known as "Doom Buggies" take patrons around the mansion, through winding haunted hills and over creepy specter-filled swamps, past emerging corpses in old deserted graveyards, finally culminating with a ghostly ballroom complete with dancing phantoms and other delightful spooks. And the patron even gets to see a hitchhiking ghost sitting next to him in the Doom Buggy at the journey's end . . . free of charge!

Even though Walt Disney World has grown considerably since the early days of the park, the Haunted Mansion remains one of the favorite attractions. Thousands upon thousands have gone through the ride, and it is a must-see every time I go to the park. The Haunted Mansion ride certainly puts some of the magic in the Magic Kingdom, but many seem to believe there is another kind of magic taking place here . . . a magic that has a life of its own.

Ghostly Legends and Haunted Folklore

Legend suggests that the Haunted Mansion may have been cursed from the very beginning. Apparently, there were problems with its construction, as well as the overall planning, and everything was eventually put on hold in the early 1960s. Then, to make things worse, Walt died in 1966, leaving his masterpiece unfinished until 1969. Legend also says that the Haunted Mansion was redesigned before its official opening because someone actually had a heart attack and died during the trial runs, so it had to be downgraded a bit so as not to be too frightening. But that's only a legend . . . right?

Of the genuine spirits amid all the puppetry exists a formal phantom known as "the tuxedo ghost," who has a knack for sneaking up behind some of the Mansion's employees and casting shadows. His identity is a mystery because there were no buildings or homes on the land before the Haunted Mansion was constructed, and no one wearing a tuxedo had ever died in the Mansion itself. It is theorized that he may have been a friend or coworker of Walt Disney during construction, or that he was a shareholder who never made the opening reception in life. Either way, this spook certainly enjoys frightening all who encounter him.

On one occasion, this formal phantom scared a worker right out of the building. Apparently, a young college girl, who was working part-time at Disney World, was tending to her duties at the end of a long day. She said that she saw the shadow of a man walking behind her, who then appeared in a mirror on the wall in front of her, but when she turned around quickly to see who it was, no one was there. This was scary enough, but when she felt a cool breeze pass by her and a cold icy hand on her shoulder, that was it, and out she went!

Another ghost, who appears to be disabled—in addition to being dead, of course—limps around the mansion long after closing. According to oral tradition, sometime in the 1940s, a small plane crashed very near to where the Haunted Mansion sits today. The crash killed the pilot instantly. Many of the employees believe that the disabled spirit is that of the of the doomed pilot, seen and felt in the mansion at closing and during the early morning hours. Known as "the man with a cane," this spirit is seen limping in the darker regions of the ride, staring pathetically at those who spot him. His gaze and demeanor are enough to give some of the employees second thoughts about working alone in some areas of the Mansion.

Although this limping phantom has not posed a threat to those who see him, he does, nonetheless, cause a bit of a fright. Incidentally, according to my research, the body of that doomed pilot was found several yards from his wrecked plane with a stick clutched in his hand, held in a death grip, as if it had been used in his last moments to aid a crushed leg. Coincidence?

Another ghost is said to be that of a small boy who died before his time. As the story goes, after the death of this child, the mother, who knew her son loved the Haunted Mansion ride in life, decided to have his ashes sprinkled inside. Disney officials had rejected her request due to legal and sanitary reasons, but the mother had her own personal funeral regardless. Apparently, the spirit of this child did not want to be interred in the Mansion as the mother had hoped, and is sometimes heard crying at one of the exits, as if unable to get out. Some have even claimed to have seen this sad apparition sitting on the ground with his face cupped in his hands.

The final ghost believed to walk these spooky halls is the result of a fatality that actually took place within the Haunted Mansion a few years ago. Disney World annually hosts a special event for high school seniors known as "Grad Night." Although the seniors have a good time, sometimes, just sometimes, a few of the students get a little too rambunctious and get into trouble. On this one particular Grad Night, while a group of the seniors was traveling in the Doom Buggy, the Haunted Mansion's mechanical system broke down. As it sat for a few moments, one of the boys decided to get out of his Doom Buggy and take a closer look at the scenery. . . .

Apparently, the boy was fascinated with one of the Mansion's scenes known as the "Séance Room." This scene has many floating objects and a ghostly face inside a crystal ball, and it is believed that this boy wanted to get close to the ball to see how it worked. What this boy didn't realize is that the walkway leading to the Séance Room had a large gap between it and the Doom Buggy's tracks. There was a fifteen-foot drop into a mechanical pit, and the boy fell and broke his neck, killing him instantly.

Although it is not certain that this doomed high school senior walks around the Haunted Mansion in the dead of night, or taps people on the shoulders or even makes himself known, there is some kind of general activity that hints at his presence, and to this day, the Séance Room feels even more ghostly than Walt Disney originally planned.

Long after closing, faint music can sometimes be heard echoing through the walls, in the mechanical pit and around that general area. Also, this portion of the ride has a tendency to break down a lot, leaving the inhabitants of the Doom Buggy stuck, forced to stare at the Séance Room in total darkness until it is manually repaired (I know from personal experience). Maybe this ill-fated high school senior is reaching out to those who pass by where he died. Perhaps he's trying to get a little attention, or perhaps he's just being playful. Who knows? But one thing is for certain: the Haunted Mansion at Walt Disney World operates on more than just smoke and mirrors.

Afterthoughts

Although the wonderment and excitement at Disney World is as large and infectious as a child's imagination, we sometimes exclude some of the things we see as merely part of the show. And, even though we grownups can let our hair down and have some fun at this imaginative masterpiece, many of us are still unwilling to see things that are all around us and have always been there.

The employees at the Haunted Mansion see the incredible devices of technology and magic on a daily basis, and are certainly accustomed to the surroundings. The noises—the shrieks of ghosts and zombies, the thunder and lightning booming in the background—are all just part of the illusion, and so such things should not be too frightening to the average worker. But, when they claim to see and feel the things that they have, we must look beyond the obvious and take note.

The man with the cane who limps around in the wee hours staring pathetically at those who see him, the well dressed ghost wearing a tuxedo who has an affinity for spooking the female staff, and the sad, childlike spirit heard weeping near the ride's exits, all indicate that there is something going on in Disney World that Walt never included in his original plans.

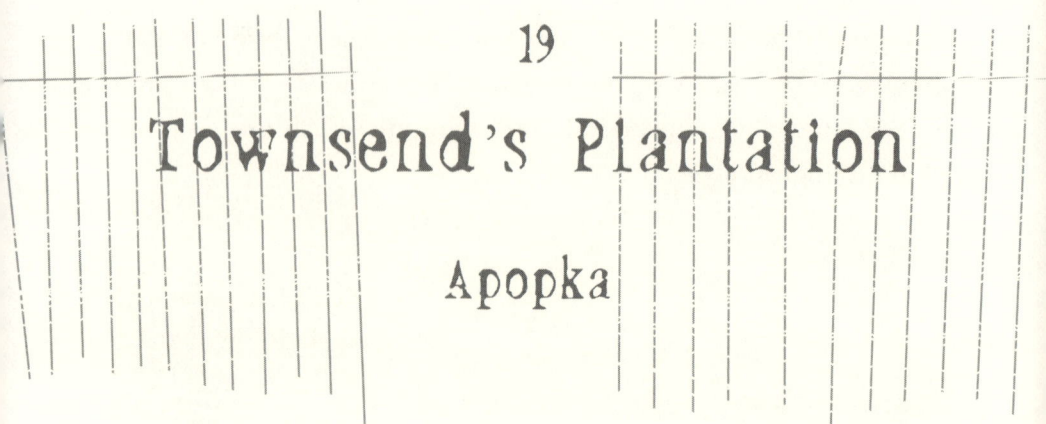

19

Townsend's Plantation

Apopka

A Light in the Attic and the Lady in White

A Little History

No matter where you go, in every town, village, or city across America, there's always one location that is considered haunted or has some kind of ghostly legend attached to it. I can remember several reputedly haunted locations when I was growing up in south Florida, and after all, what kid didn't believe at least one deserted old house in his or her home town was haunted? For the young imaginative mind, the thought of ghosts in creepy old houses feeds the imagination for sure. And, although most of these deserted houses are no more haunted than the next house up the street, every town does seem to have a least one haunted house in it. In Apopka, Florida, just northwest of Orlando, sits one such haunted house: the old McBride home, or, as it has become known, Townsend's Plantation.

The remains of Townsend's Plantation are located at 604 East Main Street, on Route 436 adjacent to State Road 441. This romantic, Queen Anne–style country home was built in 1903 for the Eldredge family, one of Apopka's original families. In the early 1920s, Dr. Thomas E. McBride, one of Apopka's first practicing physicians, bought the stately

home for his medical practice and residence. This 4,000-square-foot, eight-room home served the good doctor for countless years, as he delivered babies from one generation to the next, cared for the sick, and assisted those at the time of death. Dr. McBride was and still is considered by many of Apopka's residents to be a local hero and patriarch of the town, and after devoting a long and fruitful life to healing others, he passed away peacefully in his home in 1978. The beautiful home, which has seen so much over the years, sat silent and undisturbed until 1985, when a prominent Orlando attorney, Clay Townsend, bought the home with plans of restoring it and turning it into a fine restaurant. Though the house originally sat next to one of Apopka's oldest cemeteries, Townsend had it divided into four sections and slowly moved to its current location. The home was enlarged by more than 10,000 square feet, to accommodate the main section of the restaurant, the elegant and appropriately named Townsend's Plantation.

In addition to offering a fine dining experience, two separate buildings were constructed for holding festivities and family gatherings. In 1989, Mr. Townsend had a replica of an nineteenth-century carriage house constructed across from the restaurant. This wood-plank structure served as a quaint chapel for weddings and other gatherings. The renovated country mansion, now an elegant and picturesque restaurant, served excellent cuisine for many years. Sadly, however, after rumors of bankruptcy and foreclosure, Townsend's Plantation Restaurant finally closed its doors in the late 1990s. Although the chapel, restaurant area, and grounds may be leased for private functions, the old Townsend's Plantation sits quiet and relatively deserted.

Not long after the restaurant closed its doors, the Orlando Historical Society purposed to buy and preserve the building before it was destroyed. They turned the stately home into a commercial haunted house attraction to operate during the Halloween season. And it was successful, at least at the beginning. Unfortunately, however, the Haunted Townsend's Halloween experience later failed. The building was once again cursed to sit eerily alone, covered by the shade of the ancient oak trees and blanketed with dead leaves. Townsend's Plantation, this antique, alabaster hulk of yesteryear, appears to be forgotten. However, it is anything but still.

Ghostly Legends and Haunted Folklore

1999 was a good year for spooky things. Potential computer glitches threatened the mass mindset with chaos. In the theaters, films such as *The Sixth Sense, Stir of Echoes* and remakes like *The House on Haunted Hill* and *The Haunting* had everyone in the mood for something uncanny. And, in the little township of Apopka, Florida, Townsend's Plantation was open once again for a limited Halloween engagement. From 7:00 P.M. to roughly 1:00 A.M., Townsend's ushered in hundreds of people from all over central Florida to tour its elegant and creepy halls. I was one of the many people fortunate enough to get a peek inside.

The home had a natural Hollywood flare to it: chandeliers dusted over with cobwebs and massive bookshelves filled with dusty old tomes. The mood was set. The glass curio cases were filled with Dr. McBride's medical equipment and other surgical paraphernalia, including a genuine human skeleton. The house was overlaid with fake cobwebs and filled with fog. The atmosphere was accompanied by flashes of lightning and the rumble of thunder from special effects machines. But even the actors jumping out from behind every corner couldn't draw my attention away from the grandeur of the architecture and furnishings here, and I knew that I had to find out more about Townsend's, its history and its haunted reputation.

About a month later I called Mr. Townsend and asked for his permission to look around the property. He graciously approved my request. Although he had little information to give us about any specific spirits that might inhabit the old house, he did say that he'd heard rumors about the property being haunted, yet he himself didn't believe them. Regardless, he had nothing against my associate and I having a look. So we went to Apopka to investigate the property and interview the locals. And in fact, what we found was more than what we had hoped for.

Our first stop was Liggetts, a small five-and-dime store and diner right across the street from Townsend's. There, the woman at the cash register, a lifetime resident of Apopka, was very helpful in relaying the most common ghost stories of Townsend's Plantation she had heard over the years. She reminisced about her childhood, when she and her sister would walk around the old house and through the cemetery that lay next to it. She remembered hearing stories about the old home being haunted by a ghostly lady in white who would often be seen peering through the second-floor window, then fading away.

The woman told us about a friend of hers who worked at

Townsend's during the Halloween event in 1999. She said that this girl had many weird feelings while setting up for the event, and that even stranger things happened there after closing. She spoke of hearing strange noises throughout the house, especially on the upper floors. She said that there is a room on the second floor that is always chilly, unusually cold even when the air conditioners are not running and the weather outside is hot and humid. Moreover, the door to this room will absolutely not remain closed. Even when the door is latched, a short time later it will be found halfway open.

Additionally, the woman at Liggetts told us that the third floor is off limits to everyone, including the staff, and has been for years. This section is apparently used as a storage space today, but there are rooms there once said to have been used by Dr. McBride for the sick, then later as housing for boarders during the 1960s. Why they are locked and off limits today is a mystery I have yet to solve.

Our next destination was to explore Townsend's itself. As we walked around the perimeter of the home and between the carriage house and chapel, it was easy to see why many believe it to be haunted. The awning over the main driveway was shrouded with ivy and cobwebs, the windows were dark, and there was a thin layer of soot and mold covering the walls, giving the entire place a look of isolation and secrecy. The road that leads up to the plantation is surrounded by tall oak trees, which give full shade even in the middle of the day. As you look at the house, you notice an obvious darkness to it, something cold about its very nature. As we walked around the chapel, dodging the nets of spider webs, we could see from the thick dust covering everything inside that the building had not been used in some time. There were small electric candles on the sill behind each window. As we approached, we both noticed that one of these electric candles was flickering, ever so slightly. Then it went out altogether. None of the other lights were on, and though this could be explained in a simple, logical manner, the event was odd, nonetheless.

As we walked around the main house, we noticed that the drapery in the second-floor window was drawn back, as if someone were looking out the window. We didn't think anything more of it, but as we were leaving the front yard, we both turned around for one last look, and noticed a strange thing: the curtains in the second-floor window were now completely closed. Thinking that there might be someone inside, we dismissed the observation and continued on our way.

Just as we were turning to leave, however, we noticed a police car driving up to meet us. The officer politely asked us our business there, which we were happy to describe, saying we had permission from the owner. The policeman then told us just to be careful and not to try to go inside. He also told us that a lot of people come to Townsend's and look around hoping to see a ghost, which naturally opened up a conversation.

I told the officer that I would love to hear any stories he might have. He smiled and said he'd never seen a ghost there, but that the alarms are always going off for no reason. He told us that Townsend's has an excellent security system inside and outside, complete with cameras and motion sensors throughout the interior, which would notify the security company and inform police dispatch that there might be an intruder inside. He said that the Apopka Police Department was always receiving calls from the security company regarding the alarms going off. Every time an officer arrived, however, the doors would be locked and there was never any sign of vandalism or robbery—just a dark, creepy house with no life in it. After a while, the police suggested that the security system be checked, which it was. In fact, an entirely new, even more advanced security system was installed, only to respond in the same manner. The oddity continues to this day.

This was certainly good information, but the officer told me one more detail, which I found most interesting. Once as he was working the overnight shift, driving on main street past Townsend's around 3:45 A.M., he noticed a light in a second floor window. Knowing full well there was no light on earlier during his shift, he decided to call it in and sit with his headlights off in the driveway, waiting for backup to arrive. As he sat there, looking for movement in the second-floor window, he saw nothing. Then the light went out, leaving a blackened window in its place. Needless to say, the officer was pleased when two patrol cars entered the driveway a few moments later. Because Mr. Townsend is concerned with his investment, the Apopka Police have a set of keys for just such an occasion.

The three policemen walked around the house, flashlights scanning the entire area. Unlatching the doors, the policemen entered, anticipating the worst. What they found, however, were the flashing lights of the security system and the high-pitch scream of the klaxon. They walked through the entire house, that is except the third floor, which was padlocked from the outside. The second floor, where the light originated, was dark. A thin layer of dust lying over everything appeared to have been undisturbed for some time. This was intriguing enough, but when the officer turned to me with a smile and offered the final piece of his story, I realized that there truly was something more to Townsend's Plantation. You see, when the officers were looking through the room on the second floor to find the light, they found only one lamp there, and it hung from the ceiling. He shined his flashlight on the lightbulb and felt it to see if it was warm, but it was cold to the touch. Upon closer examination, he noticed that the bulb's filaments were broken and the bulb blackened from the inside. The light could not have gone on in the second-floor room; it had long been burned out. The police officers logged their investigation and went about their duties. The officer offered no answer when I asked him if he believed the house was haunted; he just continued to smile and shook his head.

I thought it would be hard to find a better story than the one the policeman gave me that afternoon, but I was fortunate enough to find via the internet a woman who worked at the restaurant from 1988 to 1989. After researching countless ghosts- and haunting-related websites and writing email after email, I received a letter from a woman I'll refer to as "Marisa." Marisa was very open about her experiences working at Townsend's Plantation, stating that she enjoyed her work, but that she always had uneasy feelings there, especially at closing time. Apparently, when the restaurant closed its doors for the evening, and after the cleaning was done and the money counted, several of the workers would sit and have a drink and talk. Sometimes the employees would sit and relax into the wee hours, as the setting was certainly enjoyable. It was on one such occasion that Marisa and two of her coworkers clearly heard a woman's voice from either the second or third floor. As it was very late, somewhere around 3 A.M., it was strange to hear someone's voice coming from upstairs, especially when all the guests had gone home hours ago and the remaining employees were all sitting in the lounge.

The chef and a bartender decided to check it out. Marisa, not wanting to stay in the lounge alone, went upstairs with the two men. The voice, she told me, was a clear-spoken woman's voice that sounded as if the woman were asking someone a question. The chef said he thought that one of the female guests might have gotten lost upstairs or had fallen down up there and was crying for help, but when they arrived, looking around in every room, they found nothing. Just as they were starting to head back downstairs, however, all three off them distinctly heard the woman's voice again. They heard the words, "Oh dear!" as if this phantom lady were mildly perturbed. The voice clearly came from one of the old offices of Dr. McBride in the second-floor turret.

The three of them looked at each other in confusion and headed for the room that they were just in moments ago. They entered the room cautiously, not knowing what they were going to find, but it was completely empty, except for the antique furnishings. But the room was icy cold, almost like the inside of a refrigerator, which was especially strange because this was the middle of July and the air conditioners were set for 78 degrees.

Marisa was kind enough to wish me luck with my research, and she said she hoped that Townsend's Plantation would open again someday, as she had enjoyed her time there. Marisa also told me that she is an avid believer in ghosts because of her experience that early morning so many years ago. She also told me some of the stories she had heard from others over the years. Evidently, many have claimed to have seen a mature woman dressed in a white nightgown standing at the window of the second-floor turret, her face fixed with concern as if confused or contemplating. I eventually heard this same story from at least ten of Apopka's residents, all claiming to have seen a woman standing at that window holding the lace curtain in her hand, staring into space. It wasn't too much of a surprise to me when I was informed that Mrs. McBride died in that room many years ago. She died early in the morning and she was wearing a white nightgown.

In addition to this lady in white being seen in the second-floor window, some have said they've seen the almost completely white specter walking around the mansion. As the legend goes, you might see this pensive apparition silently strolling on the sidewalk or the main driveway late at night, visible from an almost iridescent glow. If someone sees this swaying specter and tries to get a closer look, she will simply walk past a column or behind a wall and promptly disappear . . . just one more elusive spirit in Townsend's Plantation.

Afterthoughts

The fate of Townsend's Plantation is unknown. Many believe that because Apopka is growing rapidly, the highway may expand to accommodate further building scheduled for the area, and Townsend's may very well be moved again. Others believe that the stately old manor will be bought and turned into a bed and breakfast, which would certainly create even more ghost stories in the future. In either case, the legend of the lady in white and other oddities will undoubtedly live on. When we look at the fascinating and colorful history of this house, it may answer many of the ghostly questions we might have.

Dr. McBride dealt with his patients right in his own home. As many parts of central Florida were still small country towns back then, it was natural for a doctor to treat his patients in his home rather than a big hospital, which was more likely to be found in a much larger city. Many of Dr. McBride's patients died in that home. It is believed that several members of the Eldredge family passed away there, too, and some suspect that more than one vagrant was found dead inside the home when it lay abandoned during the late 1970s and early 1980s. Still others have suggested that when the house sat at its original location near the cemetery, wandering, restless souls took refuge there as well.

Today, you will find an empty Townsend's Plantation sitting just west of State Road 441, also known as Orange Blossom Trail. If you plan on walking around this location, don't be surprised if you meet a policeman—Townsend's is well looked-after by the Apopka Police Department. And don't be surprised if the alarms go off, as even if there is no living person inside, something seems to trip the security system from time to time, regardless of the building's apparent emptiness. Townsend's Plantation is a beautiful example of architecture for sure, and we can only hope that it will be saved rather than scrapped for Apopka's growth and progress. Perhaps in the near future we will be able to dine there again, or perhaps stay the weekend in Townsend's Bed & Breakfast. Who knows? What many of us do know, however, is that this structure is haunted, pure and simple. If you're driving down Main Street late at night or early in the morning, and you peer over to this charming, if not spooky, house covered in a light mist of fog, don't be too startled if you see a light go on in a second-floor window . . . and don't be surprised if you too catch a glimpse of the lady in white.

20
Woodbridge Cemetery
Fern Park

Forgotten Souls and a Spirited Supermarket

A Little History

About ten miles east from Orlando, just west of route 1792 on Woodbridge Road in Fern Park, lies the barren Woodbridge Cemetery. Although there are only a few graves actually visible—mostly homemade tombstones, and a scattering of two or three cement crypts—this cemetery is in fact quite large. Originally extending for almost two blocks, the area was once used primarily to bury slaves and poor pioneers of Florida's past. Now, the remains of this once well-used cemetery are nothing more than a huge sandy field laden with sinkholes where caskets once sat.

Although the city of Fern Park is small, consisting mostly of strip malls, pawnshops, and fast food restaurants, there seems to be a hidden past here, a particularly dark history that holds a level of regret that cannot be mentioned in any real estate brochure. Many of the people who live in Fern Park may only know that the city was once almost completely covered with many varieties of fern plants. Some may know it for the part it played during the Civil War, or for the many pioneers of the mid-nineteenth century who settled here, but

what few remember is that many slave trades also took place here. In effect, the dark past lies in the disrespect, the mistreatment, and the degradation of the human spirit that once took place where this tiny town now rests.

Woodbridge Cemetery's history is not listed in many records. Indeed, finding the history of the cemetery and its past seemed close to impossible. Fortunately, with the aid of several of Fern Park's luminaries and long-time residents, some of the cemetery's basic history has finally been found. Apparently, there was a small settlement here in the 1870s, consisting of both white and black settlers. Each lived in their respective areas, tending to their own farming, cattle, and textile trading, living a meager, rustic lifestyle.

At the turn of the century and up into the 1920s, Fern Park served as nothing more than a small residential community, a suburb of an equally small Orlando. Woodbridge cemetery was one of the only burial grounds, outside of private family graveyards. As many brought their dead here, it grew to encompass nearly two town blocks. By the 1950s, more residential homes were being built, many around the Woodbridge area, and the cemetery unfortunately stood in the way of progress, so plans had to be made in order to continue the advancement of the city. Because the majority of the people who had once buried relatives here were themselves now dead, no one complained about what would take place next.

During the fifties and sixties, a road leading into a newly built housing community was constructed. Across the street, just footsteps from the cemetery, a strip mall was in the plans. It would have many shops and eateries, a grocery store and a drug store, too, but during the preparation of the land for the laying of the foundation, a terrible rumor began. Evidently, workers were digging up bones and even some rotting remains and coffins when their bulldozers were churning up the earth. Some of the Native American workers refused to work there, telling their foreman it would be unwise to disturb the dead, let alone build over their graves, but no one listened.

Today, the Main Street Square strip mall offers a moderately sized Winn Dixie supermarket, pizza and Chinese restaurants, a travel center and a few other common shops. Of course, it pales in comparison to the super malls and industrial-sized grocery centers being built today, but it still serves many local families. The old Woodbridge Cemetery across the road seems as dark and as lonely as any forgotten graveyard anywhere else in the world, and those who shop here pay little mind to the location, if any notice it at all. If they only knew they were walking over the forgotten dead. . . .

Ghostly Legends and Haunted Folklore

Though this forgotten cemetery seems to be just an abandoned empty lot, the area is actually quite active, at least on a supernatural level. You see, Woodbridge Cemetery's history is less than peaceful, filled with hatred and disrespect for the living as well as the dead.

Of the several ghostly legends I have heard about Woodbridge over the years, the one that stuck out the most was the story of dark figures walking around in the back of this cemetery. Apparently, the witnesses to these events, while going for a stroll or walking their dogs, reported seeing these dark shapes shambling around in the bushes and under the low-hanging trees after dark. Although the majority of these witnesses think the shapes are actual people, possibly vagrants finding a spot to sleep for the night, some claimed to have seen these shapes vanish before their eyes. On occasion, a sheriff's deputy will shine his spotlight back there just to make sure there is no illegal activity going on, but will usually find nothing more than empty land. Yet, there are still others who have actually captured fantastic visual evidence for the existence of something quite extraordinary in this location.

Terri Mestre, a security officer and now an amateur ghost hunter, has had a particular interest in the Woodbridge Cemetery for some time. Terri lives close to the cemetery, and has complained about the poor shape it has been in for years. She finally decided to take matters into her own hands and began a cleaning regimen of her own. Mowing the outer perimeter and trimming the unsightly weeds around the tombs was one thing, but cleaning up the trash, the discarded beer cans and bottles, as well as people's old junk, was also a necessary part of the routine. The cemetery was just too close to her home and the lack of respect for the property was troubling, so Terri happily cleans and maintains the old graveyard as her way of showing that proper respect.

Late one night, when she was having difficulty getting to sleep, she decided to walk down to the old cemetery to see what it looked like during the early hours of the morning. She brought along her new digital camera to see how it worked in low light. It was a cool morning, and there was a low, flowing fog that slowly moved over the stones and what seemed to be a vacant field in the distance. The glow from the florescent lights in the nearby supermarket lit up the old cemetery ever so slightly, just enough light to take a few photos . . . and what odd photos she got!

As Terri was walking through the field, stumbling in pits and sink-holes, she managed to capture the creepy images of the bent and gnarled trees as well as the eerie fog that was present that early morning. Thinking there was just enough fog to add to the already spooky atmosphere, she continued her photo session, then headed back for home. She had hoped to get a few good photos of the cemetery and the spooky atmosphere, but never thought she would have captured the strange images she did that morning.

When Terri returned home, still unable to sleep, she decided to check her digital photos on her computer to see how they turned out. It was no surprise that some of the photos where just too dark to make out and others where completely black. Yet, there were two images she had captured that simply made no sense. After a little more investigation, she got a very scary feeling. To this day, even after being completely investigated by state-of-the-art equipment, these photos still defy logic. One image showed what looked like a small campfire about one hundred yards ahead of her. She was certain there had been no fire that morning, or any light at all for that matter. When she enlarged the photo on her computer, she found that it didn't look like a camp-fire at all, but more like a bright red sunrise, as if from far away. And to the left of that there appeared to be a bed frame without a mattress. Although this made no sense at all and Terri was very curious, she decided to wait until morning to go back and ascertain what these images could have been.

The other photo was even more bizarre. This image at a normal size shows a classic orb hovering over a crumbling crypt. Having heard of orb phenomena, she felt that this might point to a haunting in the cemetery, so she decided to examine it more closely. When she enlarged it to fifty times its normal size, she found that it looked somewhat misshapen, not exactly round. At one hundred times its size, it began to take on definite features and when enlarged at one hundred and fifty times, an amazing thing took form: a man's head!

When Terri saw this, she didn't know what to think. Was she acting on her imagination or was this image truly there? Dumbfounded and mistrusting of her own eyes, she decided to show the image to some friends for confirmation. Sure enough, everybody saw what looked like a man's face, complete with a mustache and a sad, morose expression. When Terri returned to the cemetery during daylight, she found no evidence of there ever being a campfire in that area, or anything resembling a bed frame. In addition, the crypt where the orb was photographed was completely dilapidated, bearing only the remnants of where a name once existed. Who could this unfortunate spirit be?

That some of us might become disembodied, melancholy, floating heads after we die is a dreadful thought to say the least. However, some paranormal investigators believe that these images may only be the recordings of feelings or emotions of the dead, rather than actual sentient spirits, and that theory is a little more comforting. Others believe that orbs like this one are a primary form of transportation for spirits, allowing the spirit in question to save energy that may be needed at other times during its existence, such as when manifesting into another form. Although pure conjecture of course, these theories offer at least some explanation.

As Terri and I continued our research into the history of Fern Park's forgotten cemetery, we found that the strip mall across the street covered a good portion of the original cemetery of the 1870s. In fact, the Winn Dixie there is apparently built directly on a larger section of an old cemetery. However, when we asked several town officials if this was true, many said either that there was absolutely no cemetery there, or that they just did not know. Some of the older residents, however, those who have lived in Fern Park for thirty years or more, said they could remember when the digging took place and the many delays that hindered the construction. A few of these residents remembered the rumors of caskets being dug up when the construction teams were digging the building's foundations; some remembered the bones that lay exposed and the expressions of the construction workers.

With this new information, I decided to ask some of the proprietors of the stores there if they had ever experienced anything odd or out of the ordinary. And although some of these people said no, and some even looked at me strangely when I asked such a question, some said yes. Of the oddities reported, many had experienced audible phenomena, such as disembodied voices or footsteps when no one was around. On some occasions, there had been reports of cold spots or waves of air passing by when there should be no such gusts of wind. Yet, the most reported event was the feeling of being watched. Some were even unwilling to venture to the back rooms of their stores during the closing hours on late nights, as they always would think someone was going to jump out at them. When I walked over to the Winn Dixie one dark, rainy night in search of information, I was delighted to find a plethora of spooky events . . . events that have some of the late-night employees unwilling to go in certain rooms by themselves.

Going to the Winn Dixie to find a ghost story was a good idea, as there was more than one employee to have had an experience to tell. One employee named "Carla" was very open with me regarding her experiences. She told me that during late nights, when closing the store for the evening and stocking the individual departments for the next day, many strange events would take place.

Carla works in the deli section on the second shift, so she is expected to close the deli when the store closes, then clean and prepare the deli for the next day. When doing this, she oftentimes has to walk in the back sections of the building to retrieve condiments and other supplies for the next day. Sometimes, she will hear unusual echoes coming from the dark corners of the corridors, and sometimes she has even heard voices. Occasionally, cold spots will be felt where there should be none, and she has gotten intense feelings of being watched or followed. Needless to say, extremely unsettling feelings occur in this section of the store.

Apparently, the bakery is quite haunted, too, as the employees working there have experienced some downright frightening things. Sounds of someone walking on the catwalks above them after closing hours are certainly odd because these catwalks, which are high above the ceiling panels that stretch in all directions, are for the most part closed off. Absolutely no one is allowed there up there outside of management, security, or maintenance personnel. Because these sounds are heard long after anyone should be up there, and the entry hatches are found secure and locked, such noises can be quite unnerving. Moreover, when one ex-employee felt what she described as a cold hand resting on her shoulder, substantiating her fears, she left for the night and never returned. Other events like bread falling off the counter by itself are also common, and from time to time the sound of a man's low voice saying "hey" can be heard when no one is around. All in all, there seems to be far more than just dinner rolls and dough-nuts in the bakery section of this supermarket.

As I continued my research throughout the supermarket, I found that many of the heavy metal doors throughout the building will sometimes open and close by themselves, and cash registers will often cease functioning altogether. The sensors above the main entrances will sometimes go off, opening the sliding glass doors even when no one passes in front of them, and an overall feeling of dread and the feeling of being watched are common. More than a few employees will say in no uncertain terms that this Winn Dixie is quite haunted. Though most are usually unable or unwilling to talk about such things, I have found that with a little finesse and honest questions, people will open up with their experiences. And so it seems the Woodbridge Cemetery and the nearby supermarket are actually one and the same.

Afterthoughts

Woodbridge Cemetery endures as nothing more than a huge sandlot brimming with straggly bushes and sticker thistles. The majority of the graves are now just empty holes. This is a cemetery, although out of sight and out of mind for most, that still manages to get a little attention from time to time. Just recently, one of the homemade above-ground crypts was broken into, the casket torn to pieces and most of the human remains missing. Though the police investigated the incident, minimal effort was put forth, as the person who once occupied this grave died more than ninety years ago, and no surviving family members could be found. Were the bones taken by a ghoul, or was this just an accident, a car that backed over the crudely made crypt, the bones carried off by animals years ago? No one knows.

The Woodbridge Cemetery is one of those places that stays hidden until someone stumbles over it. It remains an enigma today, and it certainly isn't much to look at. Although some people, usually the extremely poor, continue to bury their dead here, this land remains a burden for Fern Park, and will soon attract private builders and business owners. The question might be, would they move these graves or build on top of them as before? Will apartment complexes and residential homes rest where the dead once rested? We may find out soon enough, but in either ending, it seems the restless, forgotten souls of Woodbridge Cemetery will continue to roam until they find peace.

If you ever go to Fern Park's Winn Dixie supermarket, don't forget to pick up the eggs and a carton of milk, and when you go to the bakery to buy a loaf of bread, try to remember what happened to one of the employees there. Perhaps you will hear the echoing footsteps overhead on the catwalk, or maybe you will feel a cold draft pass by. Maybe, just maybe, you will take someone or something home with you when you're finished shopping.

21

Interstate 4

Sanford

Tread Not on Us!

He was wearing odd clothes, kind of tattered and certainly out of style—
he wore a round hat with a wide brim, like the actor in Little House
on the Prairie. *But the thing I remember the most was his color. . . . He*
looked as if a bluish light was being shined on him, and when I passed
him, I looked back, and would you believe it? He was gone!
—Florida trucker

A Little History

Interstate 4, or I-4 as it is known, is the main highway running from
Tampa Bay on the west-coast area to Daytona Beach on the east. I-4
gives motorists access to every city and township in central Florida,
from Polk County to the bustling city of Orlando to the spring-break
haven of Daytona. As central Florida's only east-west interstate, I-4 is
certainly a benefit for Florida's residents and visitors alike. However, it
was only designed to support a modest population. Since its construction, central Florida has grown dramatically—officials estimate
that the population has tripled since the 1960s, when Walt Disney
gave new life to Florida's workforce, tourism trade, and commerce,

generating new towns and cities in the process. Let's take a moment and think about what was here before the days of these modern roads and businesses.

Many of the people I have interviewed over the past year, especially in Orlando, can reminisce about the old days of central Florida's past. They have related to me that Orlando was once a small series of dirt roads and quaint orange groves. Many of the older people I have spoken with have a less-than-friendly attitude toward the vacation wonder that is Walt Disney World. Many feel that central Florida was compromised to big business for Walt Disney's dream, which took away the small-town essence Orlando and the other nearby cities once had. Those small towns either grew to metropolises like Orlando or vanished altogether, and the Florida of the past is just that: the past.

Unfortunately, when a township dries up and its inhabitants move on, or when progress runs through a small town and its surroundings, the most personal part of the town may be covered up or even destroyed. One such part of our pioneer past was a small colony, which included a farmhouse and a tiny cemetery in its backyard that were obliterated by the progress of I-4's construction. Near the St. Johns River, a family—a father, a mother and two children—died of yellow fever, and were buried behind their log cabin in a small plot under a camphor tree, surrounded by a rustic wooden gate. This family was one of about four families who settled near the St. Johns River in November of 1886 as part of a religious colony. The physical remains as well as the very legacy of this small colony are gone now. Yet, something is said to remain there, something not quite right.

In the late nineteenth century, the Department of Agriculture and the governor of Florida formed the Florida Land and Colonization Company. This government agency was created to establish populations and commerce in all areas of the then frontier state. The organization offered a beautiful spot of land to the Roman Catholic Church for colonization. The church was of course delighted with the home-steading offer and immediately began designing what would become St. Joseph's Colony. Father Felix Prosper Swembergh was designated to lead St. Joseph's Colony and began administering God's word to all the residents of the colony. Father Swembergh was soon called to Tampa, however, to assist those stricken by a yellow fever outbreak, and sadly, after only a short time on the west coast, Father Swembergh himself contracted the sickness and died within a few weeks. As ill fate would have it, the yellow fever epidemic came to St. Joseph's Colony, killing an entire family in a matter of days. Father Swembergh was dead, so there was no one to give last rites to the dying, and the four victims were quickly buried without any formal ceremony. With no family gathering and no absolution, it was a sad farewell indeed.

The Seminole County Historical Archives have little other history from that point on regarding the colony and its survivors, but it is assumed that the colony disbanded, the remaining colonists fleeing back to the northern states. Some of the land the colony originally used eventually became the township of Lake Monroe, and by the early 1900s, a farmer by the name of Al Hawkins, along with his wife and family, bought a large portion of the colony's land. The farmer quickly began clearing the now-overgrown fields in order to plant orange groves and celery. While clearing the dead center of the field, the farmer found four small graves, marked by four small, wooden crosses, eerily reaching out of the tall weeds and thickets. Weathered and falling apart, the wooden markers were preserved by the farmer, who respectfully farmed around the graves instead of plowing over them. "The Field of the Dead," as it became known, remained as it was for many years, until the farmer died in 1939.

By the 1950s, the field began to get overgrown again, returning to its original form. Although the farmer's widow continued to live on the land until 1960, Florida's government wished to purchase a great portion of land by the St. Johns River for the creation of a "super high-way." Now quite elderly, the farmer's wife decided to sell her property and move closer to her children in another state. She was assured that her land would benefit Florida's growth, especially with the promise of a great attraction being planned by a man named Walt Disney. This all sounded so wonderful—her land would help so many in the state she'd lived in most of her life, so it just had to be the right thing to do . . . or so everyone thought.

Although the state engineers and land surveyors were alerted to the existence of the tiny cemetery, they decided that because the graves were so old and decayed, and because there were no living relatives to speak up for the remains, it was most beneficial to expedite construction by ignoring the graves and building over them. After all, as one engineer apparently said, "It's not ancient Indian burial grounds. They're just a few old bones." Needless to say, this cavalier attitude had negative consequences that continue to this day. According to the legend, the very day workers began plowing over the graves, piling dirt on them in order to elevate the land for construction, one of Florida's most deadly hurricanes crossed the state. Hurricane Donna still strikes fear in the hearts of those who survived it; the storm caused millions of dollars in damage to many areas of central Florida and was responsible for many lost lives, not to mention the delay of I-4 construction. Many believe that when the graves were disrupted, a bad thing took place. The hurricane came and the curse of I-4 began.

The colony, the log cabin, and then the farm and its celery fields have since rotted away. What stands in their place is Interstate 4 and the roar of cars and trucks speeding by. The march of progress continues over this one-time pioneer's homestead and the remains of the unfortunate family that once lived there. It is on this spot where the family rests that strange things are said take place. Tales of pioneer ghosts standing by the busy highway at night, ghostly voices coming over radios, CBs, and cell phones, and radio stations going dead while crossing the gravesite are just some of the oddities that take place on central Florida's haunted highway.

Ghostly Legends and Haunted Folklore

I discovered the story of this haunted site was while searching the Internet. I found a web page called *Charlie Carlson's Strange Florida*, and first encountered the legend of the cursed Interstate-4, which Mr. Carlson refers to as the "Dead Zone of Interstate-4." The haunted part of the road is located toward the southern end of a bridge that crosses over the St. Johns River in Seminole County, just west of the city of Sanford. This section of road and bridge, which covers only a quarter of a mile or so, has been dubbed the "Dead Zone" because the primary supernatural events involve the failing of electrical equipment, such as radios and other communication devices. However, there has also been an unusually high number of traffic accidents and fatalities on this section of the road, all well documented by the Florida Highway Patrol.

The electrical disruptions are particularly mysterious because there are no radio or cell phone antennas nearby, nor any microwave emitters from local weather or television stations in the area, so logical explanations are hard to find. One of the most common creepy complaints involves cell phones that cease to function properly when crossing the bridge, as well as car radios going to static, or going silent altogether. This may not sound too frightening or fanciful, but when tape players and CD players do the same thing, one must take notice of such phenomena.

Other complaints include hearing voices crackling over the static of the radios, which are said to sound like a man calling out "Who's there?" or "Why?" Sometimes when truckers cross the bridge, they hear the same thing echoing over their CBs, and when the trucker answers back to what he thinks is just another driver, he gets no response. On occasion, some have heard what sounds like the giggling of two girls playing in the distance, as if from a playground, eerily echoing over the radio. Some have even claimed to see ghostly hitch-hikers on the eastbound side of I-4, as well as the shapes of people walking on the banks of the river. Now, these could be ordinary people walking near the road at night, but one person claims to have seen something far more disturbing late one evening.

A Floridian trucker who delivers produce emailed me via my web site in October of 2002 to tell me the story of his ghostly encounter while crossing the haunted stretch of I-4. He caught a glimpse of something so strange it made him lock the doors to his cab. Apparently this trucker, whom I will refer to as "Pete," was making a run from St. Petersburg to Orlando and then on to Daytona Beach. This routine trek takes him right though the Dead Zone. As the state was widening this part of I-4, there was still a lot of construction equipment on the sides of both the east- and westbound lanes, and Pete took care in driving safely over the dark bridge. It was there, at the start of the bridge that the country music station he was listening to began to break up. Pete thought that was strange because his radio was a particularly expensive, state-of-the-art model, able to pick up the most distant radio stations, and this station was just out of Orlando, only about 13 miles away. Regardless, he remained patient, hoping his station would return once he'd crossed the St. Johns River. It was that moment, when he was near the top of the bridge, that he says he spied what looked like a man walking toward him on the shoulder of the road.

As Pete got closer to the man, he could see that he was tall and slender with a big beard. His features were dark, especially his eyes, almost as if there were no eyes, just empty sockets. He was wearing odd clothes, kind of tattered and certainly out of style. He wore a round hat with a wide brim, a hat similar to the actors on the TV show "Little House on the Prairie." Certainly, driving trucks for a living can introduce someone to a lot of strange things and even strange people, but what Pete saw was more than just something strange. What he remembered most was the color surrounding the image, as if a faint bluish light was being shined on the roadside man from nowhere. Pete admitted that the whole event was weird—weird enough to give him the shivers and weird enough to make him lock the cab doors. As he passed this glowing man, he got the urge to look behind him as best he could, for just one more look, but when he did, he saw absolutely nothing—the ghostly wayfarer was gone!

Pete's email was brief, and he expressed that he was not a fanciful man prone to, as he put it, "spook stories," but that particular night he began to think just a little differently. Pete continues to drive over this stretch of road, as he has done for the last ten years. And, although he has not written back to report any other encounters, I'm sure that he will always keep a lookout for a ghostly glow, or an odd man walking on the side of I-4. And I suspect that Pete might just continue to lock the doors to his truck when crossing the graves on those dark, moonless nights.

Afterthoughts

To this day, people are reporting more and more that they are having problems with their communication devices and radios along that stretch of road, and others have witnessed ghostly hitchhikers like the one that Pete saw, as well as other strange things creeping near the river. Some people even claim to have stopped their vehicles to call the police or an ambulance because these hitchhikers look so dejected and sick. When they pulled over to help, however, they found no one, just the breezy wake of passing cars and trucks.

Indeed, because the reports of these roadside phantoms have become so common, and have been written about in many ghost hunter web sites, those claiming to be psychics have gathered in hopes to release these particular tormented souls. Some have come to the Dead Zone to apologize for the cruelty and greed of the past, and for ignoring the resting places of the dead. While investigating, several of these psychics have reported that there are many cold spots or "portals" near and around this location, and they also say they've heard voices coming from the bushes and river area, only to yield no sign of people. And, although some have left flower wreaths where the graves are believed to be, the state will still not acknowledge or officially recognize the site where the colonists still lay buried under the rushing traffic of I-4.

When traveling to see this site, it's best to drive east on I-4 and get off at the Sanford exit, going right. Once there, travel east again until you reach the St. Johns River, then go left until you reach the I-4 eastbound exit directly on the riverbank. If you decide to park, take caution, as I-4 is not for the timid. Because accidents do happen here quite often, the area is always dangerous. The best way to investigate is to drive over the bridge late at night with your radio on and your cell phone handy. See for yourself if ghostly voices echo through your radio station, or if your cell phone flickers and fails in mid-conversation, and maybe, just maybe, you'll glimpse a ghostly hitchhiker walking alone on the darkened road. Perhaps you too will lock your doors while crossing over the entombed pioneers on central Florida's haunted highway.

22

Stetson University

DeLand

Ghostly Lovers and Their Little Dog, Too

A Little History

Stetson University is one of the oldest privately funded universities in the state of Florida, and was originally known as the DeLand Academy in 1883, developed by then-entrepreneur Henry DeLand, the same man who was largely responsible for the creation of the city bearing his name. After financial hardships as a result of a winter freeze, which destroyed many of DeLand's citrus crops, Henry DeLand was forced to consider other options for survival, as keeping the school afloat was becoming nearly impossible.

As Henry DeLand was good friends with the university's president, John Forbes, and a Philadelphia hat-maker by the name of John B. Stetson, he made the proposal for help with his financial situation, and in 1889 the DeLand Academy became the now renowned Stetson University.

The bell tower, known as Hulley Tower, was finished in 1934. This beautiful 116-foot, red-brick structure, designed and overseen by the university's own professor of mathematics and engineering, was a gift from Dr. Hulley and his family to Stetson University and all of

DeLand. Oddly enough, Dr. Hulley died the year construction was complete, and to honor him, the university moved its original bell set from another section of the campus and placed it in the apex of the new tower. But Hulley Tower was intended as more than just a housing for the bell ensemble; indeed, the building was to serve another purpose altogether.

The eleven-bell chime set, called a carillon, sits at the inner housing of the tower's top, and was appropriately named the Eloise Chimes in honor of Eloise Mayham Hulley, the doctor's beloved wife. At the bottom of this impressive tower, facing the street, is a double-door which leads into a room measuring nineteen feet square and twenty-two feet high, and therein lies the tower's second purpose. While Hulley Tower serves to announce commencement and other special occasions to the campus, as well as to all of DeLand's residents, it also acts as the permanent resting place for Dr. Hulley and Eloise. You see, this unique structure is much more than just a bell tower, it's also their crypt.

Ghostly Legends and Haunted Folklore

Dr. Hulley served Stetson University as president from 1904 until his death in 1934 and was placed in the bell tower's bottom section, now an elegant stone mausoleum. Mrs. Eloise Hulley lived another twenty-five years, passing away in 1959 at the ripe old age of ninety-two and finally joining her husband in the tower for all eternity. That is, most of eternity.

It has been Stetson's local legend for many years, almost since Dr. and Mrs. Hulley's departing from this earth, and it has become the custom of every Halloween season to initiate freshman with Stetson's own personal ghost story.

Now, no one knows the exact date in history that the good doctor and his bride began taking nocturnal walks, but the legend of their earthbound existence has been passed down for at least forty years,

according to some local historians and other DeLand luminaries. Apparently, the two enamored spirits are seen walking the grassy grounds around the tower and under the trees, sometimes walking arm-in-arm, sometimes moving more somberly as Dr. Hulley walks a small dog, described as a white or golden terrier. And even though these two spirits seem to frequent the general area around the bell tower, they have been seen in other parts of the campus as well.

According to some of the students and even a few professors, the silhouette of an elderly couple is sometimes seen walking slowly behind Cummings Gym or glimpsed gazing into the university's fountain late at night. Moreover, on occasion in the wee hours, some of the night-owl students will catch a glimpse of a couple in period clothing walking around the dorms. At times, a courageous student or two will go in search of the phantoms, only to find an empty courtyard permeated by an eerie coldness.

Although this haunted love story has certainly been of interest to many of Stetson's students over the years, it seems they are not the only ones to have caught the spirited couple walking the grounds. According to several of DeLand's residents who live in a neighborhood across the street from the university, the ghostly couple has been seen on residential lawns near the bell tower late at night. One resident tells of a night when, while walking his dog, he spotted an older couple walking their little dog near the Holiday House restaurant, one of DeLand's historical eateries, directly across the street from the university. Although it was late at night, and the restaurant had long been closed for the evening, this gentleman decided to walk over to the couple and start a friendly conversation. As he got closer, he noticed that they were dressed in an older style of clothing, and thought that maybe they were just a bit eccentric, or perhaps had just returned from a costume party. They were looking at the restaurant's fountain, bubbling away as usual. He was preparing to comment on the fountain when his dog began to tug away from him, unwilling to walk ahead. Although this distraction took only a few moments, when he finally looked up to say hello, the couple was gone, as if they were never there. Now, it's hard to say whether or not this was Stetson's ghostly couple, but when the gentleman walked around the fountain, he saw no one, just an empty parking lot and the usual traffic from North Woodland Boulevard between the restaurant and the university. Not a soul in sight.

Apparently, this is not the only account from a person outside of the university who has seen or felt a presence off the school's property, as several of the townspeople who have lived there for many years have claimed such experiences. In fact, there are a few who actively investigate the legend of the bell tower and the ghosts who haunt it. Many have had direct paranormal experiences during these investigations. Some of these investigators claim to have detected the strong scent of flowers while walking on the sidewalk passing the bell tower, where there should be no such scent. Some have had the feeling of being watched when walking through the university's antique hallways, suggesting that the Hulleys might like to explore beyond the confines of their bell tower crypt. Perhaps there are other spirits haunting Stetson University.

Some students have told of strange experiences in other buildings of the university as well, such as DeLand Hall, Elizabeth Hall, Cummings Gym, and the Stover Theater. When I approached some of the students about this phenomenon, most were unaware of any alleged hauntings outside of the time-honored legend of the Hulley spirits. Yet with persistence, I found a few who offered some startling stories.

DeLand Hall, known as the "Grand Old Lady," built in the late nineteenth century, is a glorious example of French Second Empire architecture. It is the oldest academic building on the campus and is even listed with the National Register of Historic Places, so if there are ghosts on this campus, this building should certainly be a busy location.

According to one female student, while sitting on a couch inside DeLand Hall, going over her homework, the grandfather clock to her left began to chime, then stopped after three strikes. Immediately after the chimes stopped, she heard loud, deliberate footfalls on the staircase directly behind her. As she looked up, then over her shoulder to see who was there, she found no one. Needless to say, this student felt

DeLand Hall

very uncomfortable and left for her apartment straight away. Later, after telling her experience to one of her professors, she found out that the clock in DeLand Hall hasn't been wound in years and could not have just chimed on its own, thus adding to Stetson's strange phenomena.

Elizabeth Hall is another wonderful structure that also seems to have a noisy spirit walking up and down the old wooden staircase in the center of the building. Apparently, custodians and students will hear the unmistakable sounds of fast-paced footfalls, creaking and popping as if from an unseen student making his way to a phantom class. Just across the street stands Cummings Gym, which is said to be the home of shadowy figures that dart back and forth in the bushes. People have also spotted a certain ghostly couple walking their little dog there.

In Stover Theater, a beautiful brick building directly behind Cummings Gym, it is said that faint echoes of clapping and laughter from the audience area and balcony can be heard, as well as the sound of running footfalls from the stage. As one student told me, while in the building late at night working on a project for an upcoming theatrical production, he noticed a cold breeze blowing down the center part of the house. Realizing that it could be the air conditioning, he didn't think anything more about it. Then he heard what sounded like a child running on the stage behind him. Still keeping his cool, he walked around to see if the two other students working that night were playing a trick on him, but he found no one inside. As he walked through the lobby, he could see his companions sitting outside smoking a cigarette, and when he confronted them about his experiences, they denied playing any tricks on him and claimed that no one else was in the building. Just another school spirit, perhaps?

Afterthoughts

The whole ghost-hunting affair while researching Stetson University has been somewhat amusing. In my quest to find information about Dr. and Mrs. Hulley and their spiritual, nocturnal walks, I found a plethora of ghostly folklore that seems to coexist with the university's most popular legend. And it stands to reason that such an elegant and stately university should indeed attract a spirit or two.

Although Stetson has earned quite an honorable history over the years, and certainly should be proud of what its staff and students have accomplished in the past 100 years, we must not forget the tragedies and hardships that have taken place there as well. As with any university, Stetson has housed active and spirited lives. And, after a century's worth of such life and activity, it also stands to reason that some of those spirits may have chosen to remain at the place that was so important to them during their lives. Stetson is certainly no exception to this possibility, as these stories seem to indicate.

I find Stetson University to have that enchanted feeling to it, the kind of feeling that quietly expresses the Florida of years past, and a good feeling as far as that goes. I do not have a bad impression of the ghostly goings on there, either. I believe that Stetson University, and all of DeLand, has a special quality to it that should not be missed when looking for that small-town, homey feeling. When visiting the city of DeLand and the gorgeous campus of Stetson University, enjoy the restaurants, the antique stores, and of course, the old Florida charm that it has throughout. And when walking past the university late at night, listen for the chimes of the old grandfather clock echoing through the walls of DeLand Hall, and keep an extra lookout for a nicely dressed couple walking their little dog. Who knows? Maybe they will walk over to you for a polite conversation, or maybe they'll quietly slip away without a word.

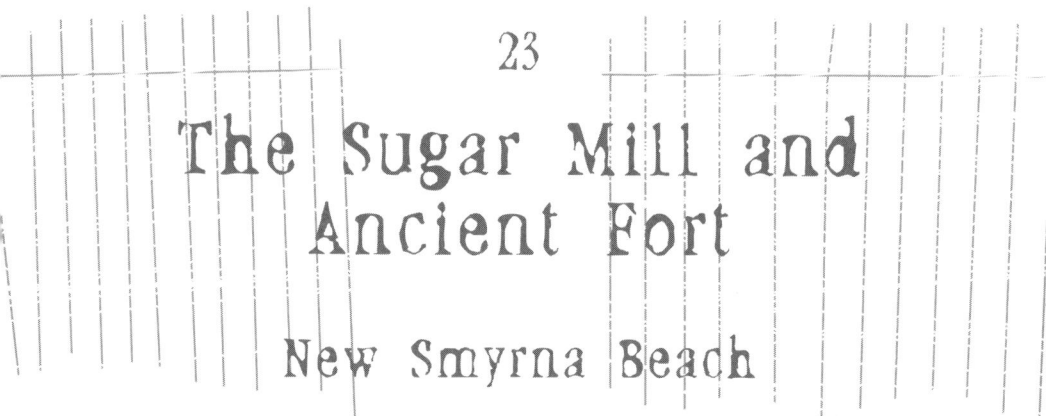

23

The Sugar Mill and Ancient Fort

New Smyrna Beach

Shadow People

A Little History

It's hard to imagine that New Smyrna Beach could have so much intense history in its past, especially British history. Just as St. Augustine is known as the oldest city in the United States, New Smyrna could be known as the location of the largest British colonization attempt in North America; in fact, it was more than three times larger than the first settlement in Jamestown, Virginia.

In this region, you can expect to find the small Florida neighborhoods, fine restaurants, little cafes, and of course, the world-class beaches that have the same beauty today that they did when Native Americans walked freely on them centuries ago. New Smyrna is just one of those Florida cities that makes everyone proud to live there, or proud even to visit.

New Smyrna Beach seems to have two ancient mysteries that to this day have not been completely explained. The sugar mill, located on Mission Drive off State Road 44 and the ancient foundation of what is thought to be a Spanish fort on Washington Street and North Riverside Drive remain enigmas for many archaeologists and historians.

The sugar mill is believed to have once been a major sugar and syrup processing location that was burnt down during the Second Seminole War in the 1830s. And although there are huge iron pots and even the remains of a motorized steam engine left for all to see on the property, many people feel that this was originally the location of a seventeenth-century convent. Some believe that this was the location of a chapel built by Christopher Columbus himself during his second voyage. This was the most common theory for many years because archaeologists unearthed many religious artifacts such as alters, candlestick holders, and various crucifixes all over the property. Whatever its history, this location is certainly a spooky one, to say the least. Still surrounded by dense woods and shaded under a canopy of ancient trees, the sugar mill hasn't changed much in centuries and is a must-see when visiting the New Smyrna area. These ruins and the surrounding forest have been dubbed sacred and enchanted by many Native Americans today, a description closely tied to the ghostly phenomena that have been witnessed there.

The mysterious shell foundation on Washington Street is just as interesting as the sugar mill, and for good reason, as many archaeologists still debate its past and purpose. The remains are in the shape of a cross, fifty-five feet by eighty-six feet, and may be those of a structure used for the storage of gunpowder and other perishable supplies. One popular belief is that these are the remains of a Spanish fort that predates the oldest masonry fort in North America, the Castillo de San Marcos in St. Augustine. The New Smyrna fort is believed by some to have been built on an even older settlement—a shell mound from an ancient Native American tribe dating from around 500 C.E.

The second theory for this ancient mystery is that it was once the foundation of the Turnbull mansion. Dr. Andrew Turnbull was a prominent eighteenth-century Scottish physician and founder of the New Smyrna Colony. He is known to have had a large mansion made of coquina (a popular shell-based building material at the time) that overlooked the inlet. Although Dr. Turnbull was a well esteemed man of his day, the collapse of the colony in 1777 may have made any records of his home, and the colony itself, disputable. As a result, many scholars and historians over the years have debated the true origins of this mysterious foundation.

Regardless of these uncertain histories, stories of the "haunted wood," shadowy people darting and dancing near the old Sugar Mill, and a ghostly Spanish soldier on the old coquina ruins have continued throughout the centuries.

Ghostly Legends and Haunted Folklore

Beginning with the area around the sugar mill—"the haunted wood," as the locals referred to it a few generations ago—the legends speak of spirited Native Americans who, for whatever reasons, still run and hide in the heavily wooded areas at dusk and during the wee hours of the morning. Perhaps these spirits are just re-living their raids of long ago, or perhaps they are restless because they still mourn the loss of their sacred land and the desecration of their burial grounds. Whatever the reasons, many people today still claim to hear and see these evasive specters.

Visitors have traveled from all over the nation and even the world to see these enigmatic ruins that have sat relatively untouched for hundreds of years. Many of these visitors claim that they have heard the rustling of trees and bushes and have even seen what some described as "people dressed as Indians" hiding behind trees and sprinting through the foliage as if in flight. Many who witnessed these entities believed that they were nothing more than historical re-enactors recreating a battle for them, like the ones they may have seen when they were visiting Saint Augustine. But we know better. There are no re-enactors at the sugar mill, just protected state land, meant to educate and fascinate those who visit New Smyrna.

Although these fast-moving spirits are indeed intriguing for anyone fortunate enough catch a glimpse of them, there is another brand of entity reported at the sugar mill that is less desired. According to local legend, there are dark spirits that many have dubbed "the shadow people." These shadow people are described as very dark, almost black shadows that creep through the dense trees at dusk and climb on the walls and rubble of the ruins when the sun begins to go down in the evening. Most frightening, these shadow people seem to be sentient, as if they watch the people who visit the ruins . . . as if they were alive.

One rather spooky story about the shadow people involves a family from Great Britain visiting Florida one summer a few years ago. As this family walked through the park, they were astounded and then even frightened when they encountered these misty shadow people. Apparently, while the mother a father were taking photos of their two children who were standing against one of the shell walls, the shadowy figure of a large man was clearly seen moving near the two children.

Acting on instinct, both parents looked behind them to see who was approaching, only to find no one there. Then, looking in all directions, they were still unable to find anyone else at the park, and there was no explanation for the strange shadow. When they looked back at their children, they saw the shadow moving away on the other side of them! This understandably had the visitors a bit shaken, but they dismissed the event as a trick of the light through the trees. They continued their journey through the ruins, taking photographs of their Florida visit. Soon the dark clouds and the sound of thunder told of an approaching late-afternoon storm, a common occurrence in Florida summers. But this time, the storm would bring something else with it, something far more frightening.

As the family was finishing up the photo session, the storm was fast approaching: the thunder claps were getting much louder and now there were flashes of lightning, which signaled that it was time to leave the park. The family wasn't quite finished, however, and decided to take just a few more photos before calling it a day. As the father was taking the last set of photos, they again saw the shadow person, this time moving on the eastern wall, as if climbing upward. Once again, there was no logical answer for any shadow of a man being there, or any shadow at all, considering the sun was now almost completely hidden by storm clouds. Although a little unnerved by this mystery, they were not overly excited—that is until there was a bright flash of lightning and a loud boom of thunder. All at once they saw what appeared to be two or three shadows of people on the wall in front of them. Needless to say, the family hurried out of the park as fast as they could.

This particular story is one of the more popular ones I have heard, but according to a few of the park rangers, and many of the locals, the shadow people still make their presence known to visitors from time to time. One of the popular theories is that the shadow people are the disgruntled spirits of Native Americans killed in the Seminole Wars of the mid-1800s. If this theory is true, these people, who fought to protect their homes and their families, may still look at visitors to the area as threatening intruders. Perhaps when this English family was walking through the ruins and taking photographs, these spirits were reminded of British imperialism. Or perhaps they came to life, so to speak, when the storm came. Either way, the shadow people can certainly raise the hair on the necks of those who are lucky enough to experience them . . . although "lucky" may not be quite the right word.

Another ghostly legend is that of the portly Spanish soldier that walks the old fort on Washington Street, overlooking the marina and bay, as if waiting for the enemy to arrive. Although no one knows who this soldier could have been in life, it's fairly clear that he was a Spaniard: he wears the steel breast plate and morion helmet commonly used by soldiers during the sixteenth and seventeenth centuries when Spain ruled Florida. This specter appears on dark and rainy summer days. The old portly soldier has been seen standing on the remains of the eastern wall of the ruins, hunched over and staring intensely at the water, as if a ship were approaching. And, on some stormy occasions, when people are driving between the fort and the marina, they have seen the shape of this soldier through the thick mist of the rain, looking for something out at sea.

One of the most frightening aspects of this specter is that his face is rarely seen. Most of the people who witnessed him claimed to see the basic shell of an ancient uniform and gray metal armor, and what appeared to be a thick, dark goatee and only dark circles where eyes should be. The image was only a rudimentary outline—no eyes, no nose, and no mouth. Others who have seen the man have said that, standing on the wall of the ruins, he looked like an ordinary man. Some did not think he was a ghost at first, they just thought he was out of place. After they passed him, however, they thought it strange that someone would be standing there during a terrible lightning storm dressed in such a costume. And it was especially weird if they noticed that this man didn't seem to have face, just a thick black beard.

Although no evidence yet has clearly shown the origins of this site, there are those who believe that it must be the foundation of a Spanish fort because they have seen the portly ghost of the Washington Street ruins. Who was this vigilant Spanish sentry, and why does he still haunt this location? Was he the victim of a pirate attack on a Spanish settlement of long ago? Did he fail to warn his troops of an approaching ship that eventually attacked? We may never know, but there is no doubt that something happened at these ruins, especially for those who have seen the ever-ready Spanish guard who stands on duty, even during the most horrific weather, and never complains.

Afterthoughts

When visiting New Smyrna, be sure to enjoy the beautiful white sand beaches, dine at one of the many fine restaurants, and enjoy the grand beauty this ancient land has. But do take the time look at the remaining wilderness, and try to recall the ancient memories that still resonate in the shell-encrusted walls of the old sugar mill. Take a good look at these forests and estuaries—they may still look as they did centuries ago, but time may not wait much longer. Florida is always growing, and even though we promise to save our history, time and the elements may have different plans.

As for the odd specters that creep and climb the walls of the old sugar mill, we will probably never know what they truly are, or from where they came. They may be desecrated dead from the Seminole wars, or something that has lived in these woods since the dawn of time.

When you visit the old fort on Washington Street, keep a lookout for the silent, solitary sentry that stairs out to sea. Whether during a still night or a raging storm, you might just catch a glimpse of this sad but vigilant guard. Try to hear the commands of the soldiers that once stood ever watchful on the walls and docks, looking out for invading forces. But if you visit these ruins, take a friend, and always depart before the hot summer wind blows in a storm. It is always a good idea to leave before the thunder and lightning descend upon you . . . just before the shadows start to fall.

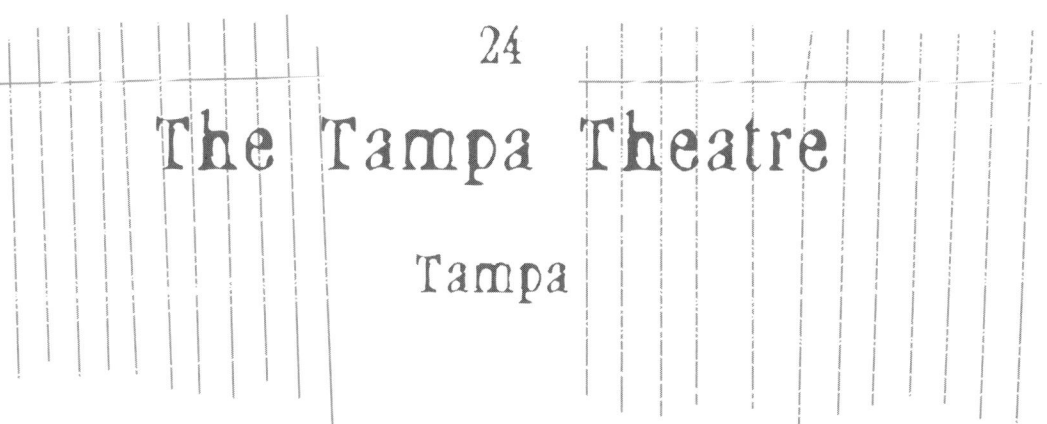

24

The Tampa Theatre

Tampa

A Tapping on My Shoulder

A Little History

The majestic Tampa Theatre is located at 711 Franklin Street in downtown Tampa. A unique example of classic architecture, the Tampa Theatre was designed by architect John Eberson to honor the unique styles of the Italian Renaissance, as well as Spanish, Mediterranean, Greek Revival, Baroque, English Tudor, and even Byzantine styles. Construction cost more than $1 million and took over a year to finish. The building opened its doors on October 15, 1926, and the first film to be played at the Tampa Theatre was a silent film called *The Ace of Cads*, starring Adolph Menjou, a heartthrob of the day. This film, which cost only twenty-five cents to see, began a long and happy era for movie and stage connoisseurs that would last more than eighty years.

The Tampa Theatre set a new standard of excellence for entertainment, hosting lavish vaudeville shows, concerts by the Tampa Theatre Symphony Orchestra, silent films as well as full-sound pictures by 1929. With the advent of sound pictures, the Tampa Theatre presented all the latest Hollywood "talkies" and put Tampa on the cul-

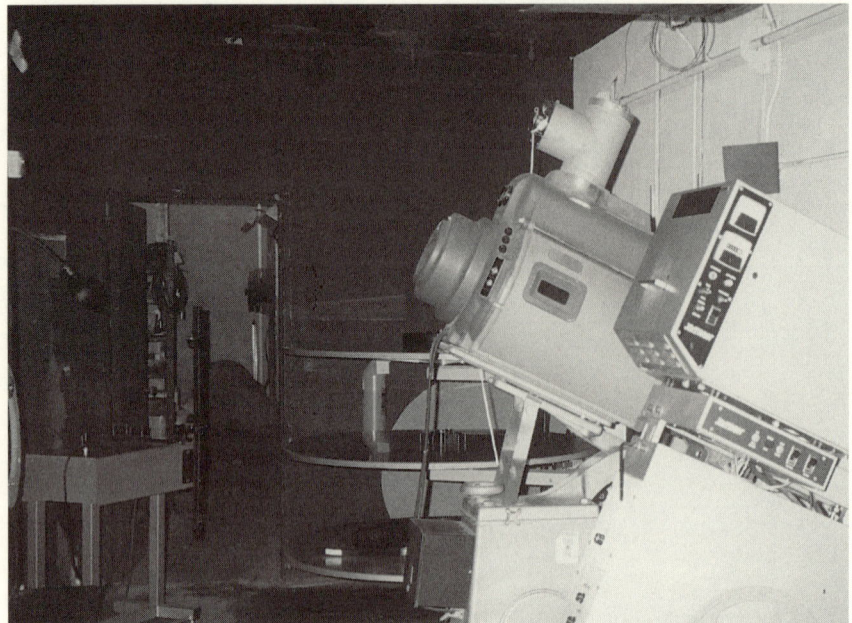

Projection Room

tural map. The theatre was also one of the first public buildings with air conditioning, a major advancement during the early twentieth century, especially in a state like Florida. With such amenities, the Tampa Theatre remained an excellent source for entertainment for years, but by the 1960s culture had changed. A dwindling city population, due to the new suburban lifestyle, was having a negative effect on urban life all across Florida.

Many of the stately movie palaces were torn down due to the value of the land. Because land in areas like downtown Tampa was needed for parking lots, large theatres were in the developers' sights—and the Tampa Theatre seemed to be facing a similar fate. Fortunately, by the early 1970s, the City of Tampa stepped in and assumed responsibility for the theatre's leases, and the Arts Council of Hillsborough County took the role of management. Tampa's residents volunteered to support the theatre's cause and helped restore the Tampa Theatre to the joy of yesteryear. Today, Tampa Theatre has a full schedule of films, foreign and domestic, as well as concerts, special events, and even hosts tours for the public, teaching history and the importance of preservation to young and old alike.

The Tampa Theatre, Inc., is a private organization that funds maintenance and restoration, as well as the theatre's repertoire. It survives from the ticket and concession sales, rental fees for private functions, and donations. The extra support in the form of grants from the City of Tampa, the Division of Cultural Affairs, and the Florida Department of State certainly help. The Tampa Theatre became listed in the National Register of Historic Places in 1978 and is a member of the League of Historic American Theatres of the United States.

Inside this glorious movie palace you will find an amazing second-floor balcony, which hangs by support beams and cables that were revolutionary in the 1920s. There are 1,446 seats, and just behind the stage stands a genuine Wurlitzer theatre organ. With close to 1,000 pipes that fill the theater with superb sound, the organ can complement any Errol Flynn movie with ease. Painted clouds and tiny sparkling lights in the ceiling are a 1930s special effect that still amazes after all these years. Even though the antiquated fog machine once used to emulate clouds is no longer working, the general feeling of romance and awe is still there. All in all, the Tampa Theatre is just as beautiful as it was at its grand opening. When I first had the opportunity to experience this wonderful theatre, I went there to see *It's a Wonderful Life*, and I must admit, although this is one of my favorite films, I too often found myself in awe of the sheer beauty of the theatre itself. The Tampa Theatre is so beautiful and relaxing I didn't want to go home at the end of the film. Apparently, I am not the only person to have felt this way over the years, as this theatre seems to have a permanent resident who never wanted to go home either: the spirit of Foster "Fink" Finley.

Ghostly Legends and Haunted Folklore

It's hard to imagine a building like the Tampa Theatre not having a haunted history to it, as so many theatres around the world seem to attract spooks. Tampa history tells us that a man named Foster Finley, or "Fink" to his friends, was one of the theatre's movie projectionists. Fink began working as a projectionist in 1930 and worked there until the early 1960s. He was described as a small, slightly overweight, quiet man. He was balding and wore thick-framed glasses that always seemed to be foggy, as if permanently affected by the humidity of the projectionist's booth. Although he may not have looked like a Hollywood playboy, he was an honest, dedicated man who took his business seriously and almost never missed a day, manning his post in the small booth until the film was run with no mishaps. He was a heavy smoker, however, and addiction would ultimately cut short his life. It is possible that he suffered a series of small heart attacks throughout the 1960s, finally culminating when he collapsed while running a film in the summer of 1965. Although he went home in hopes of recovering and getting back to the theatre and the job he loved so much, he died only a few months later. Fink Finley was securely laid to rest, but he is believed, even by the most skeptical, to be behind some very strange episodes within the theatre, and he continues to be an active spirit to this day.

Unusual incidents and strange noises abound in the theatre's seating area, as well as in the projectionist's booth. Odd feelings, smells, and cold spots are the most common events, yet objects will disappear and move themselves, too. Occasionally, one might feel a tap on the shoulder, only to find an empty theatre behind him. And from at least the 1970s, there have been reports of various other preternatural incidents. Many paranormal investigators and parapsychologists have come to the Tampa Theatre in order to prove the existence of an entity or haunting, and many of them have found sufficient evidence.

Several local ghost-hunting organizations have gone to the theatre equipped with the tools of their trade. With equipment such as electromagnetic field (EMF) detectors, portable hands-free thermometers, sensitive voice-activated tape recorders, cameras with infrared film, and an assortment of other ghost-hunter devices, these amateur investigators were ready for the extraordinary . . . and their findings were extraordinary, too.

Many of these self-styled investigators of the paranormal have collected intriguing evidence of a ghostly presence. The digital hands-free thermometers have recorded many variations in temperature throughout the theatre, with no obvious cause for such variations. Cold spots are common, too, even in areas where the air conditioners do not operate, or when the air is off altogether. Moreover, people watching movies commonly detect strange scents, like old cologne. Cool drafts will sometimes occur when no one is around and no doors have been opened.

I have had personal experience with the cologne phenomenon. While I was watching a film at the Tampa Theatre in December of 2002, sitting on the second floor in a somewhat isolated section of the theatre, I caught a whiff of a cologne that smelled old and unfamiliar. Now, of course, I could be mistaken, but there were no other men sitting even remotely close to me, and I am certain my girlfriend wasn't wearing men's cologne. She even commented on the strange scent, and both of us looked around for a possible explanation. Unless there is another logical explanation to the strange odor, someone interested in the paranormal may assume that it is a scent of the past, somehow caught in the fabric of our present. Perhaps it was Fink walking by, checking up on things in the theatre.

Along with strange smells, many claim to hear the sounds of keys dropping or rattling as if hung on a worker's belt, the noises originating in the lower sections of the stage area and around the old orchestra pit. Footsteps are sometimes heard along the walkways, and on occasions, the screen will shimmer as if someone were touching it from behind. And, though these things are definitely odd, the most peculiar occurrence and undoubtedly the most frightening, is the appearance of what many believe to by Fink himself floating across the screen when a film is being played. Although I have not been blessed with a personal appearance by Fink Finley, many people to this day have claimed to see the apparition of a man resembling Fink's description floating across the screen during a matinee. The hazy image is often seen gliding silently with its hands behind its back and leaning forward, almost as if it were ice-skating. Moreover, patrons and staff, including projectionists, have seen this fanciful apparition, yet no one has ever said they had bad feelings about the event, just the feeling of watching something that may have already taken place, like an instant replay, or a clip from an old film.

Although some feel that these events are more to be associated with the poltergeist phenomena, due to the psychokinetic events like the moving of objects, others believe the theatre shows evidence of a classic haunting, because of the longevity of the haunting-like circumstances. As most poltergeist outbreaks last for only a short time, the classic haunting theory seems to make the most sense, as these events have been going on for many years. Either way, however, there seems to be something supernatural taking place in the Tampa Theatre.

If one wishes to witness these strange events, the best time appears to be either in the early morning, or late in the evenings, and almost assuredly after hours. As with the saying, "A watched pot never boils," the specter of Fink Finley will not perform on command, but will instead go about his routine when he feels like it, and that can be at any time. When looking for evidence of ghosts at the Tampa Theatre, the best approach is just to enjoy the venue and hope to feel something out of the ordinary. Cold spots, strange or out of place scents, as well as disembodied sounds are the most common, and if you're especially fortunate, you might catch a glimpse of the spirit or spirits of this magnificent theatre. Incidentally, at a drug store not long ago, as I was looking at after-shave lotions, smelling several different brands, one lotion in particular caught my eye, or should I say, nose. "Lilac Vegetal" immediately took me back to that afternoon in the Tampa Theatre when my girlfriend and I noticed the strange-smelling cologne. Upon closer inspection of this after-shave, I noticed that it has been sold since the 1800s. When I asked the store clerk about it, he told me that only older men and barbers use it.

As I investigated further, going to a barber in the nearby plaza, I was told that Lilac Vegetal was a very common and popular cologne used during the early part of this century, and it was used today primarily as a skin tonic for older men. Whether or not there was an older gentleman wearing this somewhat rare cologne that day in the Tampa Theatre is speculative, due to the fact that no one was around us. And, because this was a popular item for men to wear during the 1920s and 1930s, it would be quite a coincidence to encounter someone wearing it today. Personally, because Fink was a clean-cut, clean-shaven man, always dressed properly and even somewhat dapper, I think there is the possibility that the Tampa Theatre's patron ghost continues his hygiene habits even from beyond the grave.

Afterthoughts

It's important to understand that the history of a location is just as important as the people who have lived there, worked there, or died there. The Tampa Theatre is no different. Over the years, many have come to this theatre, to work or to enjoy the shows, and some have even died within its walls, as historical documents show. The full gamut of emotions that has taken place over the years may account for the equally vast array of paranormal events that have occurred. As many students of the metaphysical world will agree, hauntings are the result of massive and intense human emotions. Happy occasions may repeat themselves as if they were old movies; horrific murders may recur on the anniversaries of those events. If the spirit of Fink Finley is truly haunting the Tampa Theatre, it may be likely that he is a self-evident entity, or a spirit that goes about a routine completely on its own. As Fink appears to do just that, this theory would seem to make sense, which means that his spirit is in some way sentient, regardless of his being dead for almost forty years.

The Tampa Theatre is without a doubt an icon of a more romantic time, when buildings were not just containers for people, but works of art. Even if you don't go to the Tampa Theatre to find a ghost or to spot Fink Finley floating across the silver screen, go there to witness the elegy to one man's talent and love of his trade. Whether or not the theatre is haunted, it remains an important part of Florida's heritage and growth. And who knows? You might just see more than a classic film at the Tampa Theatre . . . you might just get to meet Fink Finley himself.

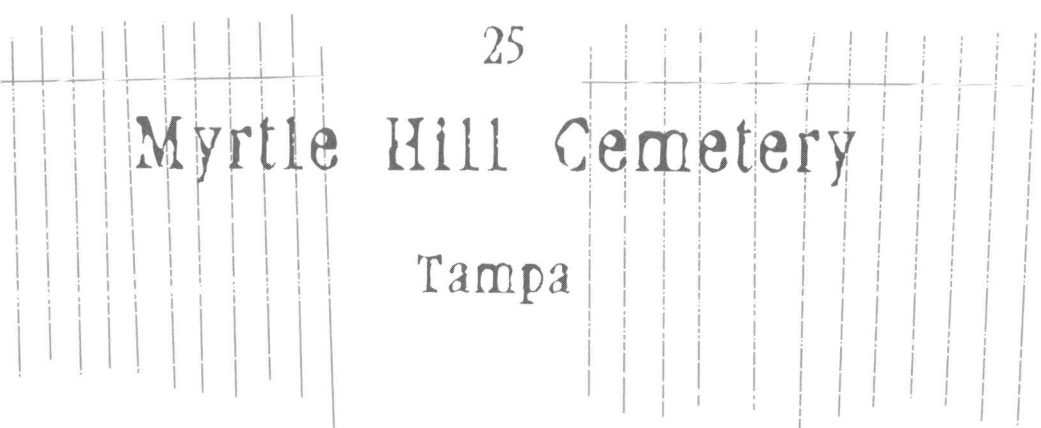

25

Myrtle Hill Cemetery

Tampa

The Mausoleum

I opened the doors slowly. Immediately a wind of rancid, decaying air hit us in the face. Standing there, we both turned to each other with looks of utter disgust as the air within was like that of an open tomb. As we looked inward, we spotted shadows flitting around on the walls and heard what we thought to be whispers and low talking, and, after a moment, we both heard two distinct voices, a man and a young girl. . . .

A Little History

Myrtle Hill Cemetery and the Garden of Peace is located in Hillsborough County, near Ybor City, just east of Tampa. Ybor City, a nineteenth-century Cuban settlement, was once one of the largest and best organized cigar manufacturers in the United States. Today, Ybor City still resonates the feeling of history, but is known mostly for its fine dining and nightlife. When the sun goes down, the roads are rerouted by the police and the once sleepy streets and cozy storefronts become packed with partygoers and bar-hoppers. This town is well known for its festive nature, but just northwest of this busy, bustling area, outside of the laughter and mayhem, lies a place known for the flowing of another kind of spirit . . . the spirits of Myrtle Hill.

Ghostly Legends and Haunted Folklore

Myrtle Hill Cemetery is without a doubt one of the most spiritually active cemeteries I ever investigated. While traveling through the Tampa, Ybor City area, another investigator and I happened upon the burial grounds merely by accident as we were en route to a hotel for the evening, but somewhat lost, I might add. Just like a scene from a surreal motion picture, it was raining hard outside, the sky filled with the bursts of lightning and the sound of rolling thunder all around us.

As we passed the cemetery, we saw the lightning reflect on the headstones and the massive walls of the mausoleum, which sent shivers of excitement down our spines. We never found the hotel we were originally looking for, but stopped at a little motel far off the beaten path. Filled with intrigue after we secured our room for the evening, we decided to go back and investigate this delightful cemetery. That's when the fun began.

From the very start of this initial investigation, we felt there was something strange about this particular cemetery. Myrtle Hill is so big we got lost driving around the many lanes and cul-de-sacs within the grounds, which wind and turn in all directions. Huge monuments, obelisks, sepulchers, and tombs adorn every turn, and the flashing of the lightning upon these structures just added to our curiosity, as well as to our confusion.

When we arrived in front of one mausoleum, we stopped the car, trying to get a good look into the dark, glass-windowed doorway of this huge structure. After a while we gathered enough nerve and decided to go on in. As we reached the front doors, an instant feeling of dread came over us. I couldn't explain this feeling, and trying hard to ignore it, I opened the doors slowly. Immediately a wind of rancid, decaying air hit us in the face. Standing there, we both turned to each other with looks of disgust, as the air within was like that of an open tomb. As we looked inward, we spotted shadows flitting around on the walls and heard what we thought to be whispers and low talking, and, after a moment, we both heard two distinct voices, a man a young girl. Needless to say, we both hurried out of there in considerable haste, not so much in fear of ghosts, but of transients lodging within the mausoleum for the night.

As we got back in the car, we waited to see if anyone would rush out the doors or at least make some movement within, but nothing moved. After a while we decided to drive around throughout the grounds. We came along another structure in the middle of the cemetery with a large, illuminated steeple at its center. As I got closer, I realized it housed niches to store the ashes of the cemetery's cremated residents. This structure has niches on the inner circumference as well as the outside and is adorned with a steeple on the roof, which reached ominously upward into the night sky. The inner section is used for religious gatherings, and like the mausoleum, it was left wide open. Unlike the mausoleum, however, there was a single chandelier eerily lighting the area. We walked around the inside of this unique structure, taking the time to read the names of the departed, and looking at the many photos hanging from the walls. The air was still and filled with the scent of decaying flowers. As we talked about our last experience at the doors of the mausoleum, we both heard two muffled thuds sounding from the back wall. Needless to say, we both decided to leave for the motel and call it a night.

This intriguing impromptu investigation constitutes our initiation to Myrtle Hill Cemetery. And, because of our experiences that night, we have added this location as an active and ongoing investigation site, which will continue to be investigated, photographed, and subjected to various scientific research, such as electromagnetic field (EMF) and electronic voice phenomena (EVP) analysis, as well as thermo-variation readings every few months.

Our first experience with Myrtle Hill was unique in many ways, but we had to put our feelings and beliefs in some sort of perspective—the basic elements of that first evening could surely have encouraged our imaginations. After all, it was raining outside, the wind was blowing, and there was a huge darkened cemetery, occasionally lit by flashing lightning, in the middle of nowhere. What ghost hunter wouldn't get excited at such a scene? With an honest amount of scientific skepticism, we decided to make another investigation, this time with two other team members, as well as a camera and a video recorder.

We arrived on a Friday evening around 1:30 A.M. The cemetery grounds were quiet. Armed only with my 35 mm camera and video camera, we entered the huge mausoleum with a bit more confidence than the last time. Like before, the smell of decay was all around us, and within only a few moments we began to hear strange sounds. Some of these sounds resembled whispers, and some certainly could have been the sounds made by a settling building; nonetheless, they were strange sounds.

As I walked around in the darkness, I shined my pen light on some of the photos and names of those interred. I asked the other investigators what they were feeling—if they heard anything out of the ordinary, or if they smelled anything different, or if they simply had any feelings at all about being there. I took into account that certain places and events may alter one's perception and mood, but all the women expressed feelings of dread and paranoia, as if they were being watched. These were the same feelings we'd had when we first discovered Myrtle Hill that dark rainy night.

As we continued our tour, one of the others stopped and asked if we could hear the sound of church bells, as if in the far off distance. Standing completely still, I did indeed hear what sounded like church bells . . . but it was now 2:20 A.M. What church would be ringing their bells so early in the morning? And why? As we continued, we huddled together and stood totally still, saying nothing. Within a minute or so, I began to hear an almost silent minuet, as if from a music box behind a wall. But not wanting to plant any ideas, I said nothing. Sure enough, each of the others exclaimed that they were hearing a music box as well, ever so slightly. It was about this time the atmosphere began to change. The air, although still rancid, seemed to be getting colder, with an occasional breeze. All the doors were closed, and there were no open windows in the mausoleum. Within a few moments, the large mobile metal staircase, used for putting flowers and cards on the crypt faces, began to shake, and footfalls echoed from on top of the stairs. Stunned, we stood still. . . .

Because there was almost no light within the mausoleum, and with my handy penlight only being slightly helpful, I decided to go

out to the car and get my larger flashlight. Although this only took a few moments—I did not expect anything else to occur during that short amount of time—when I got back to the mausoleum I found the others standing together, not overly excited, but certainly cautious. When I asked what had happened, they told me that they'd heard the sound of a baby cry in the southern hallway. The cry lasted only a moment or so, but was clear enough for each to hear it. Weeks later, when I was making another visit during the day, I found a crypt in that south corridor in which a mother and child were interred together, as both had apparently died in childbirth . . . coincidence?

With all that was taking place during that morning, it was certainly understandable that we were all becoming excited, yet we were strangely calm at the same time. It seemed that these spirits, although certainly active, were not so much angry as they were sad. After a while, each of us expressed the need to get out and get some fresh air, which was certainly needed, for the stench of decay was becoming unbearable.

As we walked around the cemetery, which seemed endless due to its immense size, we were approached by three Tampa police officers while they were making their rounds. They were naturally curious about our presence in the cemetery at such a late hour, and although it is not illegal to be there, they warned us of the possible dangers of being out so late in such a dark and deserted place.

Apparently, according to the police, this cemetery appeals to those who live outside of society's norms, those who enjoy the dark and romantic aspects of fantasy, especially gothic ghost and horror stories.

The officers were genuinely interested in our safety, as well as our ghost hunting investigations that early morning. Having a pleasant conversation with the officers about our experiences with paranormal research, and even hearing of some of their strange experiences in the past, only fueled our interest in the subject. As it was going on 4:00 A.M., we decided to call it a night and left for the hotel. Again, a splendid investigation had taken place, but this time the weather conditions were mild, and because there were others involved, people who were purposefully not told of our prior experiences at Myrtle Hill Cemetery, our observations were validated. This investigation was completely successful, as we were now sure that these strange events were not the results of our excited imaginations. The second visit was a standard scientific exam complete with photographic comparisons, video, EMF and EVP testing, as well as comparisons of temperature differentials in both the burial structures and cemetery overall.

Several weeks later, a team member and I returned to make our third investigation. The night was still and the weather fair. The mausoleum was again rancid smelling, and this time, the huge chandelier lighted the inside with a dim, yellowish glow. We were ready to take our time and conduct a thorough survey. I decided to sit on the metal chairs and listen. For a few moments we heard nothing out of the ordinary, but as time went on, what seemed to be low whispers began in both corridors of the mausoleum. We looked at each other in amazement, and then looked back toward the direction of the voices. In the absence of good light, the hallways took on an even more frightening feel, and these whispers seemed to be a conversation between two people, like two elderly ladies at the end of the corridor.

After about twenty minutes of this, we both got up slowly to investigate, only to find two empty corridors. Nobody else was present in the mausoleum that night, that was for sure, so we decided to take a few photographs and try our hand with our equipment for a possible scientific explanation.

As we walked around the massive inner circumference, we took readings of every section, taking photographs and using the EMF reader to see if there were any spikes or other abnormalities. On occasion, the meter would jump and peak, then return to a steady reading. We tried to see if there were temperature differences in the building, setting up a highly sensitive temperature recorder for this purpose. Next, we set up a voice-activated tape recorder, or VOX, which would begin recording with the sound of any voice or substantial noise, and then we prepared the video camera to film the main section and the two corridors on either end.

With the bait now laid, we walked outside and began taking similar readings around the many niches lining the outside walls. Taking photographs and checking the electromagnetic field situation outside, we left no stone unturned. After about thirty minutes, we decided to check our equipment on the inside of the mausoleum for its recordings. Success on both accounts! The temperature recorder picked up several different readings throughout the time we were gone. Two temperature gauges were used at that time, placed in stationary locations, and each one picked up cooling temperatures of almost fifteen degrees in just twenty-five minutes. This test was repeated on three separate occasions, with similar results each time. There are no open widows in the mausoleum, and the air conditioning controls are not set to cool, just to circulate. A drop in temperature in the realm of parapsychology is usually evidence of something, such as a spirit entity entering a location. This is sometimes called a portal haunting, and at Myrtle Hill, this phenomenon seems to be highly likely.

The voice-activated tape recorder results were also quite intriguing. When we played the tape back, we heard several sounds of thuds, or bumps, but we were unable to attribute them to any logical source. Plus there were startling sounds of creaking from the mobile metal staircase. These sounds were very similar to someone gently walking up or down the stairs, and almost identical to the sounds we all heard on our investigation weeks earlier. Moreover, when we checked the video camera, which had a fresh battery placed in it only moments earlier, we found that the battery was completely drained, and the video itself, which began filming normally, quickly became filled with static, and went black eight minutes after turning it on.

We gathered up the equipment, we sat and discussed our findings and finished our notes for the evening. As we started to walk out the doors to load the car, the distinct sound of someone sighing, a sort of "hummm," came from the furthest corridor of the mausoleum. This sound was quite clear and had within it a hint of sadness—yet strangely we were not startled. Instead, we felt as if we were old acquaintances with the souls of Myrtle Hill. So we said our goodbyes for the evening, but just for the evening. We will definitely be visiting the spirited mausoleum of Myrtle Hill Cemetery and the Gardens of Peace again . . . but never alone!

Afterthoughts

In the years I have devoted to my research of folklore and the study of the paranormal, I have visited many reputedly haunted locations that have been featured in the ghost lore of Florida and abroad. And, although I can only claim to believe that a handful of these locations is truly haunted, Myrtle Hill Cemetery is certainly one of them. In the short time I have been investigating Myrtle Hill Cemetery, I can honestly say that there is something there, something out of the ordinary that has never failed to put my senses on full alert.

Myrtle Hill is one of those cemeteries that will stay in your mind, primarily because of the duel expression of itself. By day, the feeling of peacefulness and calm seems to resonate from every section of this cemetery. When you walk through the cemetery lawns, you notice the artistic expressions of love and family honor in the many epitaphs and the photographs of the departed, which are affixed to the tombstones. A long history is displayed here, of many faiths and cultural backgrounds, all culminated into a wonderful place of honor and remembrance.

However, the night proves to be an entirely different subject indeed. By dusk this charming cemetery seems to go through a mutation of sorts. The trees seem to sway just a bit differently at night, even the air appears to change here, and practically everyone who has experienced Myrtle Hill in the night hours will admit that the overall feeling of doom and fear is definitely noticeable. Of the people I have spoken to about Myrtle Hill, all of them generally refuse to go there after the sun sets. Even the police don't like making rounds there at night, and when they do, they never go alone.

Of the scientific evidence we have collected in the relatively short amount of time researching Myrtle Hill, there has been a substantial amount of data that certainly makes one take note. The electronic voice phenomena test proved that there was something unexplained going on in the absence of living beings, and the electromagnetic field and temperature testing proved out of the ordinary, as well. And, of the countless photographs we have taken, both inside and outside of the buildings and around the cemetery grounds, there have been large amounts of orb activity, as well as other anomalies that should not go unnoticed. As for the video recorder's battery oddly draining so quickly, this too seems to be common during such psychical incidents as the presence of ghosts.

Of the countless legends of haunted locations, it is likely that many of these stories have been exaggerated since the original tale. Although many of us would like to believe these legends as the truth, many of them are simply stories. Myrtle Hill Cemetery has absolutely nothing to gain from having a haunted legend; in fact, it is safe to say the proprietors would rather not hear of such things. Yet, almost everyone who has come to know this location on a personal basis has found a new respect for potential hauntings, even those who claim not to believe in ghosts.

Even if you do not believe in ghosts and the paranormal, I offer you this little challenge: When in the Tampa area, experience Myrtle Hill Cemetery and the Gardens of Peace for yourself. Take a walk around the beautiful tombs and monuments and visit the many ornate graves. Take time to introduce yourself to the plethora of souls that were once as alive as you and I are today. Then, wait until night falls and take that same journey again through this immense land of stone and marble, and see if your heart doesn't race a bit more than usual. Take a stroll to the mausoleum and look around inside. You might notice a change in atmosphere, or smell the rancid air of decay, and perhaps, just perhaps, you will hear the disembodied whispers echoing from these empty corridors, or hear the sounds of phantom footsteps on the staircase, and maybe you too will become a believer in the ghosts of Myrtle Hill Cemetery.

26

Sunshine Skyway Bridge

St Petersburg

Sadness on the Skyway

A Little History

The Sunshine Skyway Bridge was built in 1954 and was considered an engineering masterpiece, running fifteen miles from St. Petersburg to Bradenton, one hundred and fifty feet above the Tampa Bay ship channel. The Skyway was officially completed in 1971 after the addition of a second span, parallel to the first, for two lanes of traffic in each direction. The bridge had its share of problems over the years, but nothing to match the great disaster of 1980. It was early morning, May 9, just after a heavy thunderstorm when an empty phosphate freighter, the *Summit Venture*, ran into the south pier, ripping over 1000 feet of bridge and road from its suspensions and plunging the remains into the Tampa Bay waters. In all, thirty-five people were killed, the majority of whom were on a southbound bus headed to Miami. Seven years and $245 million later, the new and improved Skyway Bridge was introduced, and though this marvel has once again given motorists a convenient route to and from south St. Petersburg, a darker reality continues today—a reality of sadness and pain, frequently manifest in the Skyway's growing problem of bridge-leaping suicides.

Although the authorities have a quick-response system to deal with potential suicides, including twenty-four-hour cameras to monitor the bridge, there is an increasing rate of suicide deaths. In 1996, there were six reported suicide deaths from the bridge; in 1997, there were eight; in 1999, eleven; and in 2000, there were another five reported, and the numbers have continued. It seems almost as though pain and sadness are now characteristics of the bridge itself.

Ghostly Legends and Haunted Folklore

There are a few local legends about the Skyway Bridge that seem to be flourishing. One of these legends circulates among many of the local anglers on a portion of the original bridge that is now used as a fishing pier. Remnants of that disaster seem to continue to this day, and many of these early-morning fishermen have reported the sounds of car horns and screeching tires along with a loud crash. Descending

screams that stop without the sound of a splash in the bay waters below have sent some running for the authorities, thinking there was a terrible accident nearby.

Some of these early morning fishermen have even claimed to see a phantom bus plunging through the fog, complete with dim headlights and the terrified faces of those poor souls who died more than twenty years ago. This legend began when the remains of the doomed Greyhound bus were shipped to south Florida with the intent of salvage. This is said to be a common practice; although the ill-fated bus was severely damaged, it still had certain valuable parts that Greyhound Bus Lines could still use in other buses. After all, only the parts would be used, what harm could come of that? Apparently, some have claimed that the reused parts from the Skyway disaster Greyhound have done everything from burst into flames to cause other machinery to cease functioning. Because there were so many problems as a result of this cost-cutting procedure, the salvaged parts were removed and disposed of all together, which was probably a good idea.

The phantom bus is most often seen on occasions when the early morning fog rolls in, or when a storm front begins to take effect. The descriptions and stories of the phantom bus have been told and retold in the Tampa area for at least ten years, and are scary enough to make any seasoned fisherman find a new hobby. Evidently, there have been a few fishermen who have seen this horrific spectral event, saying that they could spot every detail about the bus, right down to the terrified expressions of the passengers and the sounds of their screams as they descend. The sight of these poor souls is a painful reminder of that wet and foggy morning of 1980, but the description of one particular passenger during this ghostly reenactment became the oddest part of the whole phenomenon. This passenger, described as an elderly woman, apparently sits at the rear of the bus and looks directly at the witnesses, and with a big happy grin, she waves gleefully as the bus plunges to nothingness.

Another specter that is said to roam the Skyway Bridge is that of an old woman, described as wearing something like a gray pioneer dress, or an off-white nightgown-like dress, who hovers over the waters beneath the bridge. She makes no sound and no contact with witnesses, but her demeanor is dejected, and her sad and mournful face is always clearly noted. Although no one seems to know who she might have been in life, some feel she has been there since long before there was a bridge, or even cars for that matter. Many believe she may have been a victim either of yellow fever or an Indian attack from the pioneer days. Some believe she died waiting for her husband who never came back from the sea. Whichever the case, she is certainly a sullen ghost, but then again, all the Skyway ghosts seem to be sad; that is, except for the grinning old lady on the Greyhound bus.

Although these legends are quite interesting, there is another story that seems to follow an internationally time-honored folk tale, which has adapted itself to our great state. Indeed, we should all know the story of the phantom hitchhiker, which has been told and retold with many variations over the years. As the legend goes, a hitchhiker, usually a young female, hitches a ride with a passing vehicle. This hitchhiker gets in the back seat, and when the driver approaches the general area of where she wants to be let off, the young girl simply vanishes. The legend usually has the driver going out of his way to uncover the identity of the vanishing hitchhiker, only to find that she had died many years before. Creepy indeed, yet Florida's phantom hitchhiker has led her victims to no answers.

The Skyway's version of the phantom hitchhiker seems to have no logical origin. Although this hitchhiker is described in many of the aforementioned oral traditions, she does not seem to match any of the suicides that have occurred over the years. This young specter is described as being in her early twenties, with long blond hair and wearing a white pullover sweater or white T-shirt. She is always seen in a visibly sad state, which of course directs attention to her as a girl in need of help.

Many truckers in this area have seen her, both on and near the bridge. She either fades when approached, or will vanish suddenly and completely from the spot where she was seen. And, sometimes, this lost soul will get picked up near the bottom of the bridge, only to vanish when the hapless driver reaches the other side. Witnesses say that as they reached the center of the bridge, she became frantic and asked questions like, "Is there a God?" or "Will Jesus forgive me?" Whoever she was, it seems she never forgave herself for whatever she may have done in life. Was she one of the original suicides of long ago, one that no one noticed? Was she a victim of murder, perhaps her body never recovered from the watery depths of Tampa Bay? We may never know for sure, but the legend of the Skyway's hitchhiking ghost continues to this day.

Afterthoughts

In my quest to find out who the hitchhiking ghost could have been, I decided to ask some of the locals in the St. Petersburg area. What I found seemed to vary in almost every account. Some say this phantom girl was once a young college student who was not doing well in school, or was depressed over a lost love and flung herself off the bridge. Some say she was a hitchhiker who was killed while on her way home for the holidays. And still others say she was picked up by a murderous driver and thrown into the bay waters. In any case, this sad apparition and her legend still haunt the Skyway Bridge, alone and forever wandering.

Whether it is the phantom Greyhound bus that plunges into unseen waters, the pioneer lady in gray who sullenly floats near the old pier, or the pretty young blond girl who is doomed to walk the bridge forever, the Skyway Bridge holds a magnitude of sadness and pain, as if permeating the steel beams and concrete basins. One popular idea many paranormal investigators hold is that certain buildings or structures may contain various elements within them that might attract spirits. Some believe that the reason so many castles in Europe and the United Kingdom are haunted is that the stone with which they were made was riddled with many varieties of crystals. These crystals may be absorbing the intense emotions that had occurred throughout history, thus being responsible for the ghostly manifestations and other paranormal emanations. Perhaps the Skyway Bridge is no different in that respect, as it too is made of such mineral-rich rock. Perhaps there is truth in the ancient legend that running water keeps a ghost bound behind it, and a solid object is the only way for that ghost to cross. Perhaps the Skyway Bridge is a massive transit for the spirit world.

The next time you cross this monstrous bridge in the wee hours of the morning, fighting to see through the dense fog or misty rain, remember to keep a lookout for the young blond girl, the sad soul who keeps trying to get to the other side. Moreover, try to remember all those lives that were lost on this bridge and all those souls that perhaps roll in with the unearthly fog. And always remember how lucky you are to have made it across to the other side.

27

The Don Cesar Beach Resort

St Petersburg

A Timeless Romance

Time is infinite. I wait for you by our fountain . . .
To share our timeless love, our destiny is time.
—Lucinda's deathbed letter to Thomas Rowe

A Little History

Thomas Rowe, a real estate mogul and builder, and Spanish opera singer Lucinda were players in a sad but captivating storybook romance. Most likely one of Florida's most cherished love stories, the legend of Thomas Rowe and Lucinda is as timeless as William Shakespeare's *Romeo and Juliet*. Indeed, Florida serves as the backdrop to one of the most tragically beautiful love stories known.

The Don CeSar Resort was based on a dream that Thomas Rowe had while he was in Europe enjoying an opera that revolved around a dashing hero named Don CeSar. As history tells us, while Thomas was enjoying William Vincent Wallace's opera *Maritana*, he fell in love with a beautiful Spanish diva named Lucinda. She was cast in the opera's lead role and became the object of Thomas's love the moment he saw her. Sadly, like a tragic opera, Lucinda's family forbade her to marry Thomas due to religious and class issues, forcing the couple to part ways. The heartbroken Thomas returned to America, where even his countless love letters to Lucinda were returned unopened. But Thomas's love could not be stopped so easily.

Sadly, Lucinda died in the early 1900s, which only adds to the pain and sadness Thomas already felt. But he went on with life, got married, divorced, and eventually built a real estate empire. He would never forget his Lucinda, fueling the fires of his passions through all his days.

In the early 1920s, Thomas made several visits to Florida, hoping to follow in the footsteps of famed architect and mogul Henry Flagler. Thomas too had a dream to build. When he found St. Petersburg, he had a vision once again. It was while he was standing in the sand, with the warm waters rushing over his feet, that the memories of Lucinda and the opera he had seen years earlier passed through his mind. He recalled the story of the Spanish pirate, Don CeSar, and how he pined for his beloved, the sacrifice he would make for her, and finally, the happy ending that had always motivated him. This was the catalyst that motivated Thomas Rowe to build the fabulous icon we have today, a "Pink Palace" which he christened "The Don CeSar" in Lucinda's memory.

Construction began around 1925, and was completed in 1928. This wonderful ten-story resort hotel exhibits both Mediterranean and Moorish architectural styles, with numerous balconies and terraces around the entire structure. The hotel looks like something from a fairy tale. Inside, French doors abound, hand-carved Italian crystal chandeliers hang exquisitely, and Palladian windows and French candelabras illuminate the Don CeSar with elegance.

With the added amenities of a concierge service, valet parking, golfing facilities, two swimming pools and a Jacuzzi, a fitness center and spa, and an activity center for children, there's a taste of the modern added to the old European charm of the Don CeSar. There are even huge saltwater aquariums lining the hallways. The Maritana Grille and Sea Porch Café create classy yet casual restaurant experiences for breakfast, lunch, or dinner, and the Don CeSar offers all this with a remarkable view of the Gulf of Mexico from one of Florida's most beautiful white-sand beaches.

Today, the Don CeSar Resort is listed on the National Register of Historic Places, but it was not always this charming edifice of luxury. In the early 1940s, the resort served as a hospital for the U.S. Army, and was then turned over to Veterans Affairs and other quasi-military administration offices, remaining in such service until 1967. The government moved out, and money problems and mismanagement rendered the hotel dusty and deserted, home only to mice and vagrants. It was not until 1973 that it reopened as a luxury resort, thanks to a local preservation group headed by June Hurley. The Don CeSar was saved, and once more, the Pink Palace rose in grandeur from the white sands of the Gulf.

The resort's six majestic crowning towers and archways again reached for the skies with glory. The tall ceilings came alive once more to entertain the rich and famous, the jet set, and those on romantic interludes. Sadly, Thomas Rowe, always in poor health with severe asthma and a chronic heart condition, died in his cherished hotel, collapsing one morning on the lobby floor. Although he only had a short time to enjoy living in the tribute to his Lucinda, his spirit is believed to continue its residence. Ghost hunters eventually learned of the resort's spooky history, and came to visit this magnificent structure as well. Of course, they come to experience more than just the fabulous amenities this resort has to offer . . . they come to find ghosts.

Ghostly Legends and Haunted Folklore

It should not be too much of a surprise to find out that the Don CeSar is haunted. After all, this hotel was built out of a dream, made with the passion of love lost, how could it not attract ghosts? In the early 1970s, after a long hiatus when the resort was being renovated, the first rumors of ghosts were heard. The construction workers would often tell their superiors that an older man dressed in a cream-colored suit and sporting a white Panama hat would often stop by to check up on them. This nicely dressed gentleman could be seen standing in the shadows of the hotel, eerily smiling to the workers, only to fade back into those shadows when approached.

Today, many people report smelling mint or menthol cigarettes wafting through the hallways, which is quite strange since smoking is not allowed inside the hotel to begin with. This would be a total mystery indeed, but several of the long-time residents of St. Petersburg, and Don CeSar historians in particular, will tell you that Thomas Rowe was prescribed menthol cigarettes as a medication when he was alive, a common treatment for asthma in the 1920s. The phantom smoke may be detected at almost any time within and around the grounds of the hotel, and although no one can be certain, many feel that it's Thomas himself checking up on the staff and guests at his cherished Don CeSar.

Many people over the years claim to have been approached by a nice-looking gentleman who asked, "Is everything to your liking?" or simply greeted the guests with a smile and a polite nod. When these witnesses would ask the bellhop or bartender who the gentleman was, they might receive a prolonged stare, or perhaps a smile and a response like, "That was Thomas Rowe just making sure you're having a good time."

Another commonplace paranormal event is the unassisted movement of the chandeliers. Many people say they can see the crystals move for no apparent reason, even when all the French doors are closed and there are no air vents near the chandelier. The individual crystal shards are said to move either erratically, swaying from side to side, almost violently, or just slightly, almost imperceptibly. Many paranormal investigators will go to the Don CeSar specifically to witness such abnormalities. Some will go away disappointed, but others will be treated to this creepy event. Patience is needed here, so keep your eyes on the chandeliers.

Thomas Rowe is said to be quite active at the Don CeSar. He is often seen walking around dressed in only the finest clothing, and always with a cheerful demeanor, from the hotel's lobby, to the conference rooms, and on most of the upper floors. Employees and guests alike have witnessed Thomas surveying the goings on in the hotel. In the hotel's lobby for instance, there stands a beautiful and accurate replica of the wishing fountain where Thomas Rowe and Lucinda would meet for their romantic interludes while in Europe. Many of the employees claim to see the two lovers walking together and holding hands from time to time, then simply fading into a mist, then to nothingness. On other occasions, an image of a man resembling Thomas Rowe is seen sitting in a chair out on the beachside courtyard, staring pensively out to sea. Indeed, in life, Thomas would often sit in the courtyard contemplating the love he could never have.

Although the primary ghostly figure witnessed at the Don CeSar is its creator, there is at least one other entity that has been making her rounds since the 1940s. This specter is said to be a ghostly nurse of the World War II period. Apparently, there have been several occasions in which employees have seen this ghostly nurse walking in the back hallways and throughout the kitchen area. She is described as wearing a white dress that ends at the knees, an old-style nurse's hat, and sporting brown, wavy hair, similar to, according to one witness, one of the Andrew Sisters.

When the hotel was used as a hospital in the 1940s, many people had been admitted there. Some got well and went home, while others never left alive. Although there is no mention in historical records of a nurse having died in the hospital, it has been suggested that a young nurse did indeed die in a car accident when leaving for home in either 1946 or 1947. Perhaps she loved her work, wandering back to the place in which she had spent so much time. The spectral nurse is believed still to make her rounds throughout the Don CeSar.

I had asked several of the employees why they think the ghostly nurse would haunt the kitchen and back room areas. Apparently those areas were once used as the main nurses' station during the Don CeSar's hospital days. Although her identity remains a mystery, the ghostly nurse is said to be as gentle and as compassionate as Thomas Rowe. And why not? She was a nurse, after all.

I was fortunate enough to pay a visit to the Don CeSar. Although I did not see his kindly apparition walking through the hallways or sitting in the courtyard, I did experience a few odd occurrences. While a friend and I were walking around the hotel, exploring every room allowed, including the conference rooms and the ballroom, we witnessed the moving chandeliers. As soon as we walked in, we heard the sound of glass gently hitting against glass. We stood in the darkened ballroom looking for the moving chandeliers, but saw nothing, just hearing the angelic tinkling sounds.

As we entered further, we decided to sit in the chairs near the wall in hopes of seeing something paranormal. As soon as we were taking our seats, a spark shot out of an electrical socket below us. My friend jumped as if she were the one getting shocked. We looked at each other in amazement. A moment later, several of the chandeliers in the center of the ballroom began to lightly sway in a circular motion. Although we never found a clear explanation as to why the chandeliers would move seemingly by themselves, as though there were an air conditioning vent blowing on them or the foundation were rocking, we decided to let some mysteries remain mysteries.

Perhaps the zap from the electrical outlet and the gentle ethereal breeze that moved the chandeliers were a result of our host, Thomas Rowe, letting us know he was still there. Perhaps this hotel, this wonderful tribute to love lost, serves as a hotel for the dearly departed, just as it does for the living. We may never know for sure, yet one thing is for certain, the Don CeSar is enchanted by the spirit of romance in every meaning of the word, especially in the romantic spirits of Thomas and Lucinda.

Afterthoughts

When visiting the west coast of Florida, be sure to visit St. Petersburg and stop by the Don CeSar for a walk through Florida's history. This hotel exemplifies old Florida class and service, and actual love, sweat, and tears went into its making.

If you decide to stay here for a romantic interlude, you will be happy you did. If however you wish simply to make a day trip for a ghostly investigation, be sure to explore the courtyards and beach area, as Thomas has been witnessed here on many occasions, either walking on the beach alone, or hand-in-hand with his beloved Lucinda. Sometimes he is seen roaming the courtyard, or gazing out to sea, so you stand a good chance of seeing him at these locations.

Several manifestations of the spiritual nurse, as well as Thomas Rowe, have been witnessed on the fifth floor, giving more than a few a healthy fright when encountered. Above all, visit the ballrooms when they're not in use and especially at night, as this area seems to attract a lot of spectral attention. Also, feel free to ask the employees about their personal ghostly experiences. You might be surprised to find that many have had paranormal experiences, especially the night crew, and most are happy to recount their stories.

Lucinda died at the turn of the century, leaving Thomas always to regret not having her as his wife, and he never let her spirit out of his thoughts. Though they never married in life, many believe they are married in the afterlife, as many have witnessed the two together today. Indeed, it is a wonderful ending to this original Floridian opera.

The Don CeSar Resort and Spa is located at 3400 Gulf Beach Blvd., St.Petersburg Beach, Florida, 33706.

Afterthoughts

In ending our preternatural journey through the dark side of south and central Florida, we should now sit back and contemplate the haunted, spirit-filled side of the Sunshine State. As amazing as it seems, the state of Florida must certainly be one of the most haunted places in the United States, although most compendiums of ghosts and hauntings from around America only have two or three Florida stories. I took it upon myself to research the darker, supernatural side of Florida. In the process, I had to track down some the creepiest places imaginable, interviewing countless people, some of them regarding me as if I'd lost my marbles, but others were only too delighted to find someone to hear their stories. In the end, I found myself a little more informed and a lot more enlightened. I hope that *Florida's Ghostly Legends and Haunted Folklore, Volume 1* did the same for you, and that it may afford you the chance to look at this great state a little differently.

Over the years, I have been fortunate enough to have listened to some of the best, and certainly the most fascinating, ghost stories right here in the Sunshine State. When I visited spooky places like the sugar mill ruins and the ancient fort of New Smyrna Beach or Myrtle Hill Cemetery in Tampa, I knew immediately that there was so much more going on. When I walked through the stately halls of the Biltmore

Hotel in Miami, and delighted in the luxuries of the Don CeSar Hotel in St. Petersburg, I felt so much more than just the antiquity of these places—I felt their silent enchantment.

Although I have not seen the quintessential Hollywood ghost floating through a hallway in any of these captivating settings, I could oftentimes feel something I could not explain, as if someone or something else were there with me.

As a scientist and a healer, it is my nature first to explore before I make a judgment in any matter. And, although I truly wish to believe in spirits and haunted places, I must do the research first, and take a scientific approach to that subject before I cast either belief or doubt. Today, I can honestly tell you that I do believe in spirits, as well as many other paranormal circumstances associated with ghosts and hauntings, even though I cannot give you an exact, scientific confirmation of such things. I can tell you, however, that my own perception while visiting some of the locations listed in this book was stirred beyond the abilities of any active imagination.

When standing on the now defunct and quite creepy remains of the old Flagler Railroad in the Florida Keys, it wasn't the ghosts racing through the wreckage that alerted my attention, nor was it the fact that I knew that many people had suffered and died in that terrible storm of yesteryear. It was the sheer presence this location possessed that made me believe there was something else there. When I sat in the massive mausoleum at Myrtle Hill Cemetery, as I patiently listened for the whispers to echo through the huge halls, the result had me believing without doubt in our haunted world. Indeed, the sounds, the echoes of whispering and the phantom voices I heard there, utterly convinced me that something unseen was about, frightening me even further, knowing I was the only living person there.

Is Florida haunted? With what I have experienced during my visits to some of Florida's alleged haunted locations, whether cemeteries, old abandoned hospitals, creepy deserted hotels, or modern supermarkets, I would have to say yes. Although the stories listed here are only a fraction of the many haunted tales told in the Sunshine State, I can honestly say that the sincerity I observed in the people I interviewed impressed me far more than the evidence I secured. More than the photographs of orbs and other anomalies that I captured on film, or the strange whispers I recorded during my visits in those mausoleums and cemeteries, I found that the true purpose of my ghostly journey was to interview the many witnesses of such hauntings. Indeed, although the atmosphere surrounding many of these locations could certainly inspire any movie director making a film about ghosts and haunted houses, I kept a scientific attitude. However, I believe there is truly something more going on in the Sunshine State . . . something downright creepy.

When visiting Florida, be sure to enjoy the many amenities the state has to offer. Enjoy the amusement parks, the fine restaurants and the nightlife, and don't forget to bring your suntan oil when relaxing on our magnificent beaches. Although you'll find relaxation, excitement, and entertainment in so many of Florida's features, just remember that there is even more than the typical attractions. As you explore Florida's haunted wonders, don't be surprised if you experience the uncanny, the strange, or the supernatural. Ghosts, haunted places, things that go bump in the night—yes, Florida has these things, too!

The second volume of my true-to-life ghost stories are gathered from the northern regions of Florida, including America's oldest city, St. Augustine. So, be sure to look for *Florida's Ghostly Legends and Haunted Folklore, Volume 2*.

Happy Ghost Hunting!

Appendices

Appendix A

Tools of the Modern Ghosthunter

The ghost hunter today, whether he or she is a highly educated scholar with a university grant to fund research, or the stout-of-heart amateur hoping to find evidence of life after death, has need of scientific equipment. Indeed, such equipment is as important as bravery when it comes to walking through deserted cemeteries in the dead of night, or when exploring the old, abandoned, reputedly haunted houses during a stormy evening. Having the proper equipment can make the difference between a successful ghost hunt and just another evening stroll.

There are only a few organizations and businesses that sell fascinating items like electromagnetic reading devices, remote motion sensors to smudge sticks for cleaning a haunted area, and even dowsing rods for finding a ghost. One of the best places to find these high-tech toys is at the Ghosthunter Store at www.ghosthunterstore.com. The following examples are tools used by many paranormal investigators in their research, and although many are expensive, most of these tools are quite common and available at many department stores today:

Air-Ion Counter: This is an expensive piece of equipment, and it is used to measure the amount of positive and negative ions in the area. Ghosts can cause a lot of positive ions because they give off high amounts of electromagnetic discharges.

Baby/Talcum Powder: Used in order to find evidence of ghostly footsteps or hand prints.

Barometer: Ghost hunters have used barometers to look for paranormal activity. Some investigators believe that some paranormal events can affect barometric pressure.

Batteries: You should always bring many extra batteries. Ghosts are believed to be electromagnetic in nature and can cause your batteries to run down rather quickly. Remember to bring batteries for both your flashlight and camera.

Cameras/Video Recorders: Cameras and video recorders are important tools for the modern ghost hunter today. A 35mm camera is an excellent camera to use because it can eliminate the chances of odd things showing up on the film, which can be caused by anomalies found on many digital cameras. Color film is the easiest to buy in stores, but black-and-white film and one-time use cameras are available as well. 400-, 800-, and 1000-speed film are the best choices. Black-and-white film and infrared films have been used for interesting results. Remember to bring extra rolls of film and batteries for the camera. Often, when you are on a ghost hunt, camera film and batteries malfunction (always happens to me) so make sure you are well stocked. You can use a camera tripod to help you eliminate moving the camera so that you can get a better picture. Make sure to advise your film developing company to develop your film as-is, as developers often think the pictures of ghosts are camera mistakes. When you are taking photographs, always remember to take off the camera strap so there is no chance it will get into the photo. Be sure to secure long hair too as this can get in the way.

Candles: If your flashlight and equipment stop working you may need to resort to candles and matches/lighters.

Cell Phone: Cell phones can be useful if you have an emergency and need to call for help, even though cell phones can also be affected by electromagnetic anomalies that can occur in the presence of a ghost, so be prepared.

Compass: Some people use a compass because the compass point may change in the presence of a spirit or ghost, and it too can be affected by an electromagnetic disturbance.

EMF (electromagnetic field) Detector: Likely the most important piece of equipment, an EMF detector will pick up electronic fields over various frequencies. A digital readout is preferred in an EMF detector, and some detectors have an alarm that will sound to alert you to sudden changes. The cost for this piece of equipment ranges from $40 to $150.

Tri-Field Natural EM Meter: Designed expressly for use in paranormal investigation, this amazingly sensitive device is one of the favorite portable instruments of researchers around the world. In the magnetic setting, the unit has a sensitivity of 2.5 milligausses, which is less than 0.5% of the earth's field. In the electric setting, it has a sensitivity of 3 volts-per-meter, which is well below the level at which static electricity (10,000 volts-per-meter) forms. This instrument has a setting that will alert the investigator to the earliest stages of paranormal manifestation. This meter can detect changes in electrical magnetic currents long before they become obvious to people. It will even detect approaching thunderstorms and the presence of a person behind a wall. The alarm tone is proportional to the amount of change in the field and can be set for any desired threshold and measures radio and microwave waves from 100 KHz to 3 GHz in milliwatts of energy.

Flashlights: Since a lot of ghost hunting is done at night in places like cemeteries and battlefields, it's imperative you have quality flashlights.

First Aid Kit: Take along a first aid kit just as a precaution in case someone gets injured on the ghost hunt. Old buildings, graveyards, and battlefields can be hazardous in the dark.

Film: Take lots of extra film with you on the ghost hunt. The electromagnetic discharges can affect your film and you may have to replace it. Use 200- to 1000-speed film, which will provide the best photographs in low light.

Gaussmeter or Cellsensor: An excellent tool for the modern ghost hunter, the *Cellsensor,* or gaussmeter, is a highly sensitive meter, which features both a cell phone frequency RF measurement, as well as a single axis ELF gaussmeter. The gaussmeter is calibrated around 50/60 Hz and also offers two scales: 0–5 and 0–50 mG. Remote probe with 2-foot extension cord allows the user greater flexibility and reach. Both RF and gaussmeter provide audio and a large flashing light that corresponds to field strength so you can hear and see in the dark when you are getting a positive reading. It includes complete documentation on how to conduct proper measurements.

Multidetector II: This measures electric and magnetic fields and is highly sensitive. It has power cables that can be extended more than one meter, and it is able to detect the presence of TVs, computers, and other electronic devices from a distance of more than three to four meters, and high voltage cables at more than 350 meters. It features an LED display, which provides a high luminosity to enable measurements even in dark areas like cellars, attics, and of course, graveyards.

Headset Communicators: Headset communicators can provide a method to communicate with your ghost-hunting party. This equipment is good for distant communication on a site and provides you with benefit of leaving your hands free to use your other equipment and to take notes.

Infrared Thermometer: A non-contact infrared thermometer emits an invisible infrared beam that reads the temperature of anything the beam comes in contact with. Researchers have found that this type of thermometer can detect cold spots, moving and stationary, in under a second.

Motion Detectors: A useful tool for ghost hunters. They work best when left in a room during the time that no investigator is present. Many motion detectors used by paranormal investigators project an infrared beam. When the beam is disrupted by spirits, an alarm will sound giving the investigator a clue that spirits may be present, and when switched to alarm mode, it will sound a siren when it detects motion up to thirty feet away. Includes optional wall-mount brackets.

Night-vision Scopes: Some people like to use night vision equipment on their ghost hunting expeditions. There are monocular and binocular types to choose from, but both are useful, especially in areas where there is absolutely no artificial light. Binocular types are a better choice because they add the benefit of depth perception. Night vision adapters are available to put on your cameras and camcorders, ranging from $200 to $1,000.

Notebook and Pen: You need a notebook and pen to record your investigation, as it is vital to describe weather conditions, the temperature, and what happened on your ghost hunt. The ghost hunter will need to document EMF and Thermal Scanner readings. The date, time, and who was present on the ghost hunt, as well as what was seen, heard, or felt, are all important things to note for future investigations.

Omni-directional Microphones: An excellent tool when investigating for Electronic Voice Phenomena (EVP). Paranormal investigators recommend external microphones and the use of these microphones will make it possible to avoid tainting the recording with noises from the internal parts of the tape recorder. Omni-directional microphones are ideal because they pick up sounds from every direction equally and can be used with standard, micro cassette, and digital recorders.

Spotlights: Spotlights are always good because they can help you set up your equipment when it's dark, and they also give you an added level of security.

Tape or Digital Recorder: Take along a tape recorder to pick up

EVP. When you turn it on and let it run for the entire hunt or investigation, on occasion, strange, ghostly voices may be heard. Be sure to speak in a normal voice, as this will prevent confusion about whether your whisper was really a ghost. You may not always hear the voices during your investigation but if you review your tape afterward you may hear voices or other human-like sounds on the tape.

Thermometer-hygrometer: This indoor thermometer/hygrometer allows one temperature reading and checks the humidity. Complete with a digital humidity/temperature gauge, and able to read a humidity range of 20% to 90%, this device is an excellent addition. As high humidity can also have an effect on your camera and cause your photos to appear to have orbs or mist on them, this piece of equipment will prove useful.

Thermal Imaging Scope: This device provides you with an actual image of what your thermal scanner sees. It provides the exact shape of a particular temperature anomaly. If, for example, someone or something is walking behind a wall, you will see that person's shape and size.

Thermal Scanner: This device measures temperature changes instantly for a specific area. As temperature changes are common in haunted locations, the importance of this tool becomes clear. Infrared thermal scanners are equally beneficial, but they will cost from $250 to $500. Because ghosts are believed to be electromagnetic in nature and their materialization requires the use of energy, a noticeable change in temperature and atmosphere will take place. There may be a severe drop in temperature that could range from twenty degrees or more. "Cold spots" are good indications of what many believe to be a "portal" haunting, which can appear and disappear quickly, so this tool would also be a good choice.

Walkie-talkies: The new and improved walkie-talkie will provide the ghost hunter with a better method of communication during the ghost hunt. It also adds a better sense of security.

Watch: You need to take a watch with you on a ghost hunt to record the time when events take place.

Web Sites (ghost and haunting related): One of the best and most effective tools is the Internet. As important as the telephone today, the Internet and the massive database of ghost research and related web sites, both professional and novice, are all excellent sources of information, regional legends, folklore, as well as an outstanding source of photographs of alleged ghosts and spirits. Because there are literally thousands of paranormal-related web sites today and at least eighty in Florida alone, I have listed a few of the most notable organizations in Appendix C.

Appendix B

Glossary and Terminology

The following category represents some of the many terms used by ghost hunters, paranormal investigators, and parapsychologists today. Although these examples represent only a few of many such subjects, I have listed what I believe to be the most common terms used today.

Agent: A human being who is unaware that he or she is directing poltergeist activity. It is believed that a poltergeist or similar entity will attach itself to a child, often a female, as an agent.

Altered States of Consciousness: Any state of consciousness that is different, either altered or reduced, from a typical state of normal consciousness.

Amulet: An object believed to have the power to ward off evil spirits or other malevolent demons. It is usually in the shape of a charm or talisman worn around the neck.

Apparition: A disembodied soul or spirit from the deceased, which may be seen or heard as a supernatural appearance. Apparitions may appear and disappear very suddenly, seemingly at will. They may pass through walls, cast shadows, or produce a reflection in a mirror. They may appear real or sometimes foggy or completely transparent. Sometimes they are accompanied by smells or produce cold spots or drafts. Most apparitions seem to have some sort of purpose, such as communicating a message, and are therefore known as crisis apparitions. These entities usually appear during a severe family crisis such as when someone has died. A collective apparition refers to an apparition that is seen by more than one person.

Apport: When a solid object manifests in different locations, without physical assistance, supposedly by a spirit.

Astral Body: The soul of a person that is projected outside of his or her body, as if attached by an invisible umbilical cord.

Astral Plane: The level of existence through which spirits of the dead pass or a level of existence in which an astral projection travels naturally.

Astral Projection: The separation of the astral body or spirit body from the physical body. This astral body may travel in the astral plane and possibly beyond.

Aura: An energy field that surrounds all living creatures, supposedly captured by Kirlian photography.

Automatic Writing: This is communication via a spirit, wherein the spirit controls the writer's hand, usually performed by a medium or psychic who writes out the messages. This medium may not be conscious of what he or she is writing.

Automatism: Spontaneous muscular movement, believed to be caused by a ghost. Automatic writing is one example of this, as well as involuntary movements or spasms during sleep.

Banshee: A spirit or omen of death, usually indigenous to Scotland and Ireland. The banshee is more often heard than seen, and is almost always due to a death in a family.

Channeling: A form of communication wherein a spirit communicates and sometimes possesses a psychic medium. Popular in the 1980s. The entity being channeled is believed to be a deceased human being, angel, or demon.

Clairaudience: The psychic ability to hear sounds and voices normally not heard by most people.

Clairvoyance: The psychic ability to see objects, persons, places or events regardless of time or distance.

Conjuring: The process of calling preternatural forces into aid or action through the use of necromancy or black magic.

Discarnate: Existing outside a physical body, in spirit form, possibly in a form of astral projection.

Disembodied Spirit: A spirit functioning without the use of the physical body.

Doppelganger: Doppelgangers appear to be the ghostly duplicates of a living person. The doppelganger will often be invisible to that person, and in some cases that person will come upon his own doppelganger engaged in some future activity. Doppelgangers are traditionally believed to be omens of bad luck or death of the living counterpart.

Earthbound: Referring to a spirit trapped on the earthly plain against its will.

Ectoplasm: An unknown substance that emanates from the bodies of mediums, correlating to supernatural phenomena.

Elemental: A lesser spirit bound to the fundamentals of nature, such as earth, wind, water, and fire, or perhaps even seen as the remains of the dead.

Entity: A term used to describe a disembodied spirit or ghost of a preternatural reality.

Exorcism: The process of expelling or removing an evil spirit by a religious ceremony. Exorcisms may be performed by a priest, minister, rabbi, or shaman, each using similar ceremonies to disrupt or banish an evil spirit or entity.

Exorcist: One who conducts the rights of exorcism, such as a priest, rabbi, witch, or shaman.

ESP: Extra-Sensory Perception, or the ability to observe things that are beyond common levels of perception.

Ghost: A ghost can best be described as a form of spiritual recording, similar to an audio or videotape. Although there is no life force left, a ghost may replay the same scene or action over and over. A ghost may be the residual energy of a person, animal, or even an inanimate object, locked in repetition. It is widely believed that if a person has performed a repetitious act for a long period of time in life, he or she may leave a psychic impression or "psychic scent" in that area. This psychic scent may stay in the area long after the person who created it has moved on or died. This paranormal event is very vivid when first encountered and appears to be sentient. Over time, this psychic scent, or spirit will get weaker over time, but is believed it can recharge itself under the right circumstances.

There are many theories of what ghosts are. Many believe that ghosts are a residual energy left behind by a person of emotional strength or a person who wanted more life. Or they might be spirits that revolve around specific, traumatic life events. Many believe that there are various specific electromagnetic impulses that pulse and expend during periods of high excitement or stress, and that this energy may last long periods of time, or even feed on similar forms of electromagnetic energy, such as a power plant or other places where high levels of electricity pass. Some believe that ghosts are telepathic images. A particularly sensitive person, such as a psychic, may pick up or receive vibrations, most likely from strong past events and from the area where they occurred. Such an event may also explain instances where a person sees a loved one at the moment or near the moment of that loved one's death—the dying one might be unconsciously projecting their thoughts to a receptive person, such as a family member. It is also believed that ghosts could be the result of time slippage, where an event that happened in the past might be seen briefly in our present time because of a fluctuation in our space-time continuum.

Ghost Hunting or Investigating: When a person or group of people investigates a location where there have been alleged sightings of ghosts, attempting to find evidence of such existence. These people will use a wide variety of equipment to capture visual evidence, sounds, etc.

Ghost Lights: These anomalous balls of iridescent or glowing lights have also been called will o' the wisps, earthlights, and spook lights. They appear largely in the south and west United States, and are specific to one area or common location. Although sometimes dismissed as nothing more than swamp gas, ghost lights are reliable throughout the year and in some places these lights have been the subject of scientific study, such as the Greenbrier Lights in Jacksonville, Florida, and the Snow Hill Road Lights in Oviedo, Florida. Of the many theories and legends revolving around these mysterious lights, the typical folk tale involves ghostly, disgruntled Indian braves, phantom trains, and UFOs.

Ghostly Sounds and Lights: Sometimes a haunting will consist entirely of the sound of footsteps or ghostly music. There are also many legends of ghost lights, often said to be caused by a ghostly lantern, a spectral motorcycle, or a phantom train. The music heard at the Myrtle Hill Mausoleum in Ybor City, Florida, constitutes a phantom sound in the form of a muted but audible music box.

Ghost Ships: Although rare, these ghostly sea vessels have been seen throughout the ages, most notably the *Flying Dutchman,* or the ghostly burning ship of Block Island, Rhode Island, and the ghostly fishing ship of Mayport Village, Florida.

Haunted: In the context of parapsychology, a building, house, or area is considered "haunted" when paranormal activity can be documented repeatedly over a period of time. Paranormal activity, however, can vary dramatically from case to case and some paranormal activity is not associated with the presence of an entity or ghost.

Inhuman Spirit: An entity or spirit of a being that has never lived in the earthly realm, such as a demon.

Levitation: The raising of a body or object without any physical or visible means, found in some poltergeist cases and hauntings.

Magic/Magick: Not to be confused with stage magic, this is the art, science, and practice of producing supernatural effects in hopes of causing change to occur. The controlling of events in nature with one's own will.

Medium/Channeling Agent: A person claming to make contact with discarnate or inhuman spirits on the astral plane.

Occult: Pertaining to the supernatural, that which is beyond the range of natural knowledge.

Orbs: fast becoming the most common aspect of paranormal and ghost research, these faint balls of transparent light resemble magnified dust spores or droplets of water, and are known among parapsychological researchers as ghost orbs, spirit globules, and spirits in transit. Orbs are believed to be the main transportation mode for spirits because they require little energy in this state. One of the primary distinctions between ghosts and globules is that ghosts are imprints of the dead bound in an endless loop of repetition. Globules, in comparison, are mobile and very much sentient entities that can change their frequencies and locations at will.

Ouija Board: Oui meaning "yes" in French and *ja* meaning "yes" in

German, the Ouija Board consists of letters of the alphabet, numbers one through ten, and the words "yes," "no," and "goodbye," and it is used as a tool for communicating with spirits. Although used by many as a game or form of entertainment, some feel that the Ouija Board is an unwise form of communication to take part in, as it may open up corridors or portals to unfriendly spirits or even demons.

Out of Body Experience: Also known as *Astral Projection,* it occurs when a person purposefully or unconsciously leaves his or her body in a spirit form.

Parapsychology: "Para" meaning "above or beyond" and "psychology" meaning the study of man, his psyche and the human condition. Parapsychology is the scientific study of phenomena that natural laws have not yet explained.

Pentagram: The magical diagram, such as the Seal of Solomon, consists of a five-pointed star, which is the representation of man, as well as the five elements. Considered by occultists to be the most potent means of conjuring spirits, the pentagram is said to protect against evil spirits.

Poltergeist: From the German meaning "noisy ghost." It is a spirit associated with the movement of objects and general mischievous activity. Poltergeists are the only spirits who may leave immediate physical traces and are best known for throwing things about and producing rapping sounds and other noises. Poltergeists often occur where there are children on the brink of puberty, and may often interact with people.

Preternatural: Associated with inhuman, demonic, or diabolical spirits or forces.

Psychic: Dealing with the ability to see, hear, feel, and sense beyond the average human ability. Includes mediums.

Psychic Cold Spot: The cold sensation received when a spirit is present, usually having defined boundaries.

Psychic Photograph: Supernatural or preternatural images appearing on a photograph, from ghostly images to orbs.

Psychical Research: The study of psychic phenomena, including earth-mysteries, ESP, and ghosts and hauntings.

Psychokinesis (PK): The movement of objects without the use of physical means, by using the mind.

Repetitious Spirits: Some apparitions are believed to repeat the same motions or scenes over and over with no apparent intelligence. Many classic hauntings fall into this category. Examples: The Lady in White seen walking the battlements of Derbyshire, England, or the Brown Lady of Raynham Hall, who is seen walking down a hallway with a swaying lantern; the ghostly seventeenth-century soldiers continuously fighting on the Marsden Moors in England and the ghostly sentry who walks guard on the Turnbull Fort in New Smyrna Beach, Florida.

Shadow People: A relatively newly discovered form of entity, said to be a nocturnal spirit, having human form, and prone to flickering on the walls and ceiling of houses and other structures. Frequently a subject of the *Art Bell Show,* the famous AM radio nighttime talk show, shadow people are believed to be evil in nature.

Specter: A ghost, or supernatural entity (see *Spirit*).

Spirit: A spirit is the actual living essence, or soul, of a person that has remained after the physical body has died. Spirits usually appear for one of three reasons. First, if a person died suddenly or with little warning, as in the case of a car accident, the victim may not actually realize that he or she is dead. Second, a person could be confined to this world by an unkept promise made to a loved one. Third, he or she may have some unfinished business, usually pertaining to a loved one. A variation of this reason would be if the person were murdered at an untimely point in his or her life.

Spirits, unlike ghosts, can communicate with the living. Usually, if a person frequents a place where the deceased spent much of his or her time, a form of psychic communication can result. Sudden and unexplained feelings of sadness or melancholy are common indications, especially if encountered only in one particular room or area. Another way that a spirit can communicate with the living is through dreams. Although much more rare, a spirit can make itself appear as an apparition or make small items physically move.

Supernatural: An activity or event believed to be caused by a spirit or ghost, or even God or his angels. Used commonly to describe anything outside the bounds of natural laws.

Talisman/Charm: Also known as a fetch, these may be drawings of various shapes and sizes, which have specified purposes of good luck, protection, health, etc., and can be worn as a necklace or key chain (see *Amulet*).

Telekinesis: Telepathic sounds and voices projected to people.

Telepathy: Psychic communications between individuals.

Teleportation or apport: Objects moved or materialized by supernatural forces.

Will o' the Wisps: Also known as ghost lights, will o' the wisps are frequently assumed to be natural phenomena, such as pockets of swamp gas that hover and rise over swamps, ignite by natural causes, and glow blue or green. Also known as corpse candles, fox fire, elves' light and *ignis fatuus,* which is Latin for "foolish fire." Some believe these lights to be omens of bad luck or death.

Vortex Phenomenon: A traveling form of ghostly energy.

Appendix C

Ghost Research Organizations

The following is a listing of the most prominent psychical research organizations devoted to scientific inquiry, parapsychology, and paranormal research today. Several of these organizations, such as the American Society of Psychical Research, are membership-based institutes, but may share resources with non-members. Several of these societies also publish online journals and printed periodicals in the field of parapsychology and paranormal research, which may be of interest to Florida ghost hunters. The Florida-based web sites herein are an excellent resource for organized ghost hunts, investigative studies, and ghost-hunting tours throughout the state of Florida.

Association for the Scientific Study of Anomalous Phenomenal:
www.assap.org

Coast-to-Coast Radio: www.coasttocoastam.com Formerly "The Art Bell Show," a great late-night AM radio show hosted by Art Bell and George Noory that offers tales of the unknown, stories of strange monsters, and of course, lots of ghost stories that will keep the listener thinking throughout the night.

Big Bend Ghost Trackers: www.bigbendghosttrackers.homestead.com

Daytona Beach Paranormal Research Group: www.dbprginc.org A good source for ghostly experiences and paranormal investigations in central and north Florida.

Florida Ghost Chapter: www.floridaghostchapter.com Great site that also offers various ghost walk information.

Florida Paranormal Research Foundation: www.floridaparanormal.com

Haunts of the World's Most Famous Beach: www.hauntsofdaytona.com

International Ghost Hunters Society: www.ghostweb.com

Nightwolf Paranormal Research: www.members.tripod.com/labtec7

North Florida Paranormal Research: www.ghosttracker.com

Obiwan's UFO-Free Paranormal Page: www.ghosts.org An excellent site with hundreds of resources for ghost hunters everywhere.

Paranormal Investigations of South Florida: www.oldeenchantments.com/paranormal

The Pensacola Historical Society: www.pensacolahistory.org

Southern Ghosts: www.southernghosts.com

Appendix D

Ghost Tours

Ghost tours, or ghost walks, have become all but customary in many cities throughout the United States today. Most of these groups are designed around the haunted or ghostly history of a particular location, usually a location of some historical significance. Sometimes, these walking tours are specifically designed to be entertaining accounts of speculative incidents that may revolve around a ghost or haunting. On occasion, these tours will cover actual, documented histories that report paranormal activity, but most often, they will embellish an existing story or legend.

This process of telling a good story, and making a little money as a result of that story, may prove to be the hobgoblin to the serious paranormal and psychical researcher, as well as the scholarly folklorist. So, with this said, I would like to recommend caution when braving the busy streets and downtowns in search of ghosts. Although your guide might be wearing a top hat and a flowing black cape, and his or her story may sound wonderfully exciting, please keep in mind that there may be more falsehoods in his anecdote than facts. Although entertaining, there is always the possibility that the story is incorrect or simply designed to capture your attention, and your money. Therefore, respectfully, unless your guide holds at least a master's degree in either folklore, history, or parapsychology, take the story with a grain of salt and do the research for yourself. You might be surprised what you'll find.

The following is a list of south and central Florida's ghost walks and haunted tours. Bear in mind, however, that some groups may have closed their businesses and new ones may not be publicly advertising yet. The best way to learn of new ghost tours in your area is by the World Wide Web or by calling your city's chamber of commerce.

Cassadaga:

Cassadaga's "Encounter the Spirit Tours" offer a fun look into the spiritual side of ghosts. "Follow your guide on a Twilight Adventure through the South's oldest and largest Spiritualist Community" is their motto. With tales of magick, séances, levitation, and the spirits who inhabit this mystical community, you will be treated to Cassadaga's unique philosophy. Finding this intriguing spiritualist camp may be difficult, but the tour will be worth the trip. The ghost tour here is sponsored by North Florida Paranormal Research, Inc., and you will be presented with a layman's view into the realm of parapsychology. For information, times, and dates of the tours, please call 386-228-2880.

Daytona Beach/DeLand:

"The DeLand Ghost Walk" is among several tours in the area that also include "Haunts of the World's Most Famous Beach" and "The Original Daytona Ghost Walk." The DeLand tour covers stories such as "The Lovelorn Spirit that Roams the Grounds of Stetson University" and "The Haunted Lake at Earl Brown Park." Find the answers to your haunting questions and listen to the ghostly tales of old DeLand. For information on this and other ghost tours in the Daytona area, go to www.hauntsofdaytona.com.

Orlando:

"Orlando Hauntings Downtown Ghost Tours" offers a fun look into Orlando's creepy past. The tour guide points out locations of haunted places and murder spots. Tours meet at Guinevere's Coffee House on the corner of Magnolia and Pine in downtown Orlando. For more information call 407-718-4462

Miami:

"Dragonfly Expeditions" offers a three-hour tour to some of Miami's most frightening and intriguing landmarks and haunted locations. From the Miami Circle, an ancient Tequesta Indian village said to emit strange disembodied voices, to the city cemetery where many haunted tales await the brave, this walking tour entertains and educates. For more information, you can call 305-774-9019.

Key West:

"Key West Ghost Tours" is a lantern-guided walk through the shadowy streets and dark alleys of Key West's Old Town. You will discover dwelling places of ghosts and spirits in Florida's southernmost city. You will learn the stories behind many of the legends of this haunted island paradise. Tours meet nightly at the very haunted Hotel La Concha on 430 Duval Street. For more information call 305-294-9255

Ybor City:

"Ybor City Ghost Walk, Inc." offers a ninety-minute tour, which is also a "portable theater" as professional local actors in costume guide people through historic Ybor City. Tours begin at Joffrey's Coffee Co., on 1616 E. Seventh Ave. near Centro Ybor.

Fort Myers

"Haunted Fort Myers" is the area's original ghost tour, researched and created for the whole family. This lantern-guided stroll (covering about a mile in approximately ninety minutes) explores topics like the haunted Mermaid Club, the ghostly sloop that roams the waters there, who was buried in a bathtub on the beach, and much more. For more information call 239-949-3644 or go to www.hauntedfortmyers.com.

Bibliography

Clearfield, Dylan. *Floridaland Ghosts.* Michigan: Prism Stempien Thomas, 2000.

Guiley, Rosemary Ellen. *The Encyclopedia of Ghosts and Spirits.* New York: Facts on File, 1992.

Harvey, Karen. *Oldest Ghosts: St. Augustine Haunts.* Sarasota: Pineapple Press, 2000.

Hiller, Herbert L. *Guide to the Small and Historic Lodgings of Florida.* Pineapple Press, 1986.

Kermeen, Frances. *Ghostly Encounters: True Stories of America's Haunted Inns and Hotels.* Warner Books, 2002.

Lapham, Dave. *Ancient City Hauntings.* Sarasota: Pineapple Press, 2004.

Lapham, Dave. *Ghosts of St. Augustine.* Sarasota: Pineapple Press, 1997.

Powell, Jack. *Haunting Sunshine.* Sarasota: Pineapple Press, 2001.

Slone, David L. *Ghosts of Key West.* Key West: Phantom Press, 1998.

Spencer, John and Tony Wells. *Ghost Watching: The Ghosthunters' Handbook.* Great Britain: Virgin Books, 1995.

Miller, Capt. Bill. *Tampa Triangle: Dead Zone.* Saint Petersburg: Ticket to Adventure, Inc. 1997.

Montz, Ph.D., Larry and Deana Smoller. *ISPR Investigates The Ghosts of New Orleans.* Pennsylvania: Whitford Press, 2000.

Moore, Joyce Elson. *Haunt Hunter's Guide to Florida.* Sarasota: Pineapple Press, 1998.

Myers, Arthur. *The Ghostly Register.* Chicago: Contemporary Books, 1986.

Myers, Arthur. *Ghosts of the Rich and Famous.* Chicago: Contemporary Books,1988.

Sources:

La Concha Hotel, Key West
Anonymous, interview by author, 2001.
Slone, David L. *Ghosts of Key West.* Key West: Phantom Press,1998.

Flagler Railroad, Islamorada
Anonymous, interview by author, 1999.

Biltmore Hotel, Coral Gables
Anonymous, interview by author, 2001.
Powell, Jack. *Haunting Sunshine.* Sarasota: Pineapple Press, 2001.
Hauck, Dennis William. *Haunted Places: The National Directory, A Guidebook to Ghostly Abodes, Sacred Sites, UFO Landings, and Other Supernatural Locations.* New York: The Penguin Group, 1996.

Flight 401, Florida Everglades
Anonymous, interview by author, 1999.
Hauck, Dennis William. *Haunted Places: The National Directory, A Guidebook to Ghostly Abodes, Sacred Sites, UFO Landings, and Other Supernatural Locations.* New York: The Penguin Group, 1996.

Art Institute of Fort Lauderdale, Ft. Lauderdale
Anonymous, interview by author, 2003.

Cap's Place Restaurant, Ft. Lauderdale

Anonymous, interview by author, 2001.

www.capsplace.com/capsplace_history.html

Hillsboro Ocean Club, Hillsboro Beach

Anonymous, interviews by author, 1986, 2003.

Ashley's Restaurant, Rockledge

Anonymous, interviews by author, 1999, 2001.

Clearfield, Dylan. *Floridaland Ghosts.* Michigan: Prism Stempien
Thomas, 2000.

Hauck, Dennis William. *Haunted Places: The National Directory,
A Guidebook to Ghostly Abodes, Sacred Sites, UFO Landings,
and Other Supernatural Locations.* New York: The Penguin
Group, 1996.

Moore, Joyce Elson. *Haunt Hunter's Guide to Florida.* Sarasota:
Pineapple Press, 1998

Powell, Jack. *Haunting Sunshine.* Sarasota: Pineapple Press, 2001.

Boca Raton Cemetery, Boca Raton

Anonymous, interviews by author, 1998, 2000.

Boca Hotel and Club, Boca Raton

Powell, Jack. *Haunting Sunshine.* Sarasota: Pineapple Press, 2001.

Anonymous, interviews by author, 2000, 2001.

The Colony Hotel, Delray Beach

Kermeen, Frances. *Ghostly Encounters: True Stories of America's
Haunted Inns and Hotels.* 2002.

Anonymous, interview by author, 2000.

Flagler's Whitehall Mansion, Palm Beach

Anonymous, interview by author, 1999.

Myers, Arthur. *Ghosts of the Rich and Famous.* Chicago:
Contemporary Books, 1988.

Clearfield, Dylan. *Floridaland Ghosts.* Michigan: Prism Stempien Thomas, 2000.

Desert Inn & Restaurant, Yee Haw Junction
Anonymous, interview by author, 2002.
Resen, Warren. *Outdoor Florida Magazine,* January, Vol. 4, Page 24–25, 2002.

Cocoa's Route 520, Cocoa Beach
Anonymous, interviews by author, 1999, 2000.

Snow Hill Road 13, Oviedo
Anonymous, interviews by author, 1998, 2000, 2001.

Sunland Hospital Central Florida, Pine Hills
Anonymous, interview by author, 2000.

Old Princeton Hospital, Orlando
Anonymous, interviews by author, 2000, 2002.

Walt Disney World, Kissimmee
Anonymous, interview by author, 2000.

Townsend's Plantation, Apopka
Anonymous, interviews by author, 2002, 2003.

Woodbridge Cemetery, Fern Park
Anonymous, interviews by author, 1999, 2000.

Interstate 4, Sanford
Charlie Carson's Strange Florida,
members.tripod.com/~UNX3/strange.html
Anonymous, interviews by author, 2002, 2003.

Stetson University, DeLand
Anonymous, interviews by author, 2000, 2002.
Stetson University Campus Historical District: A Walk with the Founders, Public Relations Office of Stetson University, 1996.

Rick Tonyan and David Carter, Halifax Magazine, *Rooms with a Boo!* October, 1998.

Caccamise, Louise. The Volusian, *Tower Chimes Sing for the City,* Sunday, October 29, 1995.

The Sugar Mill and Ancient Fort, New Smyrna Beach

Luther, Gary. *A Guided Tour of Historic New Smyrna,* Southeast Volusia Historical Society, 1997.

Anonymous, interview by author, 2000.

Old Tampa Theatre, Tampa

Moore, Joyce Elson. *Haunt Hunter's Guide to Florida.* Sarasota: Pineapple Press, 1998.

Powell, Jack. *Haunting Sunshine.* Sarasota: Pineapple Press, 2001.

Anonymous, interviews by author, 2002, 2003.

Myrtle Hill Cemetery, Tampa

Anonymous, interviews by author, 2001, 2002.

Sunshine Skyway Bridge, Tampa

Hauck, Dennis William. *Haunted Places: The National Directory, A Guidebook to Ghostly Abodes, Sacred Sites, UFO Landings, and Other Supernatural Locations.* New York: The Penguin Group, 1996.

Miller, Capt. Bill. *Tampa Triangle: Dead Zone.* Saint Petersburg: Ticket to Adventure, Inc., 1997.

Powell, Jack. *Haunting Sunshine.* Sarasota: Pineapple Press, 2001

Anonymous, interview by author, 2000.

Don Cesar Beach Resort and Hotel, St. Petersburg

Powell, Jack. *Haunting Sunshine.* Sarasota: Pineapple Press, 2001.

Anonymous, interviews by author, 2001, 2002.

Index

If you enjoyed reading this book, here are some other books from Pineapple Press on related topics. For a complete catalog, write to Pineapple Press, P.O. Box 3889, Sarasota, FL 34230 or call 1-800-PINEAPL (746-3275). Or visit our website at www.pineapplepress.com.

Florida's Ghostly Legends and Haunted Folklore Volume 2: North Florida and St. Augustine by Greg Jenkins. The history and legends behind a number of Florida's haunted locations, including thorough background information on each locale and biographies of its ghostly residents, plus bone-chilling accounts taken from firsthand witnesses of spooky phenomena. Volume 2 locations include Silver Springs, Flagler College, and the St. Augustine Lighthouse. ISBN 1-56164-328-9 (pb)

Best Ghost Tales of North Carolina and *Best Ghost Tales of South Carolina.* The actors of Carolina's past linger among the living in these thrilling collections of ghost tales. Experience the chilling encounters told by the winners of the North Carolina "Ghost Watch" contest. Use Zepke's tips to conduct your own ghost hunt. ISBN 1-56164-233-9 (pb); 1-56164-306-8 (pb)

Ghosts of St. Augustine by Dave Lapham. The unique and often turbulent history of America's oldest city is told in twenty-four spooky stories that cover four hundred years' worth of ghosts. ISBN 1-56164-123-5 (pb)

Ancient City Hauntings by Dave Lapham. This second volume of St. Augustine ghost sightings by Dave Lapham continues in the same style as his *Ghosts of St. Augustine*, presenting spine-tingling stories sure to scare you. ISBN 1-56164-307-6 (pb)

Haunt Hunter's Guide to Florida by Joyce Elson Moore. Discover the general history and "haunt" history of numerous sites around the state where ghosts reside. ISBN 1-56164-150-2 (pb)

Haunted Lighthouses and How to Find Them by George Steitz. The producer of the popular TV series *Haunted Lighthouses* takes you on a tour of America's most enchanting and mysterious lighthouses. ISBN 1-56164-268-1 (pb)

Haunting Sunshine by Jack Powell. Take a wild ride though the shadows of the Sunshine State in this collection of deliciously creepy stories of ghosts in the theatres, churches, and historic places of Florida. ISBN 1-56164-220-7 (pb)

Oldest Ghosts by Karen Harvey. In St. Augustine (the oldest settlement in the New World), the ghost apparitions are as intriguing as the city's history. ISBN 1-56164-222-3 (pb)